She Said "A Landfill Where?!"

A Dr. Mary Paul in Florida Mystery

The Dr. Mary Paul in Florida Mysteries

She Said "What?!"
She Said "A Landfill Where?!"

She Said "A Landfill Where?!"

A *Dr. Mary Paul in Florida* Mystery

Mary F. Kohnke

New Dimensions Projects

Ponte Vedra Beach, Florida

She Said "A Landfill Where?!"

This book is a work of fiction.
Any resemblance to any person, living or dead,
is completely coincidental.

© 2006 Mary F. Kohnke. All rights reserved. No part of this book may be reproduced, stored in a retrieval system or transmitted in any form or by any means, electronic, mechanical, photocopying, recording, or otherwise, without the prior written permission of the copyright holder, except brief quotations used in a review.

For information contact New Dimensions Projects, PO Box 1213, Ponte Vedra Bch FL 32004.

Published 2006
Printed in the United States of America
09 08 07   10 9 8 7 6 5 4 3 2 1

Cataloging-in-Publication Data
She Said "A Landfill Where?!" / Mary F. Kohnke – 1st. ed.
p. cm.
"A Dr. Mary Paul in Florida Mystery"

ISBN-13: 978-0-9774536-1-0
ISBN-10: 0-9774536-1-8

1. Murder – Florida – Fiction 2. Women detectives – Florida – Fiction 3. Women political activists – Fiction 4. Ponte Vedra (Fla) – Fiction 5. Environmental responsibility – United States – Fiction 6. Sanitary landfills – Environmental aspects – Florida – Fiction I. Title

PS3626.K64 2006 813.54 — dc22
Library of Congress Control Number: 2006928881

Cover Photo
Afternoon Sun in the Woods
Courtesy of Dr. Jeanne Montross.

Dedicated To

Dr. Jeanne Montross

Jeanne's kindness, generosity and skill with her photography have made the covers of my books beautiful. Her wonderful photo on the cover of "She Said What?! caught the mood and beauty of the Intracoastal Waterway at sunset.

The cover of this book captures the mood and wild beauty of the woods. These are the settings for the stories. Thank you Jeanne, for taking us there.

&

The St. Johns County Roundtable and the Citizens of Ponte Vedra and Palm Valley

I want to thank all the members of the Roundtable who worked so hard to get the commissioners to support the fight against the landfill. Special mention to Cliff Petitt and Harold Baker, two of the founding fathers of the Roundtable. Joseph Davis, Pete Peters, Larry Wells, Linda Balsavage, Baron Bartlett, Gordon Gruhn, the residents of Ranch road, Palm Valley and Ponte Vedra, as well as the parents and children at Nease High School, all made important contibutions. There are so many others; it was a total community effort.

Finally I would like to thank both Mr. Davis for allowing me to tour D.O.T., and Harry Francis for being a wonderful tour guide.

Chapter One

"Sheriff Gray, there is a Robert Hayes who says he is an assistant to Mayor Walker of Jacksonville on the phone. Can you take the call?" asks the sheriff's secretary.

"Did he say what he wants?"

"No, Sir. I asked him and he said it was private."

"Ok, put him on."

"Sheriff Gray?"

"Yes."

"My name is Robert Hayes and I'm one of Mayor Walker's assistants. I am in charge of locating a new landfill in southern Duval County."

"Yes, Mr. Hayes. How can I help you?"

"Well Sheriff, first let me ask if you had heard about our efforts to locate a landfill in the area?"

"Yes, there had been some mention of it in the local newspapers."

"Yes, the newspapers. Well, that is part of the reason that I am calling you. There seems to be some opposition in the northeast part of St. Johns County to the location of the landfill. I mean, it is not even in St. Johns County."

"Mr. Hayes, if I have the location correct, it is surrounded by the County on three sides but you are correct it is on Duval land."

"Precisely. It is not a St. Johns County problem, but there is a group of St. Johns citizens who are very vocal in opposition to this location."

"Well, Mr. Hayes, how can I help you?" Sheriff Gray repeated. He rolled his eyes to the ceiling thinking, is this man really as dense as he sounds?

"Sheriff, there seems to be one person who is leading this opposition, a Dr. Paul. Would you know her?"

Know her, thinks the sheriff. Oh my, yes! I know Dr. Paul, as he flashes back a few months to the murder case she was involved in and her almost demise.

"Yes, I know Dr. Paul," he replied.

"Well, who is she?"

"She is a St. Johns County resident who lives in Palm Valley. She also is the president of the Palm Valley Community Center," answered the sheriff.

"Why is she doing this? Why is she so against the landfill? What's in it for her?" Hayes asked.

"Mr. Hayes, that is Palm Valley where you want to locate that landfill. I hope that helps to explain their interest."

"But Sheriff, this woman has stirred up the whole Ponte Vedra Community against us. It is as if it is a crusade with her. She is a fanatic; she is everywhere."

"She is not operating alone, Mr. Hayes. From what I read, it seems that there are many people up there, including close neighbors, who are involved."

"Yes, yes, there are a few of those, some 'rednecks' who live near by. But the Paul woman is different. Sheriff, is she crazy?"

"Crazy? Why would you ask that Mr. Hayes?" Oh my, here we go again, moaned the sheriff to himself. It seems if a women doesn't jump when some man tells them to they are labeled crazy or worse. "Have you spoken with her?" Gray asked Hayes.

"No, but the people in charge of locating the site, from our solid waste department, had a meeting in Palm Valley with the locals. She was presiding. Our people asked them what they could do to help. I mean, our people made all kinds of offers about the road, added landscaping and safety features. They offered some really expensive extras that we had never put in our other sites. They thought they were making some headway. They said everyone sat there and listened and asked good questions. When the time was nearly up, they thought, 'Wow, it's going to be ok.' So in closing, they asked whether there were anything else they could do. This Dr. Paul smiled sweetly at them and said, yes, they could put the landfill elsewhere. She then asked the group to voice their opinion and each one said 'Move it!'"

"I see," the sheriff said, smiling.

"Our people said they were completely blind-sided by this woman. That they were sure it was all tied up when, out of nowhere, comes this Paul woman. Now we can't field the nasty phone calls fast enough, needless to say the letters to the editor."

"What is it you want from me, Mr. Hayes? Why are you calling me?"

"Sheriff, you know County Commissioner Lee from St. Johns County? He is working with us on this landfill. He said you may know Dr. Paul and might be able to give us some insight. You see, Sheriff, we are willing to widen Racetrack road, make intersection improvements on US 1 and greatly improve County road 210. We will really landscape these roads and make the whole area a showpiece."

"Un huh," said the sheriff. He was thinking, a silk purse from a sow's ear.

Hayes went on. "There are further benefits to St. Johns County. Your landfill, off county highway 207, will need enlarging in the next few years. The new regulations are stiffer and make building landfills a more expensive job. They have all these added liners and stricter monitoring. But if we put this one in a handy location for St. Johns County, you can use it later and not have the expense of rebuilding. It's a win-win for everyone. You see that don't you?"

"I see the Commissioner's and your position quite well."

"Good, I knew you would. Our current landfill on the south side has to be closed. That leaves the haulers only Girvin Landfill out near the beaches. It can't be expanded much, and the only other one is northwest of the city. That one is a long drive from the south and east sides so this new location will serve everyone very well. The trash haulers are fully supportive of this location. They will chip in for the aesthetic improvements along the route in the County. Sheriff, there's a lot of money involved. There's a lot riding on this site."

"Do you own the land?" asked the Sheriff.

"We are getting it through condemnation of the Davis property; you know, the Winn-Dixie people."

"They wouldn't sell it outright?"

"No, we had to condemn it. So, Sheriff, can we count on your help with Dr. Paul?"

"How do you want me to help? I really don't see how this has anything to do with our office?"

"Well, do you think she can be, how do I say this, can be bought off?"

"Do you mean, can you pay her to shut up?" Gray growled.

"Yes, everyone can use money. Some of those people in Palm Valley can't be too well off."

"I don't believe Dr. Paul has financial problems."

"In that case, can you talk to her and maybe warn her off?"

"Do you mean threaten her?" asked the sheriff in astonishment.

"I wouldn't put it so bluntly," said Mr. Hayes "but you can get the idea across that it wouldn't be in her best interest to continue her battle against us."

"How do you mean 'not in her best interest'? That sounds like a not too thinly veiled threat to me."

"Now, Sheriff, please don't misunderstand me. All we are asking you to do is, maybe, remind her that it isn't wise to be going after big city business this way."

"Mr. Hayes, let me make myself perfectly clear to you. As an elected officer of the law, it is my responsibility to protect the citizens of St. Johns County, not to be going out to intimidate them in any fashion at all. They all have the right of free speech and the right to exercise it within legal parameters. It is also my job to protect them from intimidation and threats from others. So, I suggest you just forget about Dr. Paul and go about your business. I would indeed be very suspicious, if anything at all happens to her. Whether it is in terms of threatening letters, phone calls, or so-called accidents.

"Also, let me give you a word of advice. This situation has gone way beyond Dr. Paul. She is not your major problem. It's all those well-to-do folks in Ponte Vedra who do not want a landfill on top of them. So, I do not want to hear that Dr. Paul or any other citizen in St. John's County has been bothered, at all. Do I make myself clear?"

"Now, Sheriff, don't be getting all upset. We mean no harm to the woman or to any citizen. I am really taken back by your attitude. The Commissioner, after all, referred us to you. I was under the impression he thought you would be cooperative with us."

"Are you telling me that the Commissioner told you I would threaten this woman to get her out of your hair? Because, if you are, I can assure you, I will have him on the phone the minute we hang up here and set him straight."

"No, no, he said no such thing at all, never even hinted at it. No, please, don't call him and suggest he did. This call was my idea alone. I just thought if you knew the real benefits to the County of this landfill you might see your way clear to helping us. I guess I was mistaken, or I didn't express myself well. Please don't take any offense, none was meant."

The sheriff grinned to himself, as the big city mayor's assistant beat a hasty retreat. Some of these people really had an inflated opinion of themselves. Probably thinks I'm a small county 'redneck', too. Well, now that I've had my fun with him, I'll let him off the hook. "Look, Mr. Hayes, I'm sure all this bad press you guys are getting is bothersome. I can understand your wanting it to stop. But you are just going to have to put up with it. I'm sure it will all blow over."

"Yes, Sheriff, it will, and thank you for your time. I would appreciate it if you would not mention our little chat to the Commissioner."

"No problem, Mr. Hayes, I seldom see the man. Good day to you," and the sheriff hung up.

He sat back in his chair and thought, this must really be heating up for him to be calling me.

Steve Gray was not quite six feet tall, almost fifty, with thinning brown hair and dark eyes. He had kept himself in good physical condition, not merely to set an example for his men but because he took pride in how he looked. He dressed well and his clothes fit him beautifully; he believed in good tailoring. He was well prepared for his job even if he did come up through the ranks in a small Florida county. No one would ever mistake this man for a typical Florida 'redneck'.

He was nice looking and he laughed and smiled easily. The position of Sheriff in St. Johns County was an elected one and you had to get along with people and do a good job if you wanted to stay in office. Some called him smooth, especially at budget time before the County Commission, but you had to be if you wanted to make up for what he thought were years of neglect. The pay for his officers, he thought, was terrible.

The Sheriff's phone rang, and his secretary told him Major Jeff Brown was waiting.

"Send him in," said the Sheriff. Brown was the sheriff's chief assistant.

Major Brown was a big man, well over six feet. He has broad shoulders, some gray in his hair and a beginning gut. He was about the Sheriff's age, in his early fifties. He and the Sheriff were friends, as were their wives.

Brown was happy in his position and loved all the new technology that was coming out. He pushed to keep the department up-to-date in all the latest in communication gear and other gadgets. He said some day they would have a paper-free office and even have computers in the men's cars. "Hi Steve, have a busy day? Your secretary said you've been on the phone a while?"

"Hi, Jeff. Yes, you will not believe the call I just had. It was a Mr. Hayes, an assistant to Mayor Walker in Jacksonville. He wanted me to do something about Dr. Paul."

"You're kidding! What has Mary Paul done now? No, don't tell me. It's about that damn landfill that Jacksonville wants to put in Palm Valley, isn't it?"

"You're up-to-date or is your ESP turned on?" asked the Sheriff, smiling.

"No, but since a few months ago when we got to know Dr. Paul over that mess with the dead lady tied to her dock, then nearly losing her, I sort of keep an ear out for word of her. So does my wife. What's going on?"

"You know that group of homeowners in Ponte Vedra that has ganged up to make sure Jacksonville does not build that landfill in Palm Valley. Mary Paul managed to get them to all work together as a group to use all the pressure they can to stop it. The group is made up of people from those big rich developments in Ponte Vedra. They have even enlisted the member groups of the St. Johns County Civic Roundtable. They plan to pressure the County Commissioners to pay for a lawyer to fight this."

"How did she get that bunch in Ponte Vedra to work together?" Jeff asked.

"I was told by a man who attended the meeting that she presented a good case. First, she reminded them that the landfill site was only three miles away, as the crow flies, west of the Intracoastal Waterway. Then, she reminded them what it was like in summer when the hot winds blow in from the west. Finally, she told them to go over to Girvin road where the Girvin Landfill is located and check out the aroma. They say on a warm breezy day you can smell it over five miles away. Her case was made. The group took it on and it developed a life of its own. It will go ahead now with or without her."

"Can't blame them, Sheriff. Paul's place is right on the Intracoastal. Marsh Landing is only a mile or so north of her. There is a lot of money up there."

"Yeah, that reminds me of a saying they have in Jacksonville. When people complained about the smell from the pulp mills, they called it the smell of money. You could never sell that idea in Ponte Vedra. Too much odor-free Yankee money up there."

"What did the guy from Jacksonville want you to do?" Brown asked.

"You will not believe this," said the Sheriff and he proceeded to repeat the phone conversation to Major Brown.

"You know, Steve, I swear, some of those people in Jacksonville have not progressed much beyond the old mentality of the frontier days, of carrying guns and having shoot-outs in the streets," Jeff said, with much disgust.

"There are days when I agree with that. But I'm not so worried about the white-collar city hall types. It's the trash haulers and others who have a stake in this. The man said there was big money involved here, and a lot was riding on this location. I feel sorry for the people who are living near that site, across the street and next door. They are the ones who first came to the Palm Valley Community Center for help. Mary Paul and I talked about this some time ago," said the Sheriff.

" Sheriff, what are you going to do?"

"It's getting late in the day. I'll wait until the morning and call Mary Paul and tell her about the call. I forgot to tell you, I also made it clear to the man that it went way beyond Dr. Paul. That it was now out of her hands. What I won't do is call the Commissioner."

"Do you really think he told that guy to call you and ask you to threaten Paul?"

"No, I don't think he did. The Commissioner is a smart man. He wouldn't do something that stupid. He might have been asked who this Paul was and told them that I might know her and to ask me. But that's about all. Anyhow, the man was pretty emphatic that I not tell the Commissioner about our conversation. Speaking about the Commissioner, Paul is in his district and he is the one who appointed her to the Comprehensive Planning Advisory Board. They are writing a new Comprehensive Plan for the County."

Brown laughed, "A neighbor of mine is on that Board. He said it is loaded with developers, people who work for them, land attorneys and others very friendly to the development community. I'll bet Paul and a few like her were the tokens."

"He tell you how it's going?" asked the Sheriff.

"He said hot and heavy. The actual 'citizen appointments' started out believing this was a serious effort to control growth and plan for the future. That hope vanished in a hurry and it is now a battle royal."

"Who will win?"

"The developers will come out on top. But they will have to compromise a great deal more than they ever intended to because of Paul and others like her. You know, Steve, in this last election the citizens voted to go to single-member districts in 1990. That woman in Ponte Vedra who ran against Lee and lost in the last election worked hard to get-single member districts. She will run again and this may be Lee's last term in office," Brown said.

"Isn't that interesting. Think that has anything to do with his position on the landfill?"

"Good question. Well, Steve, let's get tomorrow's plans firmed up. Do you want to see that new Cigarette boat we got from the drug bust a few months ago? They are finally releasing it to us"

"You bet. Let's take a ride in the afternoon and go visit Paul. After all, she was involved that night when we caught the drug runners. She might enjoy seeing the spoils of that case." They both laughed. The sheriff said he would tell her to expect them in the afternoon.

Chapter Two

Thursday morning

"Yes, it is just lovely here. We had a quiet hurricane season. The storms all went west, up the gulf or to the east, out in the ocean." Dr. Mary Paul said. She was sitting on her porch overlooking the Intracoastal Waterway. She was on the phone, talking to her friend, Nancy, a therapist and artist, in New York City. It was mid October and the temperature was in the eighties. Mary's three dogs, two shepherds and a Doberman Pincer, were sprawled out on the porch floor taking a rest after consuming breakfast.

"You met who?" Mary asked in surprise.

"A man named Jeffery. He came into my friend Art's gallery where I had some paintings on display. Art had a painting of you I had done, like the one you have in Florida, hanging on the wall."

"You're not selling it"? Mary asked, kind of shyly.

"No, dear, I wouldn't part with it. Art thinks I do great portraits. He wanted to hang one for some people who were coming in, who are looking for a portrait artist. He told them I was the best, but unknown in the portrait world. He told them he would get a sample of my work so they could see it before meeting me. I told him I wanted a chance to see them and hear them talk before I agreed to paint them. Also, I wanted to do this unobserved by them."

"Why? I mean, why unobserved?"

"You know how you always say, there are people you won't play golf or go fishing in a boat with because then you are trapped with them for hours."

"Yes," laughed Mary.

"Well, it's worse in a studio. It's not just a few hours, it's more. Unless you are deeply interested in the subject, or unless they are decent people, it can be pure hell. Anyhow, I arrived there early to have coffee with Art in his office. He can both see and hear the customers and not be seen himself."

"Clever," remarked Mary.

"He is clever. In a little while a man came in and was looking around the gallery. Art got up and went out to talk to him. The man was tall and handsome, deeply tanned, with smile wrinkles around his eyes. He asked Art about the portrait. Like, who was it? Who painted it? Art told him he didn't know and why was the man asking? The man said, he thought he might know the person in the picture, a dear friend of his in Florida."

"Oh, my," said Mary.

"Yes, oh, my, indeed. When I heard that, combined with his great looks, I couldn't help myself. I appeared on the scene," laughed Nancy. "One thing lead to another and we are having dinner tonight. That's why I'm calling. Oh, yes, his name is Jeffery Stone."

"Wonderful! Give him my love. What happened to the portrait people?"

"I waited and they came. They had their daughter with them, a sixteen-year old with lots of baby fat and very sullen. The painting was to be of her. She, the daughter, didn't like my work. Said it was too serious and not flattering or pretty at all. Her mother said, not to worry, the artist would paint her sweet and happy. That she, the mother, would go to the sitting with her and make sure that it would come out just right.

"I was sitting in Art's office talking with Jeffery. As you know, I could hear all this and I about gagged. Jeffery was grinning from ear to ear. The father said to tell the artist they needed this done in the next two weeks and to call him right away."

"The end of the story is that you're out of town for the next two weeks," laughed Mary.

"Precisely."

"Thank God, you don't need the art to support yourself. So, my friend, enjoy Jeffery and I will talk with you later," Mary said.

"Oh, I will. Bye and God bless." Nancy hung up.

Mary sat back in her chair and thought, what a small world. She had thought about giving Nancy's phone number to Jeffery, but knew the two of them hated being fixed up, even by friends. Especially by friends. Nancy was so much her own person. Also, Jeffery was not in New York for long periods. He traveled for many reasons, frequently and unexpectedly. He had told her relationships with ties were not possible for him because of the work he did. He always said, maybe sometime in the future. But we all need friends. She was sure the two would like each other well enough for the occasional evening out.

Just then the phone rang. "Good morning ," Mary said.

"Good morning, Mary, it's Sheriff Gray."

"Oh, how lovely to hear from you. How can I help you, Sheriff?"

The Sheriff laughed to himself. She always seemed to answer the phone by asking how she could help you. Very nice. "How is the landfill issue coming?"

"Swimmingly, Sheriff, swimmingly," replied Mary. Then she laughed and said, "You know, I have always wanted to say that to someone. It's such an old-fashioned response; I just love it. But jokes aside, the opposition seems to be moving along quite well. Why do you ask?"

"I received a call from a Mr. Hayes. He said he was one of Mayor Walker's assistants."

"Yes."

"Do you know him Mary, or have you heard of him?'

"No, neither. Should I?"

"He said he was in charge of siting the landfill in south Duval. He asked me questions about you."

"Really! How charming. You will tell me what he wanted to know."

"That's why I called. He seems to think you are the ring leader of the opposition. He wanted to know whether I could help him shut you down."

"Shut me down. Oh, my! I wonder how he meant that?"

"I informed him, in no uncertain terms, we do not stand for threats to the citizens of St. Johns County. But I will tell you Mary, these are not developers. The people involved here are trash haulers and they have a history."

"Sheriff, I am not sure I understand the difference between trash haulers and developers."

"Very funny, Mary. I know you are being clever with me, but I want you to take this a bit more seriously. I told the man that this situation had gone way beyond you. That you couldn't do anything to slow it if you tried."

"That's true. You know I'm just being smart-mouthed with you. I would never dream of equating trash with developers, at least in a public forum. I am glad that you told him it was out of my hands. But I hope you did not imply that I would cease to speak up. I will speak out on any issue, if it is needed."

"No, I didn't say anything about your future behavior. I would never presume to do such a thing." The Sheriff smiled to himself. "I also called to tell you we finally took possession of the Cigarette boat the drug smugglers were using last spring. Major Brown and I will take it for a run this afternoon. We thought you might like to see it and take a short spin with us."

"Yes, that would be nice. I have seen those boats but I have never been in one. What time?"

"How about some time between two and three? We will pick you up at your dock."

"Sounds fine. I am glad you called. I was going to call you about the Roundtable finance committee. The committee has been looking at the county's budget and the administration's operations. They were asked why they didn't look at the budget for the sheriff's office and operation? So the men decided they would. Do you have a problem with that?"

"Absolutely not. Be a pleasure to have them. We are very proud of our operation."

"Good, I'm going to be the chairman this coming year, so I was asked to call you. Now I can tell them to call you. I'm not sure who it will be, but it may be a Joe Davis. He said you had told him one day that they were welcome to come look."

"Yes, I think I told one of them, at last year's budget hearings, to come over. What else have you been up to Mary?"

"Well, I am on the Comprehensive Plan Advisory Board and that keeps me busy reading.

You know, I have no background in planning, land development or any of those things. So I have to start from scratch. It comes with a whole new vocabulary. If you don't know the language, you are lost before you begin."

"How is it coming?"

"Sheriff, to tell you the truth, it is uphill all the way. The committee was loaded with developers, engineers, planners, lawyers and a few token citizens. They want to put more and more land into development and increase densities. That is not bad enough, they don't want any words in the text that say, must and should. They want the equivocating word, 'may'. So it is a multi-issued battle."

"What do you and the other citizens want?"

"The State of Florida said we must control growth. That the infrastructure must be in place to support it. No infrastructure, no growth. That is our position."

"Sounds reasonable," said the Sheriff

"Try telling that to the developer interests. Sheriff, a man named Cliff Petitt was on the committee with us from the start. He was one of the founding members of the Roundtable. He attended a few of the first sessions. Saw which way the wind was blowing and quit. He told the Board of County Commissioners what was going on at the committee meetings. He said he refused to be one of their token citizens. That may hurt the credibility of the committee. We all debated leaving. But with the special interest money invested in politics, we knew if we did not stay and tough it out, most anything could happen."

"Do you have public support for your position?"

"Within the Roundtable, yes. Because we had to educate them to the consequence of unplanned and uncontrolled growth. But the general public couldn't care less. It isn't until the roads are in gridlock and the schools overcrowded that they suddenly say we have a problem. It's too late then. Enough of this, you have me on my soap box. I may never stop."

"No, Mary, it is really interesting. We will also have to talk about the plight of the farmers one of these days."

"Yes, that is a whole other situation. I will see you this afternoon Sheriff."

Mary thought, what a nice man, but I bet he would not be unhappy to see me knitting instead of 'raising consciousness'. She laughed at the expression. How she hated it when the pretentious ladies in the women's movement used it. She was certainly sympathetic to the sorry state of women in the professions and the business world. But, she thought, 'spine stiffening' would do more than 'consciousness raising'.

Just then the phone rang again. "Mary here," she said with a smile.

"Mary here? Well, who else would it be, unless I had a wrong number?" snapped Clara. "Are you trying out new ways to answer the phone? Are you bored? Maybe auditioning for a new part in a movie you never told me about?"

Mary laughed, "All the above. To what do I owe the honor of this call? You are supposed to be working." Clara, Mary's friend, worked as an assistant to the Dean at a middle school. Both she and her husband worked there. He was a retired Army officer and she a retired nurse and housewife. They were both bored with retirement and believed in giving something back to the community. They also both loved children.

"I needed time out, so I locked the office door, shut out the lights, opened a soda and decided to lighten my day with a call to you. So lighten away. What's going on?"

"Sheriff Gray called."

"Really? When are they coming to arrest you? I'll call the press so we can get pictures."

"Later for that. He wanted to tell me about a caller he had, who was seeking information about that troublesome Dr. Paul." Mary then proceeded to tell her about the conversation with the Sheriff.

Clara was irate. "You know, you'd expect that kind of crap in Boston or even New York. But here in sunny Florida? Never! What kind of rock do these people crawl out from under?"

"Clara, the Sheriff seems to be concerned about the trash haulers and the money involved in acquiring this particular site location.

At least, that was the message he got. They said a lot was at stake in this deal. He said he told them that I was not the central attraction. That it had gone way beyond me. I think he also told them threats would be a serious mistake as far as he was concerned."

"Well, I would certainly hope so. I'm sure the last thing in the world the Sheriff wants is more threats aimed at you."

"I agree. He also wanted to tell me they were given the Cigarette boat the smugglers used last spring. He and Major Brown are coming up around two o'clock to take me for a ride."

"Let's hope that 'take me for a ride' has a funny ring to it," laughed Clara. "I'll let you go. Call me this evening and tell me about your ride with the boys."

"I'll do it."

After Clara hung up, she wasn't smiling. She was, indeed, worried about Mary Paul. Mary had almost been killed by the smugglers. There was a crooked detective on the sheriff's force who was working with them. They had killed Mary's maid when Mary was out of town, then tied the maid's body to the dock in front of Mary's house. The maid's rotten nephews were part of the drug group. They were afraid their Aunt might get suspicious of them, so they killed her. It was pure coincidence that the killing occurred at Mary's.

The investigation had the authorities wondering if someone meant to kill Mary. A developer's lawyer, along with others, was under suspicion. The development lawyer was angry at Mary for protesting a sewage plant they wanted to put in her neighbor's backyards. The crooked detective used the confusion of the case to kidnap Mary the very night of a drug run. He planned to kill her and pin it on the lawyer. Mary's friend Jeffery, who was visiting her, and the cops arrived just in time to rescue her. It was all very scary.

Where Mary lived also worried Clara. Her house was on the Intracoastal Waterway on a large piece of heavily wooded land. She had a guest house, almost all glass, with a tenant, but it was not that near the big waterfront house nor was the tenant home a lot.

The dogs were a help and Mary kept guns at home and sometimes in her pockets and boat. She laughed, remembering one day last spring after the murdered woman was found. She had come by for a chat. After she left the car she looked up and saw Mary, coming from the dock, her shorts hanging kinda low on her nothing hips. She was about five feet five, sun bleached hair going gray and blue-green eyes, laugh and smile and frown wrinkles all at war with each other. She had seen pictures of her when she was younger. She was a handsome woman and was aging well. She had told Clara both her parents lived long and healthy lives.

Clara had asked her that day why her shorts were falling off. Mary had laughed and said that the men in her life wanted her to carry both a cordless phone and her thirty-eight pistol in her pockets when she was out in the yard. She also told her she would be glad when this mess was over so she could stop that nonsense with the gun and the phone. Well, the incident that provoked the gun and phone in the shorts was over.

However, this phone call from the Sheriff made Clara edgy. Veiled threats were a part of life for those who cared about protecting their community or the environment. It's this kind of thing that makes people skittish about getting involved in controversial things, in getting involved at all. They assume and hope someone else will do it.

I do like the Sheriff saying it was way beyond Mary by now. Let's hope they believed him. That damn landfill was the stupidest thing ever. Don't those people have a map? Did they really think Ponte Vedra would just roll over for this?

There was a certain humor in this. Mary always said, 'There is nothing like watching rich folks fight'. I just hope she stays out of the line of fire. With those final thoughts, Clara turned on the lights, unlocked the door and prepared herself for the onslaught of volunteer mothers, who were due in five minutes. Thank God for volunteers. We could never function without them.

Chapter Three

Monday morning

What a beautiful morning, thought Mary as she opened the car door. She had fed the dogs and was on her way to St. Augustine for the St. Johns County Civic Association Roundtable meeting.

She had been a member, representing the Palm Valley Community Center, for the past several years. She was vice chairman this year but the chairman would be late today so he asked her to chair the meeting,

Mary loved being a part of the Roundtable. She felt right at home with people whose concern was looking out for the best interests of the County. Each person represented their own homeowners association or community association. As a group their main interest was the county as a whole, but they also banded together to help each member association with their individual problems, if they were requested.

In the past few months, when the landfill issue first came to light, Mary and the other representatives from the Ponte Vedra area asked the Roundtable for help. The group was very receptive and told them to come back with a plan for how the Roundtable could help. The Ponte Vedra/Palm Valley members met and a plan was created. Mary and the others were presenting that plan today.

Mary was driving her big Ford station-wagon down Roscoe Boulevard. It was a two-lane road and turned west at the Palm Valley bridge. The bridge was an old drawbridge over the Intracoastal Waterway; it opened for the waterway traffic on demand. Once past the bridge it was another five miles on CR210 to Highway US 1 and then south almost fifteen miles to the county complex. They were meeting in the conference room at the county offices a mile or so north of St. Augustine city on US1.

When the men who started the Roundtable were looking for a meeting place, the county commissioners said use our facilities. Actually, it worked out well. It was not unusual for a commissioner to drop in and listen. Also, the Roundtable frequently had members of the county staff making presentations or just visiting.

Mary had been invited to appear on TV with Commissioner Lee and the Jacksonville attorney for the landfill. It was to be taped this afternoon for showing this evening. She had mentioned it to the Sheriff and then to Clara over the weekend. Neither one of them were enthusiastic about her appearance; not what they called 'low profile.' She was concerned about what she was going to say but the station moderator said not to worry. It would be informal questions and answers.

She had taken care to dress well and put on more makeup than usual. The TV camera could be brutal to a poorly made up face. The traffic was light on 210 and there was hardly any on US1. At night 210 was a long empty road except for the odd deer crossing the road. She had slowed for more than one deer at night on Valley roads. She pulled into the lot with time to spare. Mary was always on time or early.

The meeting started promptly at nine AM. When the routine business was over, Mary stated the first item on the agenda was the Ponte Vedra/Palm Valley group. They had prepared a plan of action to defeat the landfill Jacksonville wanted to put next door in Palm Valley. Mary and several of the Ponte Vedra members briefly explained the plan.

Mary summarized the major need by saying, "We realized we need the county commissioners' full support to defeat this landfill. We will need a good lawyer to help us fight this in court and maybe in Tallahassee. The fight must be led with the full authority of the county government."

"Have you gone to the commissioner in your district for help?" asked Philip from St. Augustine Shores.

Jim from the Sawgrass Association replied, "Our Commissioner appears to be in bed with Jacksonville."

Groans came from several members. Paul from Treasure Beach said, "You are going to need a good Tallahassee lawyer and I bet it will cost you over $300,000."

Larry agreed and added, "Yes, I believe you're right on the cost and on the attorney. This will probably go to the State Cabinet for final resolution. It is a fight between counties. However it is fought, it will be costly and we will need the best attorney we can get."

"Yes," said Rennie from the Players Club, "That is why we need the help of all the associations. We need the Board of County Commissioners to be the lead agency in this and to vote to pay for a good outside attorney."

Harold Baker, the Roundtable Chairman, who represented the North Shores Association, had just arrived and asked, "What plan do you have for us to help you?" Mary stood to give him the chair but he said, "No, Mary, you continue as chair today."

Jim replied, "We would like each of you to go to the Commissioner from your district and ask them to put a stop to this. Tell them it would really hurt property values in the Ponte Vedra area."

"Yes," said Larry, "They would not like to kill their tax 'cash cow'."

"That is very true," Mary replied, "But you might also say, if it could happen in the northeast it could happen to any of our county borders. If you would go back to your associations and get a full association vote, then when you talk to the Commissioners you can tell them that your whole group wants this landfill stopped."

"I agree," said Philip. "They are politicians, they can count votes and they are still all elected at large. How much time do we have Mary?"

"About a month or even two before it comes before the Commission. We need the Commissioners lined up before then."

"Mary," said Larry, "Why don't I keep in contact with each of the member representatives and see how they are doing. It will sure free you up."

"I'd appreciate that. Maybe you can share tactics with each other. You all have the membership lists and phone numbers, so you can keep in touch. You also might tell the members in the northwest.

Their commissioner, Sarah Bailey, is already very concerned. The headwaters of Durbin Creek are very near to the landfill site. That creek feeds directly into Julington Creek and then into the St. Johns River."

"She is a heavy-duty environmentalist, isn't she?" asked Jim.

"Yes," replied John, the representative from the northwest. "She also lives on Julington Creek. She will really oppose this. We can count on Sarah."

"Fine, let's move on to the next agenda item: about the request from the finance committee to examine the sheriff's operation. Joe, I spoke with Sheriff Gray last week and he said he would be delighted to have all of you come over and spend as much time as you would like with them."

"He wasn't defensive at all?" asked Joe.

"No, I think he was rather flattered that you cared to come and look."

"Gee, Joe, give him a thumbs up report and you will never get another ticket," quipped Cliff.

"Yeah," laughed Paul, "Give him the reverse and you won't drive a mile without one." Everyone laughed.

"Did he say how many of us could come?"

"No, Joe. I told him you would call him yourself and make whatever arrangements you need."

"Ok."

"Mr. Baker, you are next up on the agenda. Will you explain your suggestion to the group?"

"Yes, I will be glad to."

Harold Baker was one of the originators of the Roundtable. He had worked in TV and radio for over forty years. He had investigated county, city and state governments almost as long. He explained to the group that St. Johns County's administrative organization was not very good. By that, he said he meant, there was nothing in writing about who was in charge, or who could issue orders to the staff.

The example he gave made every one laugh. Apparently, whichever Commissioner got to the office earliest would go to the public works department. They would get their pet project moved to that day. One of the new female Commissioners, an early riser, was beginning to usurp the good old boys. Therefore Harold thought this would be a welcome time to conduct an examination of the administrative organization.

He had spoken to the County Administrator about looking at the system. He was very welcoming. Harold explained he was now here before the Roundtable Board to get permission to put together a committee and begin an examination of the administration.

There were a lot of questions about time commitment and whom this committee would answer to. Harold said, "The time commitment could be worked out in committee and they would answer directly to the Roundtable Board." Mary and the other members agreed.

"What I envision," said Harold, "Is that we can make our observation and then suggest some changes that may make for a smoother functioning organization. I will bet, without change, that the way things are headed now, there will be a blow up in the near future. So what suggestions we come up with may well be listened to."

Everyone nodded in agreement. Mary asked Harold, "How many people do you need."

He replied, "At least three or four to start."

Hands went up. Mary asked , " Will you please meet with Harold for a few minutes right after today's meeting?" heads nodded. "Harold, where are you with the impact fee committee?"

"As you know, that committee started out with the Roundtable, then the Board of County Commissioners asked us to be part of a formal county committee. Our report is about done and will be sent to the Board soon. I'll be sure you all receive a copy." Harold said.

"Good," Mary said. "That's all the scheduled agenda material. Let's open the meeting to questions and comments."

"Mary will you tell us how the Comprehensive Plan Advisory group is going. We know Cliff here resigned in disgust. How bad is it?" asked John from the northwest.

"It is not good. We still have the developer interest blocking most of the citizens suggestions. For example, in your area, John, they want to put all the land along 210 west into a development area. Meaning that a Comprehensive Plan change will not be needed to develop there. They would put the whole county in that situation if they could."

"What difference does that make, Mary? I mean, what do you see happening under their system?"

"It means you could have a whole bunch of small developments, side by side, with no overall planning for the community. You also would have no connections between them, no school sites, ball parks, libraries or fire stations located. In essence, it would be piecemeal planning, done on the cheap. However, if you make them come in with large Developments of Regional Impact' that need Comprehensive Plan changes, you could require them to plan for all the needs of the community."

"So are you saying, it might be more expensive for the developers to develop if they had to get a Comprehensive Plan Amendment to create DRIs?" asked John.

"Yes, but it would be better for the county and better for the people who will come to live there. What they wanted would give you lots of people without any roads planned or other necessary infrastructure. They also wanted higher densities everywhere.

"I've been able to keep the land in Palm Valley on Roscoe to one per acre, but they wanted two per acre on Palm Valley Road. That area is composed of large oak hammocks. At two per acre they would cut most of the trees down. I am not popular, when I accuse them of 'strip mining'. I recently started to call it 'slash and burn'."

"Does speaking out like that help?" asks John.

"Helps my blood pressure," laughs Mary.

"Finally, it's a war of words. They wanted to use only the word 'may' in the descriptive text. We insisted on 'should' and 'must'. You can squirm out of 'mays' but not out of 'musts'. It's very discouraging. We will need a lot of help from all of you when it gets to the Commissioners. We will set up a list of the worst parts and our suggestions for change. Then we'll lobby the Board, use the newspapers, and whatever other means we can. With enough public pressure we may be able to keep it to only bad instead of terrible. Also, the developers realize if they go too far they may lose too much."

"Cliff's resignation really caused a storm," said Harold.

"Yes, it did. I truly miss you," said Mary, looking down the table at Cliff. He smiled back at her, "But it did scare the developers. They have backed off some of the worst changes."

"When is your next meeting?" several of the members asked.

"Wednesday evening, starting at seven. It will run late, we must finish this thing," Mary replied. "This is a busy week. I agreed to participate in a small group session for Channel 4 about the landfill this afternoon."

"Who else will be there?" Mary was asked.

"Commissioner Lee and the attorney for Jacksonville. They said they will tape it and show it this evening."

"You give them hell Mary."

Mary laughed and said, "Oh, no, I'll be just as sweet as pie."

"Yeah, like we said give them hell," they all laughed.

"On that happy note, if there is no more business, the meeting can be adjourned," Mary said, with a smile, as she pushed her chair back to leave.

"Mary, have you a minute?" asked Larry. Jim, Joe and Rennie were with him. Mary nodded and sat back down

"We missed you Saturday at the turkey shoot at the Oar House."

"I was there, I went early. You didn't think I would miss a fund raiser to stop the landfill, did you?"

The men laughed and Larry said, "No, we heard the sharpshooting Dr. Paul had been there."

"Sharpshooting?" Mary's eyebrows shot up.

"They said you won and then refused to take the prize money. But it's not that we want to talk to you about. Although why they would think any of us would take prize money at a fund raiser for the landfill is beyond me. After you left they put up a picture of Mayor Walker to shoot at."

"Oh, my. I'm glad it wasn't up when I was there. I fear that's a step too far."

"We agree. They were talking about trying to find endangered species at the site. They said this environmentalist, a biologist, was in town and he offered to look at the site for them if they could get permission so trespassing wouldn't be charged."

"Yes, he is the younger brother of a friend of mine, from up north. He called and left a message that he was in town, but I haven't seen him and we didn't talk. Actually, I don't know him well at all. I know his older brother. I hope they get permission to go on the site. Trespassing wouldn't be good, especially if they found something. They need to be legal and squeaky clean in all they do."

"I agree, Mary. I think that's why they waited until you left, to put the Mayor's picture up and to talk about tactics."

"Why? Shooting at the Mayor's picture isn't illegal, it's just juvenile," Mary replied. "What tactics? We just had a meeting with all of us about tactics."

"You will not believe this. They acquired some paw casts of the rare Florida Panther. They are going out there to plant some fake tracks."

Mary shook her head and murmured, "They know there are no Florida Panthers any where near there. We talked about this. There are damn few anywhere in the state and none up by us."

"They are desperate Mary. The people living right across the highway from the site will lose all value in their homes. They are angry and afraid. They do not trust the authorities and elected officials. They will try anything to stop this." Jim paused, then went on, "I am also afraid there are one or two who might be encouraging them to do it." He stopped talking and just looked at Mary.

"Yes, I am aware that some people might use the landfill fight for personal gain," Mary said. She stopped and looked away for a minute. "I don't think we can do anything about that. But I do appreciate you telling me."

"Mary, we both agree with you, we cannot interfere, but we thought you should at least know. If we were in their place, we might do the same thing or worse. There are some very high-powered people in Ponte Vedra fighting this, people outside of our group; the lawyer Pennington and a developer named Osteen who lives in Marsh Landing. We tried to explain to them, on Saturday that a lot was going on behind the scenes to stop this landfill. But they just stopped talking and changed the subject."

"It is so sad."

"Mary, I believe you were right. The best hope is with the Commissioners. With enough pressure from many directions, we can turn this around." All the men nodded.

Mary looked at them and said "I don't suppose if we added prayer it would hurt. Well gentlemen, I'm off to the city. Wish me luck."

Chapter Four

Monday, late afternoon

Mary drove up to her gates and got out to open them. The dogs appeared out of the shade of the azaleas and romped up and danced about until she had them open. She told them to go up to the house. They smiled, as only dogs can, and waited until she drove in, shut the gates and started the car forward. They turned and raced her to the big house. "Clowns, you are all clowns," Mary said out loud and smiled.

Boy, am I glad this day is over, she thought. The drive into Jacksonville had been easy. They had finished the TV taping quickly, so she beat the rush hour traffic leaving the city. The station said they would show it this evening as a special feature. She thought she had done a fairly good job. She had kept her cool all the way through the interview and only dealt with facts, well, the facts as she knew them. She knew she had surprised both Commissioner Lee and the attorney with some of her remarks. She would tell Clara, who should arrive shortly, and see what she thought.

She changed clothes and fixed wine, tea and cheese and crackers when the dogs loudly announced Clara's arrival. "Well, how did it go?" asked Clara, as she burst through the door.

"Fine, I think it went fine. The time goes by so fast it's over before you know it."

"Did they act like gentlemen or were they boorish, I hope?" smiled Clara as she reached for the cheese. "You know, did they show their butts?"

"No" laughed Mary. "Everyone was very well behaved. The moderator opened by asking the attorney, John Smith, what prompted the site selection for the landfill? He did the usual.... about it being near the growing south side and away from residential neighbors."

"Did he go quickly or drag it out?"

"No, he was very brief. She then asked the Commissioner what he thought about Jacksonville locating a landfill this close to St.

Johns County. Harry gave the party line about how very few people live near by. Then he shifted immediately into how St., Johns County would benefit from the landfill, since they would need a new one in the near future."

"What did you do during all this? I mean, didn't you just want to gag?" Clara said, as she handed the cheese plate to Mary.

"Thank you. Isn't this the best cheese? Wine's even better," said Mary as she took a sip.

"The moderator finally got to me and introduced me as Dr. Mary Paul. She explained about Palm Valley and a bit about the opposition to the landfill. She said I was the spokesperson for the opposition. She asked what our problem was with the landfill. You know, as if it were every day one had a landfill next door," said Mary, rolling her eyes.

"I hope you said that," replied Clara with disgust.

"No, I smiled and first explained I was not a spokesperson for anyone. I explained about the Palm Valley Community Center and the neighbors who came to us. I quickly went on and gave the distances that the landfill was from Ponte Vedra as the crow flies and as odor drifted on a hot west wind. She looked astonished and said surely I must be mistaken."

"You mean she didn't even know how near it was located to us?" exclaimed Clara.

"No, she did not. I'm sure, Clara, that the proximity to Ponte Vedra didn't occur to many people. They did not think about the odor. It wasn't until we brought it up that people realized what a disaster was in the making. She then went back to Attorney Smith and asked him and Lee about the location and its relationship to Ponte Vedra. They said in essence we were hysterical and exaggerating the whole mileage thing. They gave the land miles to old Ponte Vedra"

"They called you a liar!" exclaimed Clara.

"Essentially. But the moderator came right back to me and said, 'What do you say to that?' I told her very nicely that the gentlemen's road mileage by car was correct. But, unfortunately, odor doesn't travel by car. That it was about two or three miles at best, on a nice west breeze, from everyone on the island. Before she could interrupt, I also pointed out how close they were to Nease High School. I mentioned that hundreds of huge garbage trucks and school buses didn't auger well for road safety. She then went back to the men with more questions."

"Did they come back to you at all?"

Mary smiled and said "Yes, at the very end she asked whether I had any final words. I smiled and said that Ponte Vedra paid about forty percent of the property tax in St. Johns County. That when the smell of Jacksonville's garbage wafted over our beaches, I wasn't sure how property values would hold up. Or how the politicians would explain the resulting revenue loss. Lee actually looked sick. He could hardly look at me when it was time to leave."

"Oh, my word, not a low profile remark, at all. The whole northeast will see this on TV tonight. Well, can't be helped, it needed saying."

"Actually Clara, I was really speaking for the benefit of the Ponte Vedra citizens who would be listening. People will respond to pocketbook issues." Mary paused and thought a bit, "Time goes so fast on the TV interview shows. When you are done, you know you left out a million important things. We never even touched on the environmental issues."

"That reminds me, how did the Roundtable go this morning.?"

"Quite well." Mary gave her a summary of the meeting and then she said, "After the meeting the guys from up here stopped and told me what they had heard at the turkey shoot last Saturday." She told Clara what they had told her. "Clara, I sure hope they don't go running around out there without permission. Never mind planting phony evidence of nonexistent creatures."

"Are you sure there are no Florida Panthers out there?"

"There are gopher tortoise out there and they are a listed Species of Special Concern. They dig these huge burrows in dry upland habitat .... the old sand hills. The burrows can be over forty feet long, and some are up to two feet in diameter. The temperature and humidity levels in the burrows are about the same year 'round. These burrows provide refuge for over three hundred other species, many listed as threatened like the Indigo Snake, and lots of other things like the Gopher Frog and Florida mouse. But claiming panthers are there is a stretch too far."

"How do you know so much about these tortoises."

"My environmental friends in the Audubon and other organizations have educated me. When you are involved in land planning anything that could interfere with development becomes a subject of interest. Any question of listed or endangered species drives the developers crazy."

"So, if they find any gopher tortoises that will stop the landfill?"

"No, but they will have to either move them or buy mitigation land. But moving them is not very successful because they try to navigate back to their original range. So they get an incidental take permit and they just plow them under, bury them or pave over the burrow so they starve to death. They can take months to die. That is very sad."

"Do they live long?"

"Yes, some live more than 60 years. Actually, the female doesn't reach adulthood until they are 10 to 15 years old. They have a long history in the south. During the depression they were a reliable food source; that has been forbidden. Harvesting them is prohibited, but for years people still hunted them. That is one of the reasons they had been disappearing. Of course, loss of habitat is the major problem now. They like to live just where the developers want to build, high, dry, sandy soil so they can dig burrows. They also like to be in sunny places with lots of plants to eat."

"Have you seen them?"

"Oh, yes, you will see them crossing the road. I stop, put my blinkers on and carry them across the road. It's so funny, people will just sit in their cars and wait while you carry the tortoise across the road. Never have had one honk a horn or get mad. Most smile and wave.

"Years ago people in the rural areas had tortoise races. They were very popular. But the tortoises were removed from their original habitat and finally Florida prohibited these removals and races. It was in about 1978 when the decline became obvious and conservation methods became more prominent. They even created a Gopher Tortoise Council."

"You're making that up about the races, aren't you?"

Mary laughed, "No, people in this country in rural areas raced many animals: chickens, pigs, not to mention horses. In some areas, they even dressed them to race."

"This whole area was rural, wasn't it?"

"Yes. When I bought my place in the early seventy's there were even moonshine stills in the woods. People lived in what you would call shacks. They had a pump in the yard, an outhouse and some even cooked over an open fire in the yard. They had a few chickens in the yard, a small vegetable garden and a fruit or fig tree.

"When I was young, you grew your vegetables and bought fruit and canned for the winter. That was in Minnesota; same things happened all over the country. Here, they just stayed country longer."

"When was the Palm Valley bridge built?"

"The one you see now was built in the early thirties. It is the last drawbridge on the Intracoastal Waterway owned by the U.S. Army Corps of Engineers. I understand before that there was a turnstile affair and before that a barge system. People lived out off CR 210 on Twenty-mile Road in the late 1800's or before. Mrs. McCormick told me her mother-in-law, who lived out there on the McCormick farm, proudly told her she got to go into Jacksonville twice a year."

"Mary, I read somewhere that they built the kitchens separate from the house."

"Yes, that's true. They were often connected by a breezeway. I heard it was mainly to protect the house from fire and smoke. Here in the south, especially Florida, having the kitchen separate was not a hardship. The weather was warm most of the year and so it was cooler to cook out there. Many homes didn't have windows or screens and many had wood shutters they closed in bad weather. You can still see that in some of the islands. I had a friend in Barbados whom I stayed with on visits. They did not have glass windows or screens. Don't ask about the bugs; I don't remember any. In places where they had bugs they had netting around the beds."

"How did people live without air conditioning?"

"They built under trees. When I first came to St. Petersburg, Florida, in 1952, there was no air conditioning. We had lots of fans."

"Ha, you still live that way here."

"Yes, I hate the air conditioning. It is great for the humidity and if you are working, but otherwise I do without. I just don't entertain in summer."

"You don't wear any clothes either."

"A bathing suit."

"Speaking about the McCormick's, how will this landfill affect the McCormick's farm, or is it a ranch?"

"Both. I understand he is doing everything he can to fight it. They have a lovely home at the Beaches. But the ranch is the old homesite and the family spent a lot of time there with the children. It will be terrible for them. I hear he is spending money to fight it in any way he can.

"He has land on both sides of Highway 210, so he will be greatly affected. They formerly had about 2500 acres. I was told that whenever he needed money he sold off some acreage to Mr. Davis. This went on over the years; I don't know how much he has left. Land was like having money in the bank if it were owned free-and-clear. It seemed a lot better to some folks who remembered the depression, when the banks went broke."

"Were there roads from Ponte Vedra to the beaches?"

"You mean from Mineral City; there was no Ponte Vedra. No, not in the old days. They would take their buggies to the ocean and ride north on the hard sand at low tide. They would either stay the night, or they would go before dawn on a low tide, do their business, visit and come back twelve hours later on the early evening low tide. It was easier in summer when they had longer days.

"It was a much simpler life, but a hard one. Many homes had smokehouses where they smoked hams. They canned enough in the summer to last all winter. There were winter crops: collard greens, cabbage, potatoes. They ate off the land, shooting rabbits, squirrels, deer, whatever. They had an abundance of fish, crabs and oysters. I was told that people got water out of the ocean and let it dry up to get the salt. For many, life was one long preparation for the next season just to survive."

"I'm glad I didn't have to live that way. There are still people in this country that do live this way. It may have moments of nostalgia, but I have been spoiled by the way we live. I'm not going to wish to return to those so-called 'good old days'," said Clara.

"You won't get an argument out of me. We lived on a farm when I was little, and I remember my mother working hard from morning to night; on Sunday she had to cook a big dinner. There was no working outside the home. But you know, Clara, there were women who had to do what my mother did and they also worked as servants for others. That was back breaking."

"Mary, you sort of hinted that there were others who would use this landfill issue for their benefit. What did you mean?"

"Oh, I'm sorry I said anything. Actually, it was the guys who mentioned it in passing. It's such an ungracious thing to say or even to think."

"Yeah, but who is it?"

"Clara, I just hate to say anything. You just watch and see whether it becomes obvious. Now, don't get put out. If it's true you will see it."

"Ok, I'll play detective. Listen, I've gotta go and fix Ed's dinner. You want to come eat with us?"

"Thank you, but no. It's been a long day. I'll put on a steak and kick back with the dogs and this great book I'm reading. I think I'll even watch the TV; see if I did ok."

"I'll call you after the show and give you our critique."

After Clara left, Mary sat and sipped her wine, thinking what a nice person. Clara doesn't pull any punches. She will tell me exactly what she thought of my performance.

Clara was tall and a bit heavy, but she carried herself well. She was Boston Irish and never let you forget it.

She had a wonderful reputation at the school and with the kids. She was strict and fair. She loved children and they knew it, but they never took advantage of her (as if they could.) She believed there was not much wrong with children but a lot with parents. It just blew her mind that people could do some of the terrible things they did to kids. She shook her head, looked at the dogs and said, "Well, dogs, time for dinner."

Chapter Five

Tuesday morning

"Sheriff Gray, you have a call on line one from Sheriff Sam Edward's. Can you take the call?" asked his secretary. Edwards was the Sheriff of Jacksonville.

"Yes, of course, thank you, Martha," said Sheriff Gray as he reached for his phone. "Good morning, Sam, what can I do for you this fine early morning?"

"Can you meet me out on Highway 210 at the proposed landfill site? We have a mess on our hands."

"What kind of mess?"

"One of the county workers found a dead body at the very south end of the site, across from Ranch road. It appears that he had his head bashed in. There is a truck on the St. John's County side, in the bushes, that they think is the victim's."

"Oh, boy, just what we do not need."

"Tell me about it, Steve. With all the publicity about that damn landfill in the papers and on TV you know this will be nasty. Can you come up to the site with me? I'm afraid this is going to concern both of us."

"Give me twenty minutes and I'll be there. Has anyone touched anything yet?"

"No, I told them to cordon off the whole area and stay back."

"Good, I'll see you shortly." Steve hung up his phone, called his secretary Martha and told her to get Major Brown and find Detective Hold right away. Moments later Major Brown knocked and opened the door.

"Hi, Jeff. Are Hold and a couple of his men available this morning?"

"Yes, they are all up in Ponte Vedra. He and three other officers are working up there today. What's going on?"

"Walk with me to my car and I'll brief you as I go. Martha, call Hold and tell him to meet me at Ranch Road and County Road 210 and to bring one of his officers with him." As the Sheriff and Brown walked to the Sheriff's car, he told Brown about the call he had received and what Sheriff Edwards had told him.

"He wants to drop this in your lap."

"Smells that way."

"Why? Most forces are jealous and territorial as all getout about their cases." Steve remained quiet and just looked at Brown.

Brown suddenly raised his eyebrows and said, "Oh! this may be too hot to handle alone."

"We surely will see. Now I'm just treating it like a courtesy call. You know, keeping an open mind," he said and smiled. As he got in the car he said, "By the way, did you see Dr. Paul on TV last night?"

"Sure did. She did a good job. Our Commissioner didn't look too happy when she made those remarks about property taxes, did he?" Brown said with a big smile on his face.

"He surely didn't. I'll call you as soon as I have something to tell you."

Steve thought about the TV interviews program and Dr. Paul as he drove north. Yes, she had done a good job. Low key, stuck to the facts, didn't explode when the other two suggested she was exaggerating the situation. She just hung in and repeated the facts until she got an opening, then hit them with the property tax situation. He had actually laughed out loud and his wife said 'you tell 'em, Mary.' He bet the people in Ponte Vedra and Palm Valley loved it.

He was moving over the speed limit and was soon at CR 210. He turned east toward Palm Valley. When he hit the straightaway he could see flashing lights ahead. Well, that will surely attract the press. There was a cop in the road directing traffic as well. The cop waved him off to the left, up a little dirt road. He pulled over and stopped. Hold pulled in right behind him. He got out of the car and had Officer Rogers with him. They walked up and said, "What do you want us to do Sheriff?"

"They have a body and they requested our help. Stick with me and take notes and be as accurate as if it were our crime scene. But remember, we are in Duval County, on their turf."

Steve walked toward where the Duval County officers were standing. Sheriff Edwards turned, walked up to Steve and greeted him. "Thank you for coming so quickly." He introduced him to his men and Steve did the same.

"They have kept everyone away from the site until we arrived. That is the county worker who found the body. He went right to his truck and called it in. We told him to stay in his truck until we got here." He called the man over and introduced him to Steve as Ed Jones and asked him to repeat his story.

"I was out here today to check over the site and be sure no one had moved the survey markers or messed with the monitoring wells. We had sunk two of them."

"Had people been here and moved the survey markers in the past, Mr. Jones?" asked Steve.

"Yes, Sir. We think it was the neighbors who are mad at us."

"Ok, go on."

"I started to walk up there behind those trees and that's when I saw the body laying there. There was a shovel next to it with brown stuff on it; the man was dead with his head bashed in. There were some gunnysacks lying there too. I was scared and ran for my truck and called 911. They told me to stay away from the body and wait in my truck for them. That's all I know. Can I go now?"

"No, Mr. Jones, you have to go down to the station and give us a full report and sign it. We will make arrangements for that in a few minutes. Call your bosses and tell them where you are," said Sheriff Edwards. He motioned one of his men over and told him to keep an eye on the man and in a short while he could take him in and get his statement.

"Ok, men, stay together. We don't want to be stomping all over the site. Are the evidence men here?"

"Yes, Sir."

"Ok, have them up here in front, with Sheriff Gray and me. Officers Port and James, you go ahead and check the ground as we go."

They all moved slowly forward. The ground was composed of sand and dirt and short scrub grass trampled down over time. As they came up even with the trees the evidence men held up their arms; everyone stopped. They went ahead alone. Officer James had a camera and was taking pictures as he walked. Officer Port called back and said, "give us five minutes, Sheriff." The men stood still and chatted.

It wasn't long before Port came back and by then the coroner, Dr. Black, had arrived. They all proceeded carefully. Black went forward and asked had the body been touched and whether they had all the pictures of the body they needed. They said no, not yet, and yes, the pictures were done.

The body was laying face down. You could see the hair on the back of the head was matted. They did a quick check and turned the body over. It was a young man in his mid-twenties. Nice looking, haircut a bit long, but clean shaven. He had a black tee shirt on and jeans and work boots on his feet. The men were checking his pockets and told Sheriff Edwards he had no identification, money, not even a watch on him. If the truck on the road was his he had no keys in his pockets.

"What's in those gunnysacks?" ask Sheriff Edwards, pointing beyond the body where three gunnysacks lay. Port walked over and opened the sack and tipped it up; two turtles fell out. "I hope those are not gopher tortoises," said Edwards.

"I'm afraid so," said Sheriff Gray, looking over his shoulder.

James had been expanding the ground search, with his camera, away from the body and yelled, "Sheriff, better come." Edwards and Gray walked over about fifty feet away toward a small bunch of trees. James pointed into the trees and there lay a small dead bear cub about three months old.

"Lord, I hope the mother isn't anywhere around," said Edwards.

Sheriff Gray walked over to the bear and looked at it carefully and said "No, it's been dead a few hours. If the mother was here, she is long gone now. Looks as if it were clubbed."

"Sheriff," they heard another call.

"Now what," grumbled Edwards. "Mark this site and recover that bear" he said to James. Edwards and Gray walked back to the other men.

"Sheriff, we found these plaster casts when we moved the body," said Port. There were three plaster casts lying on the ground. One was turned over, and it looked like a large cat's paw. Gray and Edward's looked at each other in silence.

"Sam, may I ask some questions and make a couple of suggestions?"

"Yes, of course, that's why you're here."

He asked Officer James, "Have you taken careful pictures of the ground all around this site?"

"Yes, Sir."

"Can you tell how many footprints were here and are any of them fresh?"

"It was pretty trampled down as we first came in but when you turn off the main path, it was clear that only a very few people had been back in here. But I couldn't swear to the number, Sir. It's pretty dry and so you don't have any mud prints. We have a great camera, and the prints may show more. We will blow them up and go over them carefully."

"After you take prints off everything, can you get the Zoo people to identify the plaster cast prints for the animal?"

"Yes, Sir, that's no problem. We have good working relationships with them. We will also ask them who could have made them."

A Duval County detective walked over and said, "Sheriff Edwards."

"Yes, Detective Cook."

"Sir, we would like to print and search the truck, but it's in St. Johns County."

"Steve, do you have a senior man here that can work with Cook? He is my senior man in the southern district. He would like to go over that truck. They think it might belong to the dead man."

"Yes, I asked my senior man from this area to meet me here." He looked around and spotted Hold. "Hold, come here please." Detective Hold looked up, said something to Officer Rogers and walked over to the Sheriff. "Do you know Detective Cook?"

"Yes, Sir, how are you, Martin?" he said as he held out his hand to Cook. The men shook hands and turned back to the sheriffs.

"I want you to go with Detective Cook and his men while they go over that truck. Get the information off it and find out to whom it belongs. Might be this guy's, he had to have come here by some means." Both men nodded and walked away.

"Sheriff Edwards, Dr. Black said we can move the body and we have finished the pictures. We still have more work, but we don't need the body."

"Yes, move it." He turned to Gray and said, "Thank God it's early and out in the country. We have lucked out so far by missing the press. Did you see that channel 4 TV interview last night?"

"Yes, I did." Oh, oh, now what? thought Steve.

"What did you think?" asked Edwards.

"That I'm glad I'm a sheriff, not a Commissioner."

"Hum," said Edwards. "That Dr. Paul handled herself well. She looked good."

"Yes, she did."

Damn, this is like pulling teeth, thought Edwards, might as well get right to it. "Do you know her?"

Steve thought, where is this going? Well, stick with the truth. He probably read the stories about her last spring. "Yes, I do. A very smart and a very nice lady. Why do you ask?"

"This murder, what we have found and its location will be a big deal. I need to talk to you privately about it. Let me go over to my car and make a quick call first."

"Ok, take your time. I'll see what the men are finding."

Sheriff Edwards got in his car and made a call to the Mayor's office. When the secretary answered, he identified himself and asked to speak with Walker. "Sheriff, what can I do for you on this beautiful day?"

"Well, it started very well, but it shortly went to hell," grumbled Edwards. "One of the city public works men found a dead body at the Southeast landfill site. A young man, no identification, and a sack of gopher tortoises."

"That's not good. What have you done?"

"I called Sheriff Gray, from St. Johns County, to meet me here and we just finished going over the crime scene. I am calling you to advise you I will turn the management and coordination of the case over to him, if he will have it."

There was a long silence that Edwards sat quietly through. The Mayor was a careful man and did not make quick foolish remarks. "Well, Sam, you know you do not answer to me and it is your prerogative to make those decisions."

"Yes, it is, but considering the location and the publicity this thing will get I believe it will be better for everyone if St. Johns County is in control, with full consultation with me, of course. I am calling you as a courtesy and a heads up before the press calls you. I know how we all hate surprises."

"Sam, I would never tell you how to manage your job. I really do appreciate your call."

"Good, you have a good day, Mayor." He broke the connection. He thought, Like hell, you wouldn't tell me how to manage my job. I just don't give you a chance. Now to see whether Steve will be cooperative. I surely am glad we have a good relationship.

He opened the door and walked over to where Steve was watching the men. The truck they were examining was parked off the road almost into the trees. It was in a place that wouldn't attract much attention from passing cars. "Steve, let's go talk." The two men walked off toward Steve's car.

Tuesday

Sheriffs Gray and Edwards climbed into Gray's car and shut the doors. "Steve, I will be blunt and ask you to do me a great favor. I want you to take over this case. We can set up a joint investigation, but I want you to run it and have the management control. You can keep me abreast of findings, but the decision making is yours." He stopped talking, looked at Steve and waited.

"You had better tell me a bit more. This is not like you," replied Steve.

"You're right, it's not, and I hate to ask you to take on this case. For starters, this whole landfill mess will make this murder ten times more difficult than normal. The people in St. Johns just hate Jacksonville right now, because of the landfill. No matter how good a job we do on this case, they will not believe anything we say. I think the investigation will involve the two counties, so having a joint team will be necessary as well as smart."

He paused, "Also, on a more personal note, I'm running for re-election this coming spring and this will only add more grief to what might be a tough year."

"You don't expect any opposition do you?"

"Not yet, but if they smell blood they will come out of the woodwork. Steve, I also am unhappy with what I see going on with this landfill location. I mean, there are too many people in the administration pushing this and pushing it hard. There is much money involved."

"Are you afraid they will interfere with your investigation in some way?" asked Steve.

"I believe if bad things can happen, they will. Your handling the investigation will neutralize most of that."

"You know we have a Commissioner pushing for this landfill," said Steve.

"Yes, but the money people are in Duval; your Commissioner is small potatoes in the whole mix. That call I just made was to Mayor Walker. I told him I would ask you to take the lead in this case. I also told him the only reason I was calling him was to give him a heads up before the press called him. He is very clear on his relationship with me; I don't work for him. He knows that."

"I can understand your position. You are right, we will need a joint task force on this. Also, there can't be two bosses. But you and I will have to work very close together. You can be our undercover man," Steve said, and he turned and grinned at Sam.

"That may not be too far fetched," grinned Sam, "but you can be sure that my men will operate with full loyalty to you. I will make that very clear."

Steve held out his hand and Sam took it. They shook and smiled. Sam said, "Before we go out and tell the men what the arrangement will be, tell me, do you have a gut reaction to what we have seen today?"

"I have two huge questions. Was he poaching gopher tortoise or did he walk up on someone else doing it? Who is he?" replied Steve with a frown.

"When you find out the who, that may tell you the what," said Sam as he reached for his door, "I have the same questions."

"Detective Cook, call all the men together, St. Johns County men as well," yelled Sam as he and Steve walked a little beyond the truck the men were working on. Cook got the evidence men who were working the site and the others right away.

"Ok, men. Sheriff Gray and I have discussed this case and how it will be run. Due to the location of the murder and the proximity of the site to St. Johns, it will concern them as much as us. Also, because this is the location of the landfill that Jacksonville wants and many locals in St. Johns don't, we have a very touchy situation on our hands. If we manage the case, there will be many who question our veracity. I have asked Sheriff Gray to take the lead role with a joint task force; he will keep me informed.

"Detective Cook, I want you to head up the Duval County group. You know the men, and you can have whoever you need. Are there any questions so far?"

"Sheriff," said Cook, "Officers Port and James have been working the site, can I keep them on? Be fewer people we have to update."

Sam looked at Steve who nodded his head and said, "Good suggestion, do you have any more? You don't seem surprised at Sheriff Edwards suggestion for who heads the task force."

"No, Sir, but I saw the TV Interview show on Channel Four last night. When I found out what we had here, I was concerned how this would look to the public."

Steve looked at Sam and said, "He's a keeper, Sam, and I think we can start with your three men we have here now. If we find we need more, you can be sure I'll ask."

"Ok, Steve, I'm going to head back to the office. Is there anything I can do for you now?"

"Yes. Can you have one of your road deputies take the worker, Mr. Jones, who found the body, in to get his report and get him printed? I don't know what, if anything, he touched, but we better have his prints, anyhow."

"No problem. He can drive his truck in, get it out of here. Oh, sorry to tell you this, but I will have all press calls referred to your office." He smiled and waved to one of his road deputies as he left. Then he called back, "I'll call you later this afternoon."

"Ok, men, let's get started. This is Detective Hold. He will head things up for St. John's county, and you all know Detective Cook. Let's start this way. Officers Port and James, you report directly to Cook and he will share information with Hold and my office. Right now, I want both of you to finish with the crime scene site. Do you need any help?"

"No, Sir. We will bag the bear cub and the tortoise and get them to the zoo people. They will be able to tell us better what happened to them. After the casts are printed, we will take them to the zoo as well. We will have a rush put on these pictures we are taking as well. Get them blown up. Should be done by morning," James said.

"Good, that ok with you Cook?"

"Yes, Sir, one of them can do the Zoo and the other can lean on the photo lab. James, you were taking the pictures so you stay with the lab. Have them really work on the shots you think will give us what we most need. Also, tell them the Sheriff wants them first thing in the morning. You don't need to say which Sheriff."

"I can get the paperwork ready for the morning when I get back from the Zoo, Detective," said Port.

"Good. You all be in my office by eight-thirty in the morning and we will see where we go from there."

Port and James went back to the site. Steve turned to the rest and said, "Ok, did you guys finish with the truck? Have you found anything?"

"Its reasonably new, I'd guess a year-old Ford. It has New York license plates. There wasn't much in the truck. We found some binoculars in the glove compartment along with a bird identification book. There was a jacket on the seat, some candy bar wrappers and an empty water bottle. Not much, Sheriff, for a truck. It was very clean," said Hold. Cook nodded in agreement. "We didn't touch anything. Do you want us to take it into the County?"

"Yes, I do. Rogers, you have the truck taken in, Get the plate numbers and call New York; find out to whom it belongs. See whether you can locate any family. When you do, have Hold call them with the bad news. Hold, when you call the family, be sure you find out why he was down here and whom he might have known here. Gentlemen, until we know who this man is we are stumped as to why he was here."

"Sheriff Gray," asked Cook, "Do you think he was poaching or did he walk up on someone else who was poaching?"

"That is a big question," replied Gray. "but my gut tells me he was not poaching."

"If not, why was he in that location?"

"Detective Hold, that is the key question. The other question becomes, whom did the casts belong to?"

"What are they for, anyhow?" asked Cook.

"Yes, indeed, what are they for?" mused Gray.

"Detective, can you get the TV press out here? I mean, can you get them here without them knowing who wanted them here?"

Cook grinned, "I'll have them here before you know it, Sir. I have a secret and discrete source."

"Good, do it now. I want them to get a picture of that truck and a brief description of the man and I want it on the TV quickly. Be sure if I'm not here that you make it clear we need to identify the man." Cook walked over to his car.

"You don't think he was in this area all by himself, do you Sheriff?" said Hold.

"No, I don't. Out of state license plates, out of the way location? No, he was here for a reason and I'll bet someone local knows that reason."

"But would they call in and identify him?"

"Depends on how scared, or how guilty or angry, they are. We can only try to see what, if anything, it brings us. Make sure you leave a phone number for them to call. Have it be our office in St. Johns. I have a feeling about this. Hold, you be sure to have our operators alert to get the name and phone number of anyone who calls. They must call you immediately, no matter how late. You decide if you need to see them tonight. Get as much information as you can and make an appointment to see them tomorrow."

Cook walked back to them grinning. "The TV crew is in Ponte Vedra finishing a shoot. They should be here shortly."

"Good job."

"I made another call. They will let the other stations know. Wanted to be sure everyone gets coverage."

"I just told Hold, when you talk to the press, be sure you both give them our office number. Hold will alert our operators to call him immediately, even at night."

"Good idea. They will recognize a St. Johns County number."

"Gentlemen, I'll leave you both to the press. You both check in with me before the end of the day. If you hit any snags at all, call. Cook, that goes for your labs. Sheriff Edwards will move them in a hurry. Oh, one final thing, I shouldn't have to tell you both, but keep all our information within the task force. Tell the others."

He walked back to his car and stopped and talked to Rogers who was standing by the truck. "There will be TV press here shortly. Be sure they get good shots of this truck. Talk to Hold."

Steve started his car and pulled out to go back to his office. He picked up the mobile phone and asked his secretary to get him a sandwich for lunch and to ask Major Brown to join him in a working lunch in thirty minutes. After he hung up, he said out loud "this is not going to be good, no Sir, not good at all."

He and Major Brown walked in to his office together. "Well, Steve, this is a first in a longtime. Not that I don't enjoy lunch with you, but in the office?"

"I need to talk about this case now, while it is all fresh in my mind. I also need to tell you about Sheriff Edwards. You were right on target. He dropped the whole thing in my lap."

"I'm not surprised. If he saw that TV show last night, that alone would spook him."

"He did and it did. He even asked me about Dr. Paul. But it was a nice harmless question. He had two very good points. One, St. Johns County residents wouldn't trust anything his group told them about this case. Two, he's thinking this is going to be nasty and he is up for reelection and would like to dodge any major assault."

"I agree with him on both counts. It's a good thing you have a good working relationship with him. Tell me what you found."

Steve went over what they found at the site. Jeff listened quietly and didn't interrupt until he was done. "Any questions?" asked Steve.

"A lot, but I suppose the biggest is, who is this man?"

"Yes, that alone will give us many answers, I think. Jeff, I have some bad feelings about this case. I'm not worried that we have control, but I'm afraid who all this will concern and even involve. That is also part of what is bothering Edwards. He said there was a lot of money involved in this landfill site. But I will say one thing. I am sure he will cooperate with us one hundred percent. He is not part of the Mayor's inside group. He did tell him he was giving over control to us. I was left with the impression that that was not going to please the Mayor."

"You know, Steve, if you think about it, having control here is good. We are a good distance from Jacksonville and none of the money players are near us. Having his staff working with us will also be good. They can do any foot work we need in Jacksonville."

"Yes, I agree from a working point of view, it will be fine. I am actually glad we can help Edwards out. He didn't pull any punches. He was out in the open all the way. I spoke with his lead detective and two of his men. They seem to be on top of things. The lead detective's name is Cook and Hold knows him."

He went on and told him about the TV coverage and asked what he thought. "I think we will get a call. This man seems kind of clean cut, not a poacher type. Someone will know him."

"I have Rogers bringing in the truck and he will have it printed, run the prints and call New York. See whether we can identify him and maybe find his family. Jeff, see whether we have another man we can free up tomorrow if we need to start canvassing the neighborhood. I told everyone to be in here at eight thirty. Have Hold come in a bit early, especially if he finds out anything important overnight."

"Ok, I'll go talk to the chief operator, make sure the other shifts get the word and treat it very carefully," said Jeff. "Steve, wouldn't you just love to be a little bird in that Mayor's aides office, when this news gets out."

"Yes, especially when he finds out Edwards turned the lead in the investigation over to us."

Chapter Seven

Tuesday, early evening

"Mr. Hayes, the people for your last appointment are here. May I go home now?" asked his secretary. She was an older woman who did her job well and always stayed late when he needed her. She didn't have a husband and kids to rush home to.

"Yes, of course, I'm sorry, I didn't realize it was getting so late. Just show them in before you go." He had been asked why he didn't get one of those cute young secretaries the other aides had. He had laughed and said because he wanted work done and done promptly; he wanted someone who wouldn't whine and pout. What he didn't say is he wanted someone who wasn't into gossip in the office. He wanted someone who knew when to keep their mouth shut. His secretary fit that bill very well.

Hayes was in his thirties and this job with the Mayor was a real plum. He was of medium height, dirty blond hair that he was beginning to lose and brown eyes. He was a pleasant man when things went his way. But he prided himself on not being a pushover for anyone. He had put this whole thing together. This whole site location was going well, thanks to him.

He looked up as the three men came into his office; he had three chairs set up in front of his desk. He stood and shook hands first with John Smith, the attorney the city had hired to work on the landfill site. Art Moore, the head of the city's solid waste department was next; he was a recent hire. Bringing up the rear was Wilber Wood, the owner of DBF Haulers, which had the contract to haul the city's solid waste. He greeted them all and asked if any of them wanted something to drink? They all shook their heads no. They knew damn well it would be sodas.

"Saw you on TV last night, John. How do you think it went?" asked Hayes.

"It went well, until the end. When Dr. Paul landed the punch about property taxes, I thought Lee would have a coronary," said John.

"I didn't see his reaction," said Hayes "they didn't have the cameras on him."

"Good thing, it wasn't pretty. I got him out of there quickly, before he could blow."

"Is there any truth to what she said?" asked Hayes.

"Hell, no," said Wood. "It's just scare tactics, trying to stir up the good people in Ponte Vedra."

"What is the direct mileage, over land, to the beaches, Art?" asked Hayes.

"Hey, wait a minute, are you agreeing with that Paul women?" Wood blurted out.

"No, Wilber. I am not. I am just trying to get the facts straight. I want to know just what kind of ammunition the enemy has," replied Hayes and he looked at Art.

"Her mileage over land is correct. In summer when you get a west wind they will smell the landfill, no question."

"Damn it, Moore, I sure hope you don't go around telling people that," said Wood.

"Mr. Wood, I work in the solid waste business and around landfills, in summer, in Florida with the heat and the humidity, they all stink," Moore replied.

"Ok, gentlemen, no more made-for-TV spots for Paul. Let's control what goes out the best we can. That's not the major problem tonight. Have you guys seen the early TV news?"

"No," said John, "but I've had the press calling me on the phone and so has the Mayor."

"What about?" asked Wood. "I was up in Georgia all day."

Hayes replied, "They found a dead man at the landfill site. Tell them, Art."

"I sent one of our men out to check the site and the boundary marks at first light. People have been out there moving them. We were also checking on our monitoring wells. He first called 911 and then the office when he found the dead man at the south end of the site," related Art.

"Who was it?" asked Wood.

"They don't know. He had no ID on him and there was a truck near the site in the trees and it didn't have any papers in it," replied Hayes.

"How do you know that, Hayes?" asked Wood. "Have you a line into the Sheriff?"

"No, but I did call him and that's all he told me, with one exception." He waited and watched them, "He added that he had turned the case over to the St. Johns County Sheriff."

"Why the hell would he do that?" asked Wood.

"I can only tell you what he told the Mayor when he called him. He said it was almost on the county line and would need a joint task force. The people in St. Johns County hate us over the landfill and wouldn't believe a thing we said about the case. So he thought it was best for all concerned if he gave the lead to Sheriff Gray," said Hayes.

"I'm not happy about that," said John. "Can you ask the Mayor to tell the Sheriff to take the control back to Jacksonville?"

"Not a chance. The Sheriff doesn't answer to the Mayor and if it got out that the Mayor was pressuring the Sheriff in this matter, all hell would break loose," replied Hayes. "To tell you the truth, it wouldn't do any good. Once Edwards makes up his mind, that's it. Anyhow, it may be best. We don't need any more bad publicity for the City."

"How was he killed?" asked Wood. There was silence. He looked around and said, "Was he killed or did he have a heart attack?"

"We don't know," said Hayes, "they aren't giving out any more information than necessary right now, " he looked around and added, "to anyone."

"Leaves us right where the public is, ignorant and guessing," said John. "Which reminds me; remember we received the request from an opposition group last week? They wanted us to let them on the site to look for endangered species. We talked about this Monday morning."

"Yeah, and I said to forget it," said Wilber. "We will have DEP and everyone else out there. Why should we let them come?"

"I agree, it could be troublesome," replied John, "but we haven't done a site examination for endangered species. It's probably something we better think about, and soon."

"I said I would pay for an environmental investigation," said Wood "I just haven't set it up yet."

"You said you were going to send an old 'redneck' you knew out there to do a quick look through before you got the accredited people to go. Did you do that?"

"Yeah, I spoke with him last week. Told him to check it out over the weekend or as soon as he could and not to be seen. But I haven't heard from him. I'll try him tomorrow. He doesn't have a phone."

"How trustworthy is this man, Wilber?" asked John.

"Hell, he is just an old 'redneck'. He grew up around the woods in Duval and St. Johns hunting and fishing. Did odd jobs for a living, even worked on our trucks for a spell. No more honest then he has to be. But he definitely knows the woods. Got no environmental degree but he knows what's there and what's not; be able to help us plan before we get the professionals out there."

"We all agreed," said Hayes, "we didn't want any surprises. We can deal with the odd gopher tortoise but anything like a panther, we are in deep trouble." Just then Hayes private phone rang. "Hold on guys, this may be important. Not too many people have this number."

"Hello? .... Yeah, tell me." Hayes listened for a minute, then said, "That's all? Ok, thank you," and hung up. "Well, that's unpleasant news. The dead guy's head was bashed in with a shovel; they found a gunnysack with gopher tortoise in it and a dead bear cub. They said the dead man was young and clean cut, but his pockets were empty."

"Was that the Sheriff?" asked John.

"No, but someone who knows, at least that much, nothing else. There has been a lid put on all information, a tight one. All findings will be kept within the task force only. If any information is to be given out, it will come from the Sheriff's office in St. Johns County."

"This won't stay quiet long," said Art. "Jones, the guy who works for me, will be telling someone. It will get out."

John had been watching Woods; finally he said, "What do you say, Wilber? You look kind of pensive, even a little green around the edges. Care to share with us?"

"What, what," said Woods, "no, nothing." He looked down and rubbed his face.

"Woods, could this be your man they found?" asked Art.

"No, my guy is older and hasn't shaved in a while. That's what I was thinking about."

"Well, it certainly doesn't look good, Wilber," said Art.

"What do you mean by that, look good for whom?" asked Wilber as he sat forward in his chair and glared at Art.

"Well, you're the only one who was going to send someone sneaking around out there. Maybe he was doing something he shouldn't have been."

Wilber rose out of his chair; John grabbed his arm and said, "Sit down, damn it, and Art, stop ragging him. Wilber, calm down. Art was only raising an obvious question. Could this have anything to do with your man?"

Wilber sat down and just shook his head and said, "Hell, I don't know. I hope not. Maybe it was just poachers had a falling out. Maybe the neighbors were putting gopher tortoise on the site so they could be found. Hell, they were the ones who asked to inspect the site. Maybe they seeded it."

"Not a bad suggestion, Wilber," said John, "I was thinking that myself."

"What do you mean, John? Do you really think the neighbors would put specimens on the site?"

"Oh, yeah, in a minute, especially those across Ranch road and the other road near there. They will do anything to stop this site location. They have even said as much. Why I heard they even put a picture of the Mayor up at the turkey shoot fundraiser they had last weekend, for people to shoot at. Oh, yes, these are not a bunch of innocents we have out there or in Ponte Vedra either."

"Are you going to call Sheriff Gray and suggest he look closer to home?" asked Hayes.

"No." Do you know him Hayes?"

"No, I only talked to him once. I called him to ask about this Dr. Paul; he was, shall we say, very protective of her."

"Why did you get that impression?"

"I asked him about her and if she could be, sort of encouraged, to drop this landfill opposition. He got huffy as hell. Flat out told me she couldn't be bought and better not be frightened by anyone. All but gave me a lecture on the subject. I really hit a sore spot with him."

"I would say! He is a real straight arrow. If you remember in the papers, he was involved with Paul last spring in a murder and a drug runner case. He has a lot of admiration for the lady I'm told. Better tread lightly in that area," instructed John.

"I wish I had known that before I called him. I should have called you first, but I didn't know you knew him."

"I'm not what you would call special friends with him but I have friends in the law enforcement business who know him well and he is well thought of by many people. He will run this case by the book no matter who is involved."

"You mean he won't be biased toward St. Johns County people?" asked Hayes with much skepticism.

"I didn't say he wouldn't have a bias, but he will be fair and careful. He also takes very good care of the Ponte Vedra people. During the TPC he will move mountains to be sure it comes off just right as far as traffic and law enforcement are concerned. I mean, hell man, that's his bread and butter."

Wilber asked, "How's his relationship with Sheriff Edwards? They friends?"

"Damn guys, I'm not an authority on Gray. But I would say, if Edwards didn't like him and trust him, no matter how much St. Johns County would be upset with him, he never would have given Gray control of a case that was in Duval."

Art said, "I've worked my way up to the new department chief position, but I've been in Duval a long time. I can tell you Edwards is as territorial as they come. He had to have more than one good reason to give this to Gray. I would also give out a piece of advice. If your source of information, Mr. Hayes, is in the police department and Edwards ever found out, that person will be toast no matter who he has as friends."

"You're serious; Edwards keeps this tight a control on information?"

"Yes sir, he hates leaks, and if Gray wants a lid on information coming out about this case, you can be sure Edwards will treat that as if he made the request himself," replied Moore.

All this time Wood had been quietly watching and listening and worrying. The more he heard, the more worried he became. I can't believe I'm being told I have two Sheriffs who are as pure as the driven snow. Or at least they have others believing they are. Just as bad, I guess. It seems that this bunch here are believers too. They are backing off applying any political pressure that might benefit us. What the hell am I going to do about this?

It's easy for this highfalutin' 'Mayor's aide' to talk about a problem as he sees it. Meaning a potential slap in the face for the Mayor if they lose this landfill site. It's a whole other thing for us. My personal reputation is on the line if this falls through, to say nothing of the increased cost another site miles away from the south side of Duval County will cost us. That's money, my money, and if we go public it will be stockholders' money. Well, I have one card in this deck! Let's see how they like it. I don't mind charging people more to haul garbage.

Hayes turned to Wood and said, "It seems the ball is in your court."

"What does that mean?" replied Woods.

"It is your man who you sent out to the site. You need to find out if he is involved in this death. If so, how?

"Wood was very composed and just looked at Hayes. "I volunteered to send a man out to the site to see whether we had an environmental problem. I did this on my own ticket. I have made an investment in this site. If it works, all of us benefit and we can make the cost of hauling garbage cheaper to the consumer by using this site. Hell, if it can't fly, we will just cooperate with you when you find another site. So don't be laying all this on my table."

"You forget, Mr. Woods, your contract with Duval comes up for renewal in another year. How high you raise the rates will be of considerable interest. I'm not threatening you, but remember, this site is of interest to all of us. So let us not forget our mutual interest and get together on what is going on. You check out your people, and we will take care of ours."

John and Art watched this interchange with interest. Finally John said, "Going after each other isn't going to help. We have an unforeseen event here. Why don't we all just calm down and each do our jobs.

"Wilber, find out about your man. Art, go about your business as usual. If you get more requests to see the site, refer them to me. Hayes, I'm sure you want to distance the Mayor as far as you can from this situation, that's your job. Why don't you have all calls about it referred to you? Keep the Mayor off the phone. I think we all need to keep in careful communication with each other, especially over the next few days."

They were all quiet; finally they all nodded in agreement. They stood up and after a few parting comments, they left Hayes' office. Hayes sat down and thought, what a bag of worms this has turned out to be. When the prospects of the south end of the Davis property came up, it looked like a win-win for everyone. It went through condemnation at a high price but that they expected. Then when Commissioner Lee from St. Johns County signed on, they knew it was a go.

There had been no controversy until they met with the Palm Valley Community Center people. Then it started and spread like a wild brush fire. All because of that damn Paul woman. The Sheriff was right, now it was way beyond her. She had stirred up the whole community, and they were not poor country people. Hell, half of the big business men in Jacksonville lived in Ponte Vedra. Now this murder. His job was clear, keep the Mayor out of it at all costs. That would be easy, the Mayor didn't even want an update.

Art was keeping his hands clean. John was being a mediator and above the fray. Woods, well that was an interesting situation. He would bear careful watching. If that guy he sent out is involved in this death; well, then anything can happen.

Where does that leave me?

Chapter Eight

Wednesday morning

It was seven in the morning. The Sheriff was on his first cup of coffee; he made it himself since his secretary wouldn't be in until eight. He had picked up his messages; one was from Detective Hold who said a man called about the truck about eleven p.m. Hold said he would be in just after seven to talk to the sheriff. Just then there was a knock. The Sheriff had left the door partly open; he looked up and Hold was standing in the doorway.

"Good morning, detective, I just got your message off the machine. Come on in."

"Good morning, Sir." Hold had a cup of coffee of his own in his hand. He sat down and put his cup on the edge of the Sheriff's desk. "I didn't call you last night because it wasn't a real positive identification. The caller was a man named Key, Bob Key, who lives out on Ranch Road. He said the truck sort of looked like one he saw a biologist from the Guana River State Park driving"

"How did he know that much?" Gray asked.

"He met him at a meeting of one of the Ponte Vedra opposition groups recently and he saw him get out of a truck like the one with New York plates on it."

"Did he say who else was at that Ponte Vedra meeting?"

" He said it was mainly the people from out around the CR 210 area but he didn't name anyone."

"He didn't by any chance mention Dr Paul did he?" Gray asked.

"Yes, Sir, he did, but in a roundabout way. When I asked if he remembered the guy's name he hesitated and said he only remembered his first name was David but if I called the Guana Park people they would know. At the meeting Dr Paul's name came up and the guy said he had met her or knew her or something like that."

"I see," nodded Gray. "What were they meeting about, did he say?"

"I asked him and he said they had contacted the Guana State Park people to see if they could get a biologist to come and look at the landfill site to see if there were any endangered species there. Apparently this guy was there visiting and checking the place out for a possible future job. He offered to go since he had some free time. The park biologist was delighted to have him go."

"Just like that, they let a possible new employee go off into the community?"

"He said he asked the same thing. The guy was between jobs and also a college friend of the Guana biologist," replied Hold.

"For someone who didn't know the guys last name he sure knows a lot about him."

"I sort of mentioned that and he said the guy told them all this at the meeting to explain who he was."

"Will he come in and identify him for us?" asked Gray.

"He said only if he had to and he didn't think he would be the best person to do that. He actually said why didn't we ask the Guana biologist. I'm afraid I had to agree with him, it would be a more positive identification."

"Yes, you're probably right. No fun looking at dead people. Go call the biologist and tell him what we have. Ask if it's possibly his friend. If so, will he come and see if he can identify him. First, call Rogers and see if he got a name off the truck license plates. That will give you a name to run by the biologist."

"Yes, Sir, I'll call Rogers now. He will be on his way into the office. We are meeting as a group at eight-thirty?"

"Yes, that's right, go ahead."

At eight o'clock, Major Brown stuck his head in the door and told the Sheriff the men were early. He had put them in the conference room. He said Hold had gotten the man's name from Rogers and had just finished talking to the Guana biologist. Hold said he would pick him up after the meeting and drive him up to Jacksonville. The sheriff told him fine, see if anyone needed water or coffee, he would be right there.

When he walked in the six men and Brown were all sitting around the table and quietly talking. "OK, gentlemen, let's start. Hold, you and Rogers go first."

Hold nodded to Rogers. "Yes, Sir, I called New York State. The car was registered to a David White with a Scarsdale, New York address. He is twenty-six years old, six foot tall, dark brown hair, and green eyes. No record or outstanding tickets. I called the Scarsdale Police Chief, told him about finding the truck and an unidentified body. He said the Whites were an old established family. The parents were alive and there were two daughters and two sons and David, the youngest, drove a truck like that. He said if we got a positive identification would we please let him know so he could be the one to tell the family. News like that over the phone was too shocking."

"Good work Rogers, let's make sure that we call this police chief before the man's name gets out to the press. Hold, you call me from the morgue as soon as you get an identification and I'll call him. Rogers, leave the chief's name and phone number with me. Is that all, Rogers?" Rogers nodded yes. "Ok, Detective Hold, it's your turn."

Hold repeated what he told the Sheriff earlier about the call he received the previous night." They asked him many of the same questions the Sheriff had.

Hold then told them about his recent conversation with the Guana biologist, whose name was Martin Stack. Stack said he went to undergraduate school with White. He then came down here, got the job at the Guana and was finishing his masters degree at the University of Florida. White went on to Harvard for his masters and had just finished work on his Ph.D. last year. He spent a year in Africa studying something to do with cats.

"Did he say where he was staying?" asked Major Brown.

"Yes, Sir, he said he was at a bed and breakfast in St. Augustine. I'll get the name and address from him when I pick him up."

"Call it into Rogers. Rogers you go to that bed and breakfast and see what you can find in his room. Continue, Hold."

"I asked him what he knew about the landfill site. He told me the same story that Smith told me last night. They had been contacted when David was in the office with him. He said he would go look if he wanted him to. He had the free time."

"What was he doing here and how long has he been here?" asked the Sheriff.

"He has been here about a week. He was traveling around to various universities and research centers to see where he wanted to settle. Apparently he was good and any university would love to have him. He liked Florida so he started here. I guess we'll find out more on the trip to Jacksonville."

"Ok, Detective Cook, you and your men are next."

"Let's start with Officer Port and the zoo," said Cook

"The bear cub had been killed with the shovel just like the man. The gopher tortoises were dead. We don't know why, or how, but they will call us. The plaster casts were of real interest to them. They were not unusual, they said. People will have them made to show prints in sand displays in zoos and museums. You know like a cat's tracks. They could resemble a Panther, at least enough to cause suspicion." reported Port.

Cook nodded at James. James had a large envelope with him. He poured out a set of photos on the table. He started to go over them one by one and handed them around. "These first ones are of the body. It is hard to tell if it had been moved but it must have been turned to empty the pockets. With jeans on it's hard to tell if the pockets were disturbed but there was nothing in them."

"Do we have an autopsy report?" asked the Sheriff.

"Yes," replied Cook, "I'll go over it when James finishes unless you want to stop now."

"No, go ahead, James."

"There were no areas on the body's clothes we could get prints off of but you see that shovel. Most of the handle is smudged and even looked to be wiped clean. But see, it has a long metal extension up from the end of the shovel itself and it almost looks new. We dusted the whole thing and down there we found one good hand- and fingerprint, but they are pointing the wrong way."

There was silence and then James continued, "I mean the little finger is at the bottom and the index finger towards the top opposite the thumb. I got to thinking about it and realized that if it was in a truck or somewhere with the blade facing you, that is how you would grab it to pull it out or lift it up."

"Damn, you're right," exclaimed Major Brown, "then you would put gloves on." He paused and continued, "Whoever hit him would just wipe it clean with whatever was handy, forgetting the metal end."

"Assuming the person who hit him is the same one who left the prints on the shovel," Cook said.

"Good point, Cook. We can't rule any scenario out this early," the Sheriff said.

James continued, "We ran the prints and will have a report later this morning. These others shots are of the ground. They were numbered and in order as we walked in; you can see they go right and then left around the body. I continued shooting to where we found the bear cub. As you can see, even with these blow ups, you can't tell much. I talked with Jones, the county worker, after he gave his statement. He said that there had been a lot of foot and even vehicle traffic all over the place the past weeks. I'm afraid, for the time being, these pictures are a bust."

"I agree, James. Good work. If and when we find out what happened, a second look may tell us more. Ok, Cook, let's hear the autopsy results."

"These are only the preliminary results and I had to twist Dr. Black's arm to get those. The skull had been severely fractured. He had massive internal bleeding and even with immediate care Dr. Black said he might not have made it. There was a white mark on his left wrist so it looks like he wore a watch at some point. There were no physical signs of a struggle. Dr. Black said we almost have to assume he was hit from the rear, by surprise, and with a lot of force. He said he would get the blood work and stomach contents tests to us as soon a he could. I gathered that Sheriff Edwards had spoken to him. He is being very cooperative."

"Good job, no surprises so far. I saw the TV coverage, you and Hold did a good job."

"Yes, Sir, we thought that if our jobs pan out we might try acting," replied Cook. "Hold's man, Rogers, did a great job keeping the traffic moving. He kept the gawkers away until we all left."

The sheriff smiled and said, "We have our work cut out for us today. Hold, you and Cook pick up that biologist and take him to the coroner's office for the identification. Play very good cops and get as much information from him about the man as you can. Also, find out just what the people who called them for help requested.

"As soon as you get the positive identification call me and I'll call the Scarsdale police chief. Hold, I'd like Cody, who is joining us, to start going door-to-door in the immediate area of highway 210, Ranch road and that other road that looks like a long driveway. Cook, I'd like one of your men to go with him." James raised his hand. "Is James ok with you Cook?" Cook nodded yes.

"I would like you to ask the usual. Did they see or hear anything that night, any people or cars? Then say something like 'Gosh that landfill site is awful close to you guys,' and see what you get. We need all the information we can get at this point. See if you can get a hint of who might suffer the most from this landfill. That won't be easy since they all will but you get the idea of where I'm going?"

"Yes, Sir Want us to split up or go together?"

"Go together and take good notes. Once we finish there and get the family notified, we will release his name and then you can start on the Ponte Vedra bunch. I'll get names for you there if you don't get them by accident today. Any questions?"

Cook said, "I sure would like to get the gossip out of the guys at the solid waste department."

Port stuck his hand up, "Detective Cook, I got on good with Jones, the county man, yesterday. He said he was going back to work in the office today. Why don't I go by and chat. I'd also like to ask his boss about possible vandalism to the markers and even the wells. Sort of ask if this mess will hold them back in the permitting and all. Maybe make a few minor derogatory remarks about activists." He looked at them and grinned from ear to ear.

Cook smiled and asked, "Do I catch a bit of fun there, Port?"

"No, Sir, you catch a lot of veiled hostility. Anyone who would kill a bear cub and mess with gopher tortoise really ticks me off. Worse, to kill a young man whose life is just getting started. I guess you could say I am real motivated to work on this case. They also will be more likely to open up to a local cop. If the grin fooled you, it sure will work on them."

Cook looked at the Sheriff, they both smiled. The Sheriff said, "I think that would be a good use of Port's time, detective."

"That about covers it. Major Brown, did I miss anything?" the Sheriff asked.

"No, only to remind everyone of two things. Whatever you find goes nowhere but here. I don't mean to insult you but you are all going to come under pressure from many sources to talk. There is a lot riding on this landfill, lots of money, lots of powerful people and politicians. "Second, if you think you have picked up anything, even of minor importance, call here if you can't reach Hold or Cook. Don't sleep on it, don't go off on your own to investigate first; the name of the game is communication. In these cases what happens in the first few days is the most important."

"I fully agree. This task force has a lid on it. Do not talk with even your fellow officers about the case, even if it's a brother. You all check with Brown and see what time we will meet this afternoon." When he finished speaking, the Sheriff pushed his chair back, motioned to Brown to follow him and left.

They sat down in the Sheriff's office. It was only a bit after nine. "Covered a lot in a hurry, Steve. I like the Jacksonville men; this task force will work well together. I'd like to ask Cook more about why Port is so angry."

"Yes, but you know, Jeff, any death bothers me. But when I heard who that guy might be and his background, it set my teeth on edge. So did the sight of that bear cub. I guess the young innocents bother me the most. For some reason, I think we may find that young man is going to turn out to be a really tragic victim. I think Port will be ok, we sure know he is motivated."

"I agree, we will see. Steve, the guy who called last night did mention Mary Paul. Are you going to call her or let her be one of Cody's visits?"

"No, I'll call her when we have a positive identification, later this afternoon. I was going to call her yesterday, about that TV interview, but the day got away from me. If this man is who we now think he is, he was not a poacher. So the big question is, what was he doing out there?"

Chapter Nine

Wednesday, early afternoon

"Mr. Hayes, the men are here for their appointment," said his secretary on the phone.

"Fine, send them in." He put the papers he was working on away and stood up as Wood, Moore and Smith came in. "Sit. Let's get started. Wood, have you found that guy you sent out to check the landfill? I didn't get his name."

"Bubba Skeet is his name, and no I haven't found him. We have the word out. We will find him," replied Wood.

"You better, and we better hope he isn't involved. Moore, did your man tell you anything today?"

"Nothing you don't already know. He and some of the others are a bit skittish about going out there alone to check the markers and the wells. I told them we would work in pairs for a week. There is a cop, part of the task force, around asking questions. He was talking to our man Jones, who was out there yesterday."

"Really," said Hayes. "Did he say anything of interest? What was he asking?"

"He asked a lot of questions about markers being moved; about wildlife, he and the guys were talking about hunting and the Davis property. I got the impression he wasn't too hot for the activists who were after us. He didn't seem to have a very high opinion of environmentalists in general."

"When was he there?"

"Right after lunch. Said they had him doing the scut work. He was asking me questions about the site and its advantages for a landfill. Then he started talking about how they found out the dead man was a biologist who was down here looking for a job. That he was helping out a friend, a fellow biologist from the Guana, who had been asked to help the Ponte Vedra people. Apparently he had met with them.'

"I'll bet that is the guy they got to look at the site for them. That's why the request to us for a site visit," said Smith.

"I thought there was a lid on this task force," said Wood.

"Yeah, so did I, so I just came out and asked him about that. He said they found out who he was and had notified his family in New York. It would be public knowledge before the day was over. He also said they had a call last night from one of the Palm Valley people who told them who the guy might be. They recognized the truck that the cops put on TV. So he said it wasn't as if he was talking about confidential information."

"Isn't that interesting," said Hayes. "Think we can develop him as a source of information? Did he mention any names from Palm Valley?"

"No. Not unless he shows up again. I asked him who these activists were?"

"He said, oh, you know, the ones on TV and in the newspaper. No names. You know, Mr. Hayes, this cop seems to be just a 'good-old-boy'. That's probably why they gave him the scut work," replied Moore

"It's that damn Paul woman. She's the only one on TV. I was having drinks with some of the large landowners in St. Johns and they said she was giving them hell on the Comprehensive Plan Advisory Committee. She needs someone to teach her a lesson. To teach her to mind her own business," said Wood with disgust.

Hayes eyed him with interest. Wouldn't I like to sic you on her, he thought? You might be just what we need to get her out of this. "How angry are they with her? I mean, have any of them confronted her and told her to mind her damn business?"

"Yeah, one of the farmers asked her why she was trying to destroy his children's inheritance. He suggested she stay home. She told him to take his suggestion to Commissioner Lee. That he was the one who appointed her to the committee. If he wanted her off he could ask her. There are a lot of unhappy campers in St. Johns. But I think they are more talk then action."

Smith was watching Hayes with great interest. I wonder what he is thinking. I hope he isn't stupid enough to go after Paul. He thought, I better step in here, "I think we better not be thinking of going after anyone. We have a murder on our hands. I suggest we just cool it and stay low. I am going to get ahold of the people who called me about a site visit and see when they want to view the site."

Hayes started to interrupt him as did Wood. "No, no, you two. We do not need anything at all stirred up right now. We need to all keep a very low profile. You too, Moore, don't be calling that cop. If he comes back and volunteers information, fine, but don't go asking." Moore nodded his head in agreement.

Wood said, "That sounds fine for you guys but I have a vested financial interest in this landfill site. I understand that tonight is the final big meeting of this committee and a lot of outsiders sit in. One of those landowners asked me to join them. So I'm going to go and sit in back and at least get a feel for this woman. You have problems with that Smith?"

Smith smiled and said, "No, I don't and I do understand your situation. I am merely suggesting caution. I spent time with Dr. Paul. She is nobody's dummy, and further, don't forget she is only one small part of the opposition now."

"Are you saying if for some reason she pulled out of the fight it wouldn't effect the others? I mean with their environmentalist dead, wouldn't this scare them off if she pulled out?" Hayes asked.

"Hayes, those are rich folks and their property values are at stake. No, they won't back off. They will just get madder. Trust me on that."

"Ok, Ok, just asking. If that's all, let's go keep our ears open." Hayes stood up indicating the meeting was over.

A little later that afternoon, Major Brown was entering Gray's office, "Afternoon, Steve. Did you talk to the Police Chief in Scarsdale?"

"Yes, I spoke with him right after Hold called me from the morgue. Hold told me Martin Stack from the Guana was really broken up. He and Cook would spend some time with him when they take him back. Cook said they would have the information on the finger prints by noon and would check out where that leads them. He also said Port had been waiting for them and had an investigative technique he wanted permission to use."

"Did they tell you what it was?"

"Yes, he wanted to drop some information on the Solid Waste manager when he went out there this afternoon. Like the stuff the guy called in about last night and who the guy was. All that will be public knowledge by the end of the day. He thinks if he sort of looks like a 'bubba blabbermouth' who might be useful to them, he might just find out something. I told Hold and Cook to go for it. Port, by the way, is no dummy. Cook told me Port is finishing his bachelor's in environmental science. Port wants to go into enforcement in the wildlife area with the State."

"That helps explain why he was angry about that bear and those tortoise."

"Police Chief Block was going out to talk to the White family. It appears they were all at the house. The mother was just home from the hospital; she had a fall while rock climbing with her daughters. Not serious, a minor concussion. He said someone would be in contact with me this afternoon. The men should be in soon so we can set up for tomorrow."

"Did you call Mary Paul?"

"Yes, she wasn't at the meeting they had with Mr. White. She had heard he was there and she was irate that he was killed. I asked if she knew him. She said she first met him at a reception she was at for some land acquisition groups, some years ago. It was held at Harvard and he was a graduate student who had been invited by someone from the Sierra Club. He was also the younger brother of a friend of hers. She hadn't talked to him since he has been here. He had called and left a message that he was in town, but they had not talked. She said it was a great tragedy, and her heart went out to his family."

"So, she didn't have any contact with him. It seems that there are several opposition groups, it is not one united operation," remarked Jeff.

"That is the message I got when I first talked to Mary about this after the mayor's aide called me. Mary said she is working with the Roundtable people to bring political pressure to bear on the Commission to fight the landfill; that there are a number of other groups doing various things. They have only met as a total group once, I think, or at the most twice."

"Sheriff, the men are here. Shall I tell them you will be in the conference room soon?" his secretary said from the door.

"Yes, that's fine, thank you," he said. He stood up and went to the conference room.

"Ok, Hold, you and Cook go first." Cook nodded to Hold to go first.

"We haven't learned much more from Martin Stark than what we told you. He was pretty broken up. Said it was his fault for letting David go meet with those people. He just told us what a great guy he was: honest, ethical, a great friend and a great environmentalist.

"When he heard about the landfill and saw its location related to Ponte Vedra, he agreed it was not a good location. He also thought it was too close to Durbin Creek and the Davis property that was essentially preservation land. That's why he went. He thought if they could find anything, he would help them. Also, his services were free. Stark said he would be available too if they needed anything else. He also said he would go out there on his free time himself if it would help." He stopped talking and nodded to Cook.

Cook said, "That's essentially it. We went back to Jacksonville and they had the prints finished. They were of a man named Bubba Skeet. He had a record of petty theft and the game wardens had tagged him for hunting out of season and with his truck lights on back roads at night. He had a spotlight and he would blind the deer and shoot, a regular lowlife.

"He did odd jobs and worked for short periods for whoever would have him. One of the guys in the office said he remembered him when they had picked him up on suspicion of car theft. He only served short periods in city jail. He had no address. He might live in one of those shacks off Pine Island road or across US1 and the railroad tracks. We can go check and see if anyone out there knows him."

"Would he be out there poaching gopher tortoise?" ask Brown.

"He could have been but that doesn't really make sense. I mean, Sir, there are better things to eat and there is no market for them," Hold said. "But he could have been removing them from the site."

"Cook, you call the City and find out if there have been any requests for site inspections from the Ponte Vedra people. If so, when did they get the first request and what have they done about it. You guys set up a time line on all of this. Then you take Rogers and go work Pine Island and any other of those back country roads. See if he has a truck registered to him."

"We already made that request, about the truck. Should know by morning," replied Cook.

"Ok, Port, how did your acting debut go today?"

"Not good or bad. After I gave the print results to Detective Cook, I went to the Solid Waste Department office and just talked to Jones, the county worker who found the guy. The department head was there and I leaked the information Cook gave me. He was real friendly. I thought I would ask him if I could tour the site with him or one of his men and look at those moved markers. Tell him you told me to; bitch and complain about scut work."

The Sheriff sat and thought a while and nodded as if he was having a conversation with himself. "Yes, you do that. Do it tomorrow. But I want you in plainclothes; I'll call the Davis's and ask for you to tour Dee Dot Ranch. I will also call the McCormick's and ask for you to tour their ranch site. Tell them we are trying to get a feel for this whole thing. Act as you think best with each group. This is a fishing exhibition. We don't know much yet so we need to scout anything at all out."

"Yes, Sir, I'll call the solid waste people first thing in morning. Suggest you want this done right now. That will give you time to get the other stuff set up. That ok with you?"

The sheriff nodded and turned to Rogers and James. "Your turn."

"We went to all the homes. There are about twelve or thirteen out there and there was someone home at most of them. They all were really bitter about the landfill. It will ruin their homes and any possibility of ever selling, if they should ever want to. They are all active in fighting it at the schools and wherever they have to. They are planning to picket it with the Nease High School kids one of the coming Saturdays," reported Cody. He turned to James and nodded.

"One of the places we went to was a ranch with a number of horses. While Cody asked questions of the woman who owned it, I sort of walked down to the barn. There was a guy cleaning out the stalls. I leaned on one of the half doors and introduced myself. I said we were just trying to get a feel for the neighborhood after the dead guy was found across the street. The guy just sort of nodded then he quit working and walked over and lit a cigarette.

"We were both quiet for a bit. I was looking at the other horses in the stalls. I asked if he lived out there. He said he bunked in a cabin by the house. I asked if he was from Florida. He said no, Texas, said he was a drifter. Then he said this was about the best job he ever had. I asked why. He said he earned enough to get a johnboat and a small motor. He ate good, fished good and the work wasn't too hard.

"I asked if this landfill mattered to him. He shook his head and said nope, but it sure as hell would kill some of the others out here. I said, unless they were planning to move, it would only be the odor. He looked at me as if I smelled bad myself. Then he said some folks had investments in land that they would want to sell some day. The landfill would make that a bad investment. The owners would be lucky to get out what they put in to it. That's about all, but Sheriff, I think we need to check out who owns what and who loses the most."

"Jeff, we have some original thinkers here. Remind me to tell Sheriff Edwards what a great job his men are doing. Ok, Rogers, what did you find at the bed and breakfast?"

"They were very kind. I got a search warrant before I went but I asked them to go with me anyhow. Sheriff, he had very little: couple of pair of jeans, two pair of slacks, a blazer, underclothes and a bathing suit; a toothbrush, shaving stuff, some road maps and an address book. Oh and a pair of loafers and a checkbook with a few thousand dollar balance.

He had paid for two weeks. He had been there one. They said he was quiet and polite. That was all."

"Thank you, Rogers. Now for tomorrow."

Just then his secretary knocked and came in, "Chief Block on the phone for you, Sir."

"You all wait, I'll be right back." He left the room and in his office he picked up the phone and said "Yes, Chief Block, Gray here."

"Sheriff, I'm sorry I'm so late but it was rather a shock for the family. The oldest son Mark, was there and after the initial shock wore off, he asked me to wait while he made some phone calls. About an hour later he asked if I would call you and tell you he would be in Florida before noon tomorrow. He wants to see his brother right after he arrives, and make arrangements for his removal to New York."

"I'll make arrangements to have him picked up at the Jacksonville airport. When will his plane arrive and what is the flight number?"

"He won't arrive at the Jacksonville airport, he will be flying into the St. Augustine airport in a private jet. He said he isn't sure of the time but it would be before noon and could he call you with the exact time in the morning?"

Oh, thought Steve, no, this will not be easy, not at all. "That will be just fine, Chief. I will have my men pick him up and take him to Jacksonville. Is there anything else we can do?"

"No, Sheriff Gray, just find the bastards who did this. This was a fine young man and a wonderful family. He will be missed by all who knew him. If there is a way you can keep me somewhat abreast of the investigation, I would appreciate it and the family would be indebted to you."

"Chief, I'll be glad to do that. We have very little to work with now but we are turning over all the rocks and what even looks like they might be rocks. We will do our very best."

"Yes, Sheriff Gray, I know you will. The family and I have had only the very best reports on your department. Thank you for your courtesy." He hung up.

Heard the best of us. How did he even know we existed, questioned Gray to himself as he walked back to the conference room.

He sat down and said, "Well, the brother will be here before noon. I want you, Detective Cook and Rogers to pick him up at the airport," he paused and added, "the St. Augustine airport."

"They will call me when they have an arrival time. You and Rogers can start on the Pine Island road search. When the call comes, you come to the office and get my car. Then take him to the morgue. From there, take him wherever else he may want to go. If you need help with reservations or whatever, call me. When you are done, call. If you haven't finished on Pine Island road, you and Rogers can go back and finish after you return my car.

"Hold, I want you to began talking to all the Ponte Vedra people involved in opposition to the landfill. You take Cody and James with you. Let them work together. Start out with the people who met with Mr. White. I asked Dr. Paul for some names today. The list is with my secretary. You know to go easy up there. Keep on the subject. We are trying to find out as much as we can about who killed this fine young man. That's it. We have busy days ahead."

Jeff followed Steve into his office. Steve sat at his desk and looked up at Jeff and said, "Jeff, call the property appraiser's office tomorrow and find out who owns the land up there around CR 210. See if you can find out if the owners live on the land. If not, where do they live and how long have they owned it? I'm looking for someone who may have bought land for resale. If you call, they will be much more cooperative then if one of the men calls."

"Good, I can do that easily. You looked kind of funny when you came back in after talking to the Chief. Something wrong?"

"The Chief said he had heard good things about us. No, he did not say from whom. He just said that and hung up."

Chapter Ten

Wednesday, early evening

Mary was in her car on the way to, what she hoped would be, the last major meeting of the Comprehensive Planning Advisory Committee. The committee had been warned this would be a long meeting, and they wanted everyone to be there at six in the evening. They were told they hoped to be done by eleven.

Mary was thinking about David White's death. She did not know him well, but she did know his older brother who was also a friend of Jeffery's. Arthur also knew the family. She hadn't tried to call any of them before she left home. She didn't know who had been informed yet, and she didn't want to be the one bringing such sad news. She would call them tomorrow, but chances were one of them would call her first.

Who could have done such a thing and why? she kept asking herself over and over. It made no sense at all. Finally, putting these thoughts out of her mind, she began to gather herself for the coming meeting. She had requested that the group go over the question of densities in Palm Valley again. She also had a few 'mays' she wanted changed to 'shoulds' in the text. That would be an uphill fight. She felt sure a couple of the other citizen members had some changes of their own.

The committee had to operate under the Florida Sunshine laws. This meant that no member could ever talk to another member outside the meeting about anything that might come to a vote. They had to discuss everything during the meeting. There were serious penalties if you were caught violating the sunshine laws. The operative point here seemed to be 'if caught'. She and the other citizen members were very careful but she wasn't so sure that some of the landowners and developer's attorneys were as careful.

She remembered one time, at an early meeting, an attorney and a large landowner were trying to make a point, almost copying each other word for word. One of the farmers, of all people, asked them why they didn't take notes of their meeting before they came so they could get it together. First silence hit, then the two men just tripped over themselves with denials. This was followed by a brief lecture, by the county attorney, on the sunshine rules. Mary smiled in remembrance of it. Cliff was still on the committee and he and Mary just grinned at each other.

She pulled into the lot. She was a bit early, but there were already a lot of cars. She had heard there would be observers. She walked in, took her seat at the long conference room table and noticed there were a lot of extra chairs around the sides of the room. The chairman greeted her and smiled. Mary looked at the chairs and said, "Expecting company, I see."

He grimaced and replied, "Afraid so." He ran a fairly tight meeting but Mary thought he leaned a bit too much toward the developer's positions.

Soon, everyone had arrived and the meeting started. They dealt with the land map first. This map designated the underlying use of the land. If it were residential, it stated what category it was. That is, would it allow one residence per acre, or two or multi family? A block of attorneys, landowners and developers continued to push to have all the land on County Road 210 West made Residential 2. A number of members objected and stated their reasons. This all fell on deaf ears. Mary, of course, chimed in with opposition to the land use; it made no difference.

They moved on to Palm Valley and Mary spoke first about Roscoe Boulevard. There was some opposition, but she got one residence per acre. She then moved on to Palm Valley Road. She used as her argument the narrow winding road, the lack of right of way to widen the road and the large oak hammocks that would be destroyed with higher densities. It was a battle royal. She lost. The largest landowner on the road had his attorney on the committee. It was so bad he said, "If Mary liked the damn trees so much why didn't she just buy the land herself." Mary managed to bite her tongue and, half smiling to herself, thinking maybe I just will. The press was just scribbling away, making sure they wrote every one of the lawyer's offensive remarks down.

They moved on to the farmers. The fight there was bitter. All the land was in agriculture, and the committee had said you could only build one home per forty acres. If the landowner wanted to sell he would need a major Comprehensive Plan change. Mary stayed pretty much out of that. The Department of Community Affairs in Tallahassee covered most of those rules. The farmers were told the DCA was trying to control growth. The farmers said yes, on our backs. The developers stayed out of the fight; wanting to develop way out in farm country wasn't yet on their horizon.

Finally, they came to the actual written text of the Plan. The Plan was divided into several areas: Land Use, Transportation, Housing, Infrastructure (which covered things like sewer and water), Conservation (which covered the coast, forest, wetlands etc.), Recreation and Open Space and finally Intergovernmental Coordination.

Each of these areas had goals and objectives and policies stating how these goals and objectives would be met. It was here that the words like shall, will, must, may etc. came in. What was important was that the policies stated clearly what the county would do and expect others to do.

The developers had gotten so much of what they wanted on the land maps that they thought they could just railroad all this stuff through in as watered down a fashion as possible. They hit a brick wall on most all the areas. They wanted language that said maybe they would do something. Most of the other members said no. It would read 'should' and in most cases 'shall'.

It got so bad that the chairman asked just what is going on here. Mary looked at him and said, "Why, Mr. Chairman, it is a very simple matter of the developers and their attorneys wanting to gut the whole plan. They got what they wanted with the land map. Now they are trying to do the same with the text. If they are successful, I for one will resign this committee and go public in writing with what has occurred and name names. The taxpayers in St. Johns County have a right to know who is ripping them off." That got the press's attention.

She had no sooner finished talking than five more members said they would sign on with whatever Dr. Paul wrote. Many of the observers loudly cheered and applauded. The chairman called for a ten-minute break so everyone could cool down. The attorneys, developers and large landowners go off in a corner. The Chairman reminded the members they were still under the sunshine laws and to be careful what they said. The press was having a ball. Moving here and there hoping they could overhear some juicy bits.

They went back to work. They went over the major areas of conflict and the advisors finally said the DCA wouldn't sit still for watered down language. The attorneys begrudgingly went along. At the break it had apparently been made clear what a huge public relation fiasco the developers would face if they kept on pushing. They also had the maps they wanted; to hell with the text, they would worry about that later.

At last the major work was completed. There was a lot of editorial work to do before it was a completed product. That product would be brought to the first hearing before the Planning and Zoning Board and then to the Board of County Commissioners. The committee members would each be sent a copy. They were asked to call the staff if they found major errors.

It was almost eleven o'clock. The committee had spent many weeks on this Plan and they were ready to go home. Several of the members asked Mary if she would go have a drink with them. She politely refused and said another day. She had a long drive home and had a long day ahead of her tomorrow. She stood around and chatted awhile with them and then went to her car and started for home, going north on US 1.

She thought, what a long day. I'm surely glad that's over. It didn't come out a well as she would have liked, but it could have been worse. She knew if they ended up with the two residences per acre on Palm Valley road that the oak hammocks would be all but destroyed. There must be a way to work with the developers to encourage them to save the bigger trees. If Paul Fletcher in the Marsh Landing development could, why couldn't they? Just make the lots bigger and charge more for them. After all, the whole Ponte Vedra/Palm Valley area was already expensive; we were not talking affordable housing.

"Damn" she said, "how annoying." The car behind her had his bright lights on. She reached up and flipped her rear view mirror to get the lights out of her eyes. She hated having to flip the mirror. It distorted the view behind her. "Calm down, Mary" she said out loud to herself. She thought, it won't be but a couple more minutes and you can turn on to 210, no traffic there. She made the turn and it seemed the car had gone ahead. She flipped the mirror back to normal. Just after the first curve she could see down the straight away there wasn't a car in sight, front or back.

She stretched her back and rolled her shoulders and thought, I am tired and tight. She had slowed down to forty-five miles per hour. It was not unusual to see deer crossing the road. Hitting one would not be healthy for the deer or her or the car. "No rush girl," she said.

All of a sudden the car was filled with light. A car was almost on her bumper. It had appeared from nowhere. She almost slammed on the brakes, in reflex. She pulled her foot back. She was even afraid to tap the brake to make the red lights come on because the car was so close to her rear end. The lights seemed to be kind of high, not like a car, more like a truck. Maybe that's why they lit up her interior so much. Where did he come from? Must have had his lights off.

She was annoyed beyond belief as well a becoming a bit anxious. Now what do I do? Is this just a stupid practical joker? A drunk? She sped up a bit and so did the car or truck or whatever it was behind her. "Not good, girl," she said out loud; "you got trouble." She thought it might be a good idea to get the gun out from under the seat and beside her, just in case. She slowed the car down to forty and reached down for the gun. It was a Taurus short-barreled thirty-eight revolver. Not a big gun but big enough for her. The Sheriff had suggested she get a revolver rather then an automatic.

She felt better with the gun. Now, how to keep from getting hit by this guy. She wanted to floor it, in fact, her whole instinct was to run, but something made her keep a lid on it. Maybe the gun had calmed her down enough to think things through. "Slow it down, Mary" she said, maybe he will get bored and go away.

The lights moved back, the truck pulled out into the next lane and then up level with her. Yes it was a truck. It began to crowd closer to her. Mary thought she should roll the window down and shoot, but just trying to stay on the road took all her skill and two hands. She was just ready to hit the brakes when the truck swerved into her; she pulled the car to the right and hit the shoulder and the brakes simultaneously. She aimed for the ditch, it was shallow, only a little dip, she could feel the rear end skid on the grass and let up on the brakes. Think snow and ice and Minnesota; don't lose it now, she thought.

The truck raced by, narrowly missing her. He was almost off the shoulder but not in the ditch. Mary came to a stop by a fence. She was shaking; she had the brake to the floor and a death grip on the steering wheel. She was aware the car was stopped. She could see the truck heading away, and then his tail lights went out. She forced herself to let go of the steering wheel and took her foot off the brake. The motor was still running. She put the car in reverse and slowly moved the car back a few feet. She was not stuck; it was dry dirt, not mud or sand.

She looked up and lights were coming at her. Oh no, not again. She knew she could not drive away. She rolled down the window and ducked down in the seat. Soon, she heard a voice call "Mary, Mary, Dr. Paul, are you ok?"

She slowly looked up and a car, not a truck, was stopped on the shoulder across the road from her.

"Mary, it's Roy, Roy Gunther. Are you ok?" He walked slowly up to the car.

Mary looked up and said "Roy, oh, thank God it's you." She opened the door and turned to get out.

He reached the door and repeated, "Mary, are you ok? What happened?" He saw the gun in her hand and stopped. Mary, with great effort in trying to control the shaking in her voice, told him what happened. He listened and said he saw a truck that had shut its lights off as it shot past him. He told her he had a two way radio in his car and he would call the sheriff's deputies. He quickly went to his car and called. When he returned, Mary had pulled herself together. She told him what had happened; by the time she had finished a sheriff's car had pulled up, coming from Ponte Vedra.

Mary repeated her story to the officer. He asked whether she recognized the truck, she said no, she hardly saw it. She asked if she could go home, she was tired. Roy offered to drive her. She said no. The sheriff's deputy said he would follow her home and go in and be sure she was ok. She agreed. She drove the car back onto the road and went home. The deputy came in and looked around and said he would sit by the entrance for a while. Mary thanked him and after he left she let the dogs out for a quick run.

She then let them in and checked the answering machine. There was a call from Clara who said if she did not call before midnight she would call the cops. It was just now midnight. She called Clara and before she could say a word Clara said, "Where have you been so late?"

Thank God, thought Mary, some things never change. She told Clara they finished late. She paused and Clara picked up on that immediately. "Yes and then what happened?"

Mary told her a shortened version of her trip home. "You called the cops?"

"No, Mr. Gunther did. The deputy came and followed me home, came in and checked things out and said he would sit by the gate for a while."

"Good Lord, Mary, do you have any idea who it might have been? Who's after you? You could have been killed."

"No, Clara. It could have just been a drunk."

"Yeah, right out of nowhere. Forget it, Mary, that was no mysterious stranger getting his kicks off. What happened down there tonight?"

Mary gave her a very brief summary and ended by saying, "I'm so tired Clara, all I want to do is go to bed (after a drink, of course.)"

"Yes, I guess you are. Yes, go to bed. I'll call you tomorrow if you are sure you will be ok, or Ed and I can come spend the night."

"No, I'm fine but thank you anyhow."

Clara hung up and thought, yeah, you're fine. A death at the landfill site and you get run off the road. That's not what I call fine. Ed called out from the bedroom and asked if Mary were ok and was Clara coming to bed? She yelled back she would be right in after she made a phone call.

Chapter Eleven

Thursday morning

Sheriff Gray walked into the office at seven. He made his coffee, laughing to himself that this early bird stuff has to stop. He checked the overnight incident reports and there on the top was the flagged report on Dr. Paul being run off the road on 210 about eleven o'clock last night. He called the night supervisor, who was still in, and asked for a full report. He asked whether the deputy who answered the call was still available and if so have him call me.

The young deputy called him minutes later. He gave the Sheriff the story just as Dr. Paul had given it to him. He ended by saying he followed her home, checked the property out and hung around the gates for half an hour. No, she did not say the color of the truck. Said it was a dark color. After a few more words the Sheriff thanked the deputy and hung up.

He thought, well, that's good; she had her gun with her. That Mr. Gunther is damn lucky she didn't shoot him when he walked up to her car. He did have to smile. It took both him and her friend Jeffery to browbeat her into carrying that gun whenever she was out at night or in the boat. He looked at his watch. It was seven-thirty. He would call her now; Mary was an early riser. Just then Major Brown walked into the office. He told him about Mary Paul and that he was just going to call her. He asked him to stay and he put on the speakerphone.

"Hello," said Mary.

"Good morning Mary, how are you this fine day... alive I hear?" asked Sheriff Gray.

"Yes, I do seem to be alive, it is a nice day and my coffee is good, too. How can I help you and do you realize what time it is?"

"Yes, I do. Major Brown is here with me and we have you on the speakerphone. I just read the report from the deputy who saw you last night. Do you have any suspicions about who could have been in that truck?" asked Gray.

"No, I told Clara last night it just may have been a drunk and she blasted me as being naive," replied Mary.

"Yes, I can see her doing that. Tell me what happened after you left the meeting?" Mary told him about the car on US1 that was behind her and its bright lights. That it disappeared after she turned on to 210, at least the lights did. Then after she drove past the curves into the straightaway the lights suddenly appeared right on top of her. "Damn fool" said Gray, "he's lucky you didn't hit the brakes."

"Yes, I thought that myself. You know, Steve, I came within a hair of doing just that. I mean it was dark and then the whole car just lit up. If I had not had those damn lights on me all the way up US1, I might have hit the brakes. It was close."

"Mary, this is Major Brown, did you speed up at all after he came up to you?"

"Good morning Jeff. Yes, I did and he sped up too. But I wasn't going fast to start with, about forty-five. Don't laugh, I know I go a lot faster but it was dark and that road at night has deer crossing it, I never drive it fast at night."

"Then what did you do?" asked Brown.

"I slowed down to about thirty-five. I was tired and was afraid to try to outrace him. I also figured he would get bored and take off if I went slowly. Well he did, sort of, get bored, but not before running me into the ditch. I also had to slow down to get my gun from under the seat. When he pulled up next to me, I couldn't hang onto the car and get the window down, or I would have shot him." Steve and Jeff looked at each other and smiled. "To tell you the truth, I didn't know whether I was more scared or angry. I just held on and when I hit the grass and the rear ended started to skid, the car was all I could handle."

"Your lucky you didn't flip over," said Steve.

"That is the virtue of that big station wagon. It sits low to the ground and it's wide. I was also lucky there are not many big trees out there, just that farm fence.

"Mary, I don't suppose you remember seeing a truck like that in the lot at the meeting?"

"No, but it was the last big night so there were a lot of observers, farmers and others. There were trucks and cars both. I pooh-poohed the idea that it was deliberate last night when I was talking to Clara, but I am not foolish... it very well could have been. I was a little annoying last night at the meeting."

"You, annoying? Say it isn't true?" quipped Steve.

"Well, they pushed me a bit," she said sounding a bit defensive.

"Mary, could it have been someone from the landfill group?" asked Jeff.

There was quiet from Mary for a few seconds. "Jeff, I don't know, I was going to say no, but in fact it could have been anyone. If they think I am the major opposition then, yes, they could have done it to scare me off. That is pretty drastic, but Steve, you said yourself these are desperate people."

"Yes, well you take care until this mess is over. I'll drop a little word in Sheriff Edwards ear so he can warn the Jacksonville people away from you. It may not work, but knowing the cops are watching can make a difference," said Steve.

"Thank you, Steve. How is the investigation going?"

"It's in the early stages. Do you remember Officer Cody?"

"Yes, a lovely young man."

"He and another officer are going to be talking to all the opposition people in Ponte Vedra/ Palm Valley today and over the next couple of days. We have several areas we are looking into for information. Lots of leg work matched with luck. Have to go now, call if you need us."

"Thank you and goodbye to you too, Jeff."

Mary had no sooner hung the phone up when it rang again. Hum, seems everyone is up early, Mary muttered, as she reached for the phone. It wasn't that she was a late riser, just the opposite, but she really wasn't up to facing the world in person or on the phone until after breakfast. "Hello."

"Mary, it's Arthur. You have heard about young David?"

"Yes, I was going to call you today. I didn't want to call until I was sure the family had been officially notified. Then, last night I was at a late meeting. I was sick. The family must be devastated."

"That's putting it mildly. He was the baby brother and the apple of everyone's eye. But I'm calling you now to tell you we will land in St. Augustine just before noon. Jeffery is coming with Mark. I'm picking them both up at a little airport outside Scarsdale in a few minutes."

"Can I pick you up in St. Augustine?"

"Thank you, but arrangements have been made with Sheriff Gray. He is having one of his men and a Jacksonville detective pick them up. They will take them to the morgue so Mark can see his brother and begin arrangements to fly him home. Jeffery will go with him. The officers will bring them back to Ponte Vedra. I made reservations for all of us at the Ponte Vedra Club."

"Good, what can I do to help?" asked Mary.

"I will be renting a car at the airport and the pilots will get their own after they get the plane settled. I would like to stop for a quick lunch with you if that's ok?" Arthur asked.

"Of course. Will a roast beef sandwich be ok?"

"That will be fine, with pickles and a cold beer. Also, I want you to let Jeffery stay with you while he is here," Arthur said a bit hesitantly.

"Well, of course, Jeffery is always welcome here, I love his company. But I sense there is something else going on here, come on, what's on your mind?"

"Mary, I am not happy about David's murder and you know I am always concerned about you."

"Really, I know that, but why is it I don't quite believe you are shooting straight with me?"

"Mary, you damn near were killed last night..."

"What! Killed? No way, I just got run off the road into a ditch, and how come you know... Oh, I see. You and Clara are secret phone buddies. How that happened I'll never know, you've never even met her. Did dear Jeffery, set that up?"

"Yes, he did, at my request. We knew you would persist in an activist role and wouldn't call if things became rocky. So we set up an early warning system. Look, we are about to land; we can discuss this some more, if you insist, over lunch. I'll call when I leave St. Augustine. Bye now."

The phone went dead and Mary sat there listening to a dial tone. So that was clever, hang up so you don't have to discuss this outrage with me now. Thinking I'll forget by lunch. She stood up muttering to herself as she prepared the guest room for Jeffery. She made a shopping list for lunch and for meals later.

She had another cup of coffee. That made three this morning; she rarely had more then two. Well, this was a difficult morning. Why is that, Mary dear? Did you have a bad night? Hum? Not in denial are you dear? She remembered back to the spring when Jeffery and others saved her life. She sat quietly for a while and thought, why is it so hard for you to accept help and concern from your friends? You had better leave this alone. It also might demonstrate a bit of graciousness on your part if you just never mention it again. Arthur has enough on his mind without you being a pain. With that she picked up her keys and left for the store.

Sheriff Gray asked his secretary to get Sheriff Edwards on the phone for him. A few minutes later she rang and said 'they are getting him now, Sheriff.' He picked up his phone and waited. "Good morning, Steve, I was hoping I would hear from you today."

"Morning, Sam. I would have called you sooner but I haven't had much to report. Detective Cook told me he was giving you a day-to-day."

"Yes, he told me last night that he and Officer Rogers were picking up the brother at St. Augustine airport some time later this morning. Using your official car as well. Are these VIP's coming in?"

"Easier to take them to your morgue in my car then putting them in the back of a patrol car. Small courtesy, that's all."

"Uh huh, I can understand that. This David White who was killed doesn't seem to be a run of the mill long haired environmentalist, does he?"

"No, I'm afraid he wasn't. He had a Ph.D. from Harvard and some interesting friends. This is going to need a lot of careful handling. I've told Rogers and Cook to take as long as they need and then to deliver them wherever they want to go. But that's not what I'm calling about.

I need some help."

"Anything at all, Steve."

The Sheriff told him what happened to Dr. Paul last night on her way home from the Comprehensive Plan meeting. "We don't know who ran her off the road. It could have been a crazy drunk jokester, someone who got angry with her at the meeting, or someone from the landfill group trying to scare her off."

"I don't buy the crazy drunk option. Sounds to me as if they were driving too carefully to be drunk. I don't suppose she recognized the truck from the meeting did she?"

"No, she said there were a lot of observers at the meeting and that she might have annoyed a few people."

Edwards laughed, "I don't suppose you have seen today's Times Union. There was a quick blurb about last night's meeting and Dr. Paul's threat to go public if the developers continued to try to gut the Plan."

"Really? No, I missed that, but I'm sure there will be something in our local paper as well. There have been hot and heavy issues throughout this whole process. I guess that, now they are near finishing, it will really heat up. However, we don't know who it was. In order to cover all bases, what are the chances that you can drop some kind of remark to warn your locals away from her?"

Edwards was quiet for a few moments. "That's a real good possibility. The Mayor's aide, Hayes, seems desperate to get information. Someone in my office leaked information from the first day to him. Nothing important and I'm working on finding out who did it. Cook told me about Port's work, I was going to ask you whether I could use him to drop a crumb here and there. If he gets to be known by certain people as a blabber mouth it might work for me.

"I have a meeting later this morning over in city hall. The Mayor and his aides will be there. I can ask for a minute afterward to update both Hayes and the Mayor on the landfill killing. I can give them stuff like the brother being in today and we are combing the neighborhoods, that kind of stuff. Then why don't I just flat out tell them about Paul last night? Suggest that someone from our landfill group is under heavy suspicion of trying to scare her off. I can add I don't know whom they are looking at but that the authorities insist they will find out one way or the other."

"Damn, Sam, that's a little heavy, but it might work. It will stir things up. I don't know what we are going to find. There are no clear patterns, the incident with Paul may not be related at all or it may be a smokescreen. I'm hoping we can get them to back off Paul, that's if it's the landfill people. We can't be sure of anything right now."

"I know how you feel, I will sound very sympathetic to the city's position and ain't it awful. Between Port and me, we can see what happens when we stir the pot."

The men chatted a bit more and Steve hung up. Steve thought, I'd bet Edwards is going to enjoy his little scene with Hayes and the Mayor.

When Edwards hung up it wasn't enjoyment that he was feeling. In fact he was angry. He knew Hayes was corrupting one of his men. Not that his man wasn't at fault. But men like Hayes could turn the heads of weak men. Letting them think they were important to the Mayor's office. That someday they would be rewarded for their confidences. Yes, he, Port and Cook would close off this leak to Hayes one way or the other. He had one or two men whom he suspected.

Chapter Twelve

Thursday

The Sheriff called Detective Cook and Officer Rogers. He told them the plane would be arriving at eleven thirty at St. Augustine airport. He would leave the keys to his official car at the desk. He told them to take the brother wherever he wanted to go after they finished at the morgue.

A short time later Cook and Rogers picked up the car; Cook said, "You drive, Rogers. Better if you mess up the sheriff's car than me. Anyhow, I'm not authorized to drive St. Johns County cars." They both laughed and Rogers said, "When we get back, let's check out that store up there on US1. See whether they know Bubba and have they seen him recently."

"Good idea. So far, people say, yeah, they know him, but no, they haven't seen him. Then they want to know why we are looking for him. I'm getting the distinct impression if they did see him they wouldn't tell us a thing."

"Well, a lot of those people we saw so far are all country people and they stick together pretty much. Probably don't have much time for cops, reminds them of revenuers. You know those woods and that whole countryside way up into Palm Valley was filled with moonshine stills. I wouldn't be surprised if there were still some around."

They pulled the car into the parking area near a small round-shaped terminal building. They walked into the center of a round room which had a small console like counter desk. They asked the man at the desk where they would meet the people who were flying in on a plane from up north. The man said he was just told that a small jet was ready to land now. It would pull up just outside if it were dropping someone off. He had been told on the radio that it would need parking and would stay a few days. They could go outside and watch if they wanted.

Cook and Rogers walked out onto a small porch area that led onto the tarmac. A plane was landing now, way up at the north end of the runway. There were a number of single engine planes of varying size parked to the right. "Nice looking planes," said Cook, "I've always wanted to learn to fly but no money."

Rogers said, "It is probably like a boat. The maintenance is what eats you up. Damn, look at that, that's no piper cub. That's has two engines and I bet it can carry a few people. Look, it has two pilots."

The man who was at the desk walked out the door. "That's a beauty, isn't it? They were here last spring in that thing. The man who owns it often flies in. He rents a car and goes up to Ponte Vedra."

"What kind of plane is it?" asked Rogers.

"Its a Gulfstream jet."

"How many people can it hold?"

"Depends on how it's configured inside. You can have conference space, sleeping space or combinations," he replied.

"Bet they are expensive," said Cook.

"Two, three million," replied the man.

"How far can you fly in one?"

"Cross-country, maybe three thousand miles, they usually have two pilots; this one has." The three of them watched the plane pull to a stop not far from them.

After the door opened, a tall well-built man about thirty with sun-bleached hair stepped down the small stairs. He was well over six-foot, six three at least, handsome in a rugged fashion. Just behind him came another man the same size, age and build as the first one. He had dark brown hair and more refined features but was equally good looking. He was followed by a third tall man, also over six feet. He was pushing sixty with gray hair and was neatly dressed. He looked like the Wall Street men you see in magazines.

The men walked directly toward them and Rogers burst out, "Well, how about that!"

He walked forward, putting his hand out to the first man who got off the plane, and said, "Jeffery, how are you, I didn't expect to see you here."

Jeffery stopped and shook Rogers hand. Rogers said, "This is Detective Cook from the Duval County police force; Cook, this is Jeffery Stone." The men shook hands.

Jeffery turned and said, "Detective Cook, Officer Rogers, this is Mark White, David White's brother, and Arthur Steel. If you can wait just a moment, Mark and I will be right with you." Rogers and Cook told them to take their time; they would meet them inside. They turned and walked back inside the small terminal building.

Cook said, "I didn't know you knew them."

Rogers replied, "I know Stone but I had no idea he would be here."

"Who's the tall distinguished man, what's his name, Steel, with them?"

"I saw him once last spring with Stone and Dr. Paul. I think that's his plane. You know the Sheriff said Paul knew the dead man. That must be the connection," replied Rogers.

Before Cook could ask any more questions, Jeffery, Mark and Arthur came walking through the door. Jeffery asked where they would leave them after they finished in the city. Cook told him they would take them wherever they wanted to go. He asked where they would be staying and was told at the Ponte Vedra Club. Cook said they would take them there when they finished.

Jeffery turned to Arthur and told him he would see him at the Club. Arthur said fine, he had a luncheon appointment. Reservations had been made for all of them already at the club. He would see them there later.

On the way to Jacksonville Jeffery asked what they could tell them about David's death. Rogers and Cook had asked the Sheriff how much they could tell the brother. Sheriff Gray said to tell him most anything he wanted to know. If they weren't sure, just tell them, the Sheriff would fill him in the next day when he met with him. So they related the history of the landfill site, the locals' opposition to it and David's offer to look at the site for the locals after they had called at the Guana. He was there that day, with his friend the Guana biologist, and offered to go for him.

Jeffery asked what they found at the site. Cook related what they found including the gunnysack of gopher tortoise, molds of cat paws and the dead bear cub. His brother spoke for the first time. "David loved animals. He would never have killed any. You don't think he did that do you?"

"No, Sir, we don't think that at all," replied Cook. "We honestly don't know what to think. We found some prints on the shovel left at the site, on the lower end on the metal. A reversed hand, as if you grabbed it with the metal end toward you to haul it out of a truck. The handle had been wiped clean or came clean with gloves on when using it. We ran the prints and have a name. We are looking for the man now."

Jeffery said, "You said found some molds of cat paws. What's that about?'

"Again, I'm sorry to say we have no idea."

The brother started to say something; Jeffery put his hand on his knee and he changed the subject. "Had David seen or talked to Dr. Paul since he's been here?" he asked Rogers.

"The Sheriff said Dr. Paul told him Mr. White had called and left a message but they hadn't connected. She wasn't at the meeting he had with some of the opposition people."

"I want to talk to Mary, Jeffery," said Mark.

"I think she is having dinner with us tonight, Mark." They all talked some more, and Mark told them a bit about his brother when Cook asked him about his education, what he had been doing in Africa, what he was doing in Florida, what kind of man he had been. By then they had arrived at the morgue.

Noon

Arthur pulled up to Mary's gates, and she was there, leaning on them. He smiled and she opened the gates for him. He drove in; she closed the gates and got in the car, giving him a kiss on the cheek. He smiled and said, "Aha, all is forgiven I hope?"

"Nothing to forgive," replied Mary.

Ok, thought Arthur, never question gifts. "Mary, I love this place. It's so simple and clean. Lots of trees, no expanses of lovely lawn to keep up and the trees make it look three or four times larger."

"Yes, people ask why my place seems so much larger than others? It's the trees, they disguise the actual size. "

Arthur replied, "But it's more, it's the house. It's an old mid-century board-and-batten with most of it on the second floor. The open-beam ceilings and large rooms also make it look bigger than it is."

"True, Arthur, but if I were an air conditioning addict I would go nuts here. When the temperature hits the nineties and I turn the air-conditioner on at full blast, it may cool the house down to the mid-eighties. Thank God for the trees and that I hate air conditioning. I just never have guests for dinner in the summer."

"Also, you don't wear clothes in summer."

"Arthur, I do so wear clothes, they're called bathing suits."

"Mary, the man married to a woman like you would never go broke putting clothes on your back."

"Not quite true; I buy value. Good, well tailored clothes don't lose value quickly. So you pay more, you wear it longer. If it is good, cut well and you keep your weight, a little goes a long way. Anyhow, I hate to shop... end of subject."

A short time later they sat on the porch over sandwiches, cold beer and pickles. Arthur had his coat and tie off. He rolled up his sleeves and actually looked as though he belonged. Mary smiled, looking at him and thought, I wonder how many people really see you like this, a charming, relaxed, lovely man without a care in the world.

He thought, how I love it here. No wonder Mary took early retirement and left New York. She loves the quiet and the solitude, I know she gets lonely but she will be the first one to tell you, better to be lonely here in God's Country than in the mean streets of a city. She has known those only too well. While they mused in silence, they both made the roast beef disappear.

Finally Mary asked, "Would you like a cup of coffee?"

"No, but hot tea would be fine."

"Yes, that's sounds like a great idea." Mary put the dishes in the kitchen and made two cups of tea. They sat and sipped and watched Mary's birds on the feeders.

Finally Arthur said, "The family is just devastated; there are just no words that will comfort. Mark is hanging on for dear life. If it weren't so necessary for him to support his mother, father and sisters, he would collapse. Duty sometimes comes to our rescue when we least expect it; it is all that's keeping him together."

"Hum, I have seen that. It's strange what comes to our rescue. What can I do, Arthur?"

"Can you call the Sheriff and get an appointment for him to see us all in the morning? Also, can you ask him to please not withhold information from Mark?"

"Yes. Why don't I call him now, then you won't worry"

"Please."

Mary came back to the porch after her call. "He said nine-thirty and he had nothing to withhold. I also told him you, Jeffery and I would be with Mark. He will also make arrangements for Mark to pick up David's belongings from the bed and breakfast he was staying at in St. Augustine. We can do that after we leave the Sheriff. Funny, he did not react to Jeffery's name or you at all. Maybe the jet gave him a large clue, or he is just unflappable."

"Good, now let's get on to other matters. There is some land I would like us to look at in southern Louisiana some time in the next few weeks. The weather is good at this time of year. It came to my attention last summer but it wasn't a good time to go. It will be lovely there now and the land is not going anywhere."

"That sounds fine, I need to check when the Comp. Plan will come before the Planning and Zoning Board and the County Commission. I won't miss that after all the time we've put into getting it done. This land, is it a single owner?"

"Yes, an older man and his wife. No kids and no other family he cares about. He made his money in oil in Oklahoma, hates what he sees happening to the best parts of his country."

"How many acres?"

"You won't believe this, over 200,000, some on the Mississippi and then west and north. Hasn't been timbered, has a nice lake and he has managed it well with controlled burns."

"Wow, almost pristine. Why does he want to sell?" asked Mary.

"He and his wife are getting older and he is afraid if anything happens to them it will go to some of the timber and development people who hound him to sell. So he wants to take care of that now."

"Where will he go if he sells?"

"That's the only catch. He will go nowhere. He wants us to make a contract that will allow him and his wife lifetime tenancy. He has enough money to afford nurses and caretakers around the clock should either he or his wife or both become bed ridden. No nursing home at all."

Mary smiled from ear to ear and just shook her head. "Think he is my long lost twin?"

Arthur laughed and said, "My first thought. They have a large home on the property, on the lake and hired help to manage the house and the land. They want us to stay with them when we come out. I had one of our people check the situation out. He said the place is lovely and about as private as you could want. The man and his wife have friends and are social, not hermits."

"Did he mention price?" asked Mary

"No, he said he would rather talk about that in person with us. He said he had aerials, as well as surveys, all recently done. Apparently, he will do a video will when we are there with his lawyer and an old friend of his who is a State Supreme Court Judge in attendance. He has made it very clear to me that no one should be able to question his action."

"Property must be valuable; sounds as though he has really been bothered to sell."

"He has but he is well known in the State and no one is going to pressure him too much. He thinks they will just wait until he dies off and then go after it. According to him, if he sells quietly now, the hounds will go seek other prey."

"We have vetted him very well, Mary, and he is a power in the state and also in Oklahoma. If we buy, he said there would be no future trouble. What saddens me is I was going to ask young David to come with us and stay there a while and do a more in-depth assessment of future management needs for us."

"Maybe Mark and Jeffery will come out with us. I would also like us to rent a small helicopter so we can see all the acreage and even what surrounds it," Mary said.

"The owner has a 'copter at his house as well as horses and three wheelers. Travel will be no problem. Now I need to go. I enjoyed lunch. This evening... drinks at six and dinner at six-thirty?" Arthur asked.

"Sounds fine, Arthur," said Mary, and she walked down to the car with him.

Chapter Thirteen

Thursday, late afternoon

Sheriff Gray was quietly working in his office when there was a knock at the door. "Your secretary must have stepped out," said Major Brown. "The men are all in the conference room."

Gray said, "Half a minute, let me finish this letter." Gray thought, I hate this paperwork. I've delegated a lot of it but that still leaves too much. But I can't complain, at least not out loud. I wanted this job.

When he walked into the conference room Cook and Rogers were telling the others about the jet the men from New York had arrived in that morning. They stopped talking when he came through the door. He had caught part of the conversation. "Nice, huh?" he asked.

"It was nice. I would love to see the inside of it," said Rogers.

"Why don't you ask that Stone guy if he will show it to you?" said Cook "You seemed to know him."

"It's not his, it belongs to the older man, Steel. Anyhow, I would feel foolish asking," said Rogers, looking sheepishly at the Sheriff.

"Ok, let's get started. Since we are on the men you picked up this morning, how about you and Cook starting," said Gray.

Cook nodded to Rogers to go ahead. "The man Jeffrey, who we met last spring and who knows Dr. Paul, was with the victim's brother, Mark White. They were with Dr. Paul's friend Arthur Steel, whose plane it seemed to be. On the way to Jacksonville, the brother made it abundantly clear that his brother David would not be poaching gopher tortoise or killing a bear cub or engaging in any unethical behavior. The brother was very upset and having trouble holding himself together.

"When Detective Cook asked him to tell us about his brother and what he had been doing the past few years it was the same information we had already heard. Jeffery Stone did make it clear that David White was a gentle young man, who would volunteer his services to help but that he would go by the book. If he, in fact, found evidence of endangered species on the site, you can bet it existed. If he did not, he would also state that clearly." Rogers finished and nodded to Cook.

"We arrived at the morgue and it was bad, like it always is. We left him and Stone alone with the body for a while. After he pulled himself together he asked about David's belongings that we found on him. We told him we found nothing, not even the truck keys. We did find an extra set at the place he had been staying.

"We asked Mark if his brother carried anything special or wore a watch. He said he wore an old watch of Mark's, one his grandfather had given him as a young boy when he was diving. It was a Rolex diving watch. David had coveted it since he was a kid. Mark said he gave it to David when he graduated from high school and won admission to Harvard. He said even if it was a Rolex there were better diving watches on the market now but David treasured that one.

"He said he also carried a small gold pocket knife that his mother had given him. He said David was never without them. He said the pocket knife had two blades; the smaller had his initials on it. You could easily miss them since hardly anyone would open that small blade. His mother had them put there since David would never tolerate them on the outside. He didn't discover them until a year later when he had a reason to use the small blade. He said David just grinned and never said a word to his mother.

"On the way to the beach he was fairly quiet. He talked a bit to Stone about their plans when they got to the Ponte Vedra Club. He thanked us for help and said he didn't mean to take his grief out on us. That's about it Sheriff. He seems like a good man who is just overwhelmed at the moment."

The Sheriff, Brown and the others had sat quietly through the reports of both men. There were no questions. "Ok, did you find anything out about the missing Bubba Skeet today?"

Cook replied, "We went to that store up on US 1 after we dropped the men off. The woman behind the counter said she had seen him on Tuesday morning. He bought a case of beer and some cans of spam, beans, bread and smokes. He didn't live around there but a lot of the folks back in the woods knew him and hunted and fished with him. She said she didn't see what he was driving."

He looked at Rogers who said, "We didn't have any luck with the people we talked to on Pine Island Road and on the road to the west. Some didn't own up to knowing him and the others hadn't seen him. I had the feeling that cooperating with the police wasn't something they did too often. There are some old families on 20 Mile Road, off 210. I thought we might just try them in the morning, if you want?"

"No, Rogers, I had Port include them in his travels today since he was going to cover the McCormick land and they are on the same road. I want you to go with these people into St. Augustine early in the morning. They are going to pick up the brother's belongings before they come back here. I told Dr. Paul you would meet them in the library parking lot about eight in the morning. You can hook up with Cook later in the morning and finish with anything you guys haven't covered.

"Detective Cook... Sheriff Edwards wants an early morning conference with both you and Port, at about eight I think he said. He also said he would have the information for you if the Mayor's people are granting landfill site visits to the opposition. Port can then head for the landfill area, and you can meet Rogers when you are finished. Port, did you find anything today?"

"Yes, Mr. McCormick is a very angry man who knows his property is going to be devalued with the landfill. It's right on top of his ranch. That is beautiful country, Sheriff, and he is a nice fellow. He is doing everything he can, legally, to defeat this site. He has some handsome horses and great pasture. I didn't see anything that could be called endangered species.

"When I left, I went to the homes on 20 Mile Road and asked about Bubba Skeet. You know, one of our deputies lives out there. His wife was home and she said she'd heard of him but didn't know him. There was one old man who knew him but hadn't seen him in a while. He wanted to know what Bubba stole this time. I missed a couple up by CR 210; no one was home. Shouldn't take long to cover the landfill tomorrow. Did you get the Dee Dot appointment for Monday?"

"Yes, you can go after our morning conference. I have a number for you to call. Ok, Detective Hold, what have you, James and Cody discovered in your interviews?"

"Well, for starters, they are not reluctant to talk to any of us. In fact, we had a hard time stopping them. Those in Old Ponte Vedra had us meet them at the Club. There were four of them, who I gathered are key Ponte Vedra Community Association members. We talked to them first as a group and they gave us a full history of the landfill fight. We then each took them separately to see whether they had more to say. One of the men told us about what happened at the 'turkey shoot' and about the talk of getting casts of panther paws and planting prints. He said none of the other Ponte Vedra men were with him. He gave us the name of the man in Sawgrass and the other two men with him and suggested we talk with them."

"The general story from all these people was about the same. The plans they were making, the politics, the marches, all of it. We split up and called the three men who were at the 'turkey shoot'. We each took one. The names they mentioned were some of the people James said he and Rogers had talked to out on Ranch Road. The other names were people on our list plus a few we didn't have. They were all consistent with the story," he stopped and looked at James and Cody.

"Yes," said Cody, " almost word for word. Even to the point about how they had shut up when they thought they might have said too much about the cat's paw prints. One of the men said they had told Dr. Paul about the story after the Roundtable meeting. How she just shook her head in regret that they would act that way."

"Sheriff," said James, "I had the fellow from the Players Club. He is one smart man. He was at the meeting when David White met with part of the group. He said that calling the Guana staff was really an initiative of the Ranch Road people. He also said that Mr. White was very pleasant and listened more than he talked. He did tell them his background and what he was doing in Florida.

"He said White made it clear they needed permission to visit the site. He told them if they didn't get permission, whatever they found would be seriously questioned and of no good to them. Needless to say, he said, he wasn't about to get arrested for trespass. He said he left the meeting but some of them stayed to talk with White. He gave us a few more names of people who were there that we didn't have."

Hold said, " I have a few local duties tomorrow but we have divided the names up and Cody and James think it would be better if they did them together like Rogers and James did on Ranch Road. I want to check out a few local bars in the valley."

"Good, I know this is slow tedious work. We don't have much to go on but something will turn up I'm sure. Keep good notes. We will need to cross check all the names with all we hear. A couple of names may pop to the surface."

"Major Brown, did you get the land ownership records?" asked the Sheriff.

"Yes, I would like to suggest we use the large white board on the wall to start a series of lists and see how they match up. I have been sitting here listening to the men's reports, and I hear duplications of names, some who were at meetings and some who live in one place or another. Now I am going to add more names of property owners. I would like to see how all these people relate to certain situations."

"What categories would you suggest Major?" asked the Sheriff.

"Cody, will you write for me? Let's start with the people who we know were at the meeting with Mr. White. We know they met him, at least once. The second category should be all the people you are currently interviewing. Then we should have one for the people who live near the site, on 20 Mile Road or Ranch Road or on the side roads or drive ways. Then, the people who own land near the site and finally, off to the side, the names of those who will benefit from the landfill. That gives us five lists. It has been bothering me that we have so many people that somehow touch on this thing."

"Good point. Before you all go today give a copy of your lists to my secretary and I will have her set the board up. Also, as you add names over the next few days, update right away with Martha. Ok, Jeff, go ahead."

"On 20 Mile Road we don't have any major landowners, just people who either own their homes or are renters, mainly of trailers. That is with the exception of the McCormicks, who use 20 Mile to get to their ranch. Across 210, on Ranch Road, some of those places are two and three or more acres in size. The larger ones have been there a while. Most of the homes are medium in size and some are trailers. I have a map here with the properties identified and labeled. I put down when they were bought. It seems a pretty stable community. On the side road west of Ranch you can see there are a couple of properties. Again, the home prices are modest.

"West of Ranch Road on 210 is a parcel that is owned by an old man and his wife. They have a trailer and once had some horses. The land has been cleared; it was pasture. The land is for sale, and they say someone has an option on it and wants to resell it to another man. A person in the Appraiser's office overheard us talking and dropped by to tell us that."

"Jeff, can you go back to the man who told you that and find out who has the option?" asked the Sheriff.

"I sure can. I'm sorry I didn't think to do it at the time.

"You will just love this next one. There is a nice house on about sixteen acres next to this one on the west. Lou Ritter just bought it."

"Wasn't he the Mayor of Jacksonville back in the sixties?" asked the Sheriff.

"That's him. He is a big time lobbyist over in Tallahassee," replied Brown.

"Do the people in Jacksonville know he bought that land?"

"Well, Sheriff, if they don't, they will in the near future. They say he knew the possibility of a landfill there and bought it anyhow. Then just down the road the next big piece is more of the McCormick property."

"Detective Cook, do the Jacksonville people have any idea of who owns land there?"

"Sir, it seems like something my old mother used to tell me that they have forgotten: 'Son, always do your homework.' I'll just bet they didn't."

"That's most of it, there are still other pieces but these are the major ones. I'll give the list to Martha," said Brown.

"Ok, gentlemen, that's it. You all know what you are going to do tomorrow. We will set up a brief meeting at the end of the day to plan the weekend. Major Brown, will you come to my office for a minute?" Sheriff Gray said and walked to his office.

They both sat down and Gray said, "Jeff, do you think Mary Paul knows this about Lou Ritter?"

"I wouldn't think so; he was before her time. But he is a power. He certainly will shake things up in Tallahassee."

"You're sure this will eventually go to the cabinet to decide?"

"Yes, when two counties are involved and especially if St. John's gets involved fighting it legally, it will go to the top. Are you going to tell her about Ritter?"

"No, she will find out soon enough. There do seem to be a lot of people involved, all doing something different. We need to focus on this murder and your idea of a board list is good. Jeff, I want to add a section off to the side on incidents. Like the cat paw casts and Mary's almost accident, the turkey shoot and other oddities. Even stick the Comp. Plan meeting in there."

"Good idea, how about the Mayor's aide calling you?"

"Yes, that too. Also, I would like you to be here in the morning when Mary, Stone and Steel come in with the brother. I am not going to withhold any information. I am going to be very honest about not knowing anything at all so far except for that Skeet's fingerprints. You agree?"

"I do, we have worked with Stone before and he has lots of official friends. He should be ok and maybe a help."

Chapter Fourteen

Thursday evening

Mary parked her car at the club. She got out and looked up at the sky. Oh, how nice, a clear evening and a moon. I love these three men I'm coming to meet. I just wish the circumstances were more pleasant. Well, chin up old girl - you know grief will fade with time. She walked into the Surf Club where Jeffery was waiting for her inside the door. She smiled at him and he hugged her and kissed her cheek.

"The others have gone on up to the Sea Foam room. I think Arthur is mulling over the wine list. It takes him a while."

"You mean I don't order the house Merlot tonight?' Mary asked with a smile.

"Afraid not, dear. Not when he is paying. How are you Mary?"

"I'm fine Jeffery, just fine, but the question is, how is Mark?"

"He's better this evening. He took a long walk on the beach alone. He was gone about three hours. Arthur got in nine holes of golf with the pilots and me; thank God, we are all addicted to the same sport. You know, Mark is very religious; he says he needed to talk with the Lord awhile and would be ok alone. He even half-grinned and said he talks out loud to his Lord and he hoped he wouldn't be arrested as a crazy on Ponte Vedra Beach. He went to the pool when he got back and swam some laps."

As they stepped out of the elevator, Mary said, "I couldn't have prescribed a better treatment and dinner with us will be ok as well. Are their rooms ok?"

"Yes, right on the beach. I have my bags at the entrance downstairs, so I will leave with you after dinner if that is ok?" asked Jeffery.

"You know my home is yours whenever you want."

Arthur and Mark stood as they approached the table by the window. Mary walked up to Mark and just put her arms around him and hugged him tightly and looked up and kissed his cheek.

She then looked in his eyes and nodded and said, "I'm glad you're here. I just wish the circumstances were different."

Mark smiled and squeezed her shoulder and said, "Yes, I do too, but your company makes it more bearable."

"I'm glad. Good evening, Arthur, I understand you have been perusing the wine list. Did you find anything acceptable?" She sat as Jeffery held her chair.

"Yes, my dear. The club has a good cellar. As a matter of fact, Mark picked the wine."

"Well, not quite, Mary, he gave me a choice of three. But after spending time with him, I have learned that the first one he mentions is really the one he prefers."

Mary laughed, "I'm glad someone else caught on to him."

"Yes," said Arthur, "But you always make an effort after you learned my tricks and then found out I was switching them around, on you."

"I have had so many bottles of wine with you that unless a really new one appeared it is not hard to pick your choice out. Anyhow, you would never let us force a bad or even just average wine on you."

They chatted a bit about Jeffery's latest adventures and Mark's final work on the land they had purchased last spring. Mark was a lawyer and an excellent biologist. He combined both fields to inspect land purchases for preservation and help design preservation plans. He worked at Arthur's office in Chicago as well as at a home office in Connecticut where he could be near his family. But he traveled so much he always said the world was his home. He was even known to have helped Jeffery on some of his secret adventures. He asked Jeffery how the project in the islands early last spring had turned out. They discussed that for a bit.

They ordered dinner, steak for Mary and fish for the men. The conversation during dinner continued in a light vein. When they were through Mark asked, "What time will we see the Sheriff in the morning?"

Mary replied, "I made a 9:30 appointment but said we would meet one of his deputies at the St. Augustine Library parking lot at

8:00 so we can get David's belongings from the bed-and-breakfast where he was been staying. I also called David's friend, Mr. Stack, the biologist at the Guana. He left word with the Sheriff that he would like to see you if possible. I told him I would tell you and, if you could, you would stop by later in the day. He said he would be there all day; to stop anytime before five."

"Good, I was going to ask whether we could see him before I left. Mary, Arthur told me about your being run off the road on Wednesday. Do you have any idea if that was related to David's death?"

"That is the same question the Sheriff asked me. To be honest, I don't know. At first, I was brushing it off as a drunk but that's probably not true. There was something very deliberate and even careful about the whole thing."

Arthur was watching her very carefully. Well, he thought, so you are finally realizing that this is a serious business. Mary could be very stubborn when it came to other's fears about her, sometimes to the point of damn foolish behavior. Not that he thought she was foolish, she was very careful with others. It was probably because she had lived by herself all her life that self-reliance was now ingrained. She had led a very active, some might say an adventurous, life but she would say no, it was just an average life.

She seemed to be a bit more thoughtful these last few years. He knew she quit waterskiing and diving and wasn't as much into horses as she used to be. He had asked her about it once and she said she noticed he had quit a few of his old activities as well. She had asked him what that said about him? He had replied that it means he was getting older and wiser and not as well coordinated. She had agreed that she was coming to that assessment about herself.

"Mary," Arthur said, "I was reading the local papers today. A couple of things caught my eye. That meeting you were at last night, they said a man told you if you cared so much for the damn trees on Palm Valley Road you should buy the land."

"Yes, I do recall someone said that."

"What did you reply?" asked Arthur. "The paper didn't say."

Mary looked down; just then the waiter came and took the plates. They all ordered after-dinner drinks; Mary had a B&B, the men had Drambuie. When the waiter left, Arthur said, "Well, what did you say?"

Mary actually grinned broadly, "Do you really want to know? Not what I said, which was nothing 'cause I was biting my lip too hard, but what I was thinking of saying?"

"I would," said Jeffery and even Mark was grinning.

"I said to myself, maybe I just will." Mary looked at them shyly. "I was so irritated that for a minute I was afraid I had said it out loud."

"You can, you know," said Arthur.

"Oh, no, Arthur I would never do that."

"Why not?" asked Mark.

She looked at the three men who were watching her intently. Do they really think I would do such a frivolous thing? Something in her expression must have warned Arthur because he said, "Mary, I do not think you would ever engage in buying land or anything else off the top of your head or out of spite. I meant that you know you can do whatever you like."

"That is not true Arthur. None of us can do whatever we like. We all have responsibilities and the more we have, the more responsible we must be. Anyhow, I do not want to own the land but I do want it developed in a manner that will save as many of those large oak trees as possible. There is a man developing Marsh Landing, and he is making an effort to save the big trees and making money on the land doing it. I decided to put my efforts into working with the developers to influence them to do better."

"Will you be successful?" asked Jeffery.

Mary smiled, "There is a small chance, maybe. If it becomes clear it is better to do a good job than to have the community calling you names in the press, they will listen. I'll try."

"What's that land on Palm Valley Road like Mary?" asked Mark.

"It was all a large oak hammock, never developed. But now they want to cut it up for development. It is not a just a question of loss of habitat for the animals and the resulting intraspecies competition. It's also the wanton and unnecessary destruction of those oaks that bugs me. The thought of saying 'the hell with you, I'll just buy it,' is satisfying but not wise or prudent."

"Let's get onto what else I read in the local paper. They said you made some kind of remark that, if the developers continued to try to gut the Comp. Plan, you would go public and name names. Is that accurate Mary?" asked Arthur with his eyebrows raised.

"It is and I would."

"Good for you," Arthur said.

"What? You approve? Say I'm not imagining this," said Mary.

"No you are not, of course I approve. I do not expect you to sit back and let developers, or anyone else, destroy a beautiful county like St. John's. Anyhow, they also said about five other committee members said they would sign on to whatever you said. That's good, there is safety in numbers," Arthur replied.

"Then Arthur, you don't think it was the developers who tried to run Mary off the road?" asked Jeffery.

"It could've been but it also could've been someone else who might've been using that as an opportunity to cloud the landfill issue," said Arthur.

"Really," said Mark. "If so, that puts a different slant on it, doesn't it."

"What do you mean, Mark?" Mary asked.

"Well, I get the impression no one knows anything, and everyone is somehow involved in this landfill site. A lot of people opposing it and a lot supporting it... mass confusion. If it becomes a big enough mess maybe someone thinks the landfill people will go away." Everyone was silent; they all looked as if they were really thinking about what Mark said. "Does that sound too far out?" he asked.

"No, Mark, it does not," replied Jeffery. "Are you suggesting David's death might have been unplanned or an accident?"

"Maybe not an accident but something that happened sort of spur-of-the-moment. I mean, hasn't anyone asked himself what he was doing out there? It seems he was there either at dusk or even after dark. Was he with someone? Jeffery, there are a lot of unanswered questions, and I want to put those to the Sheriff tomorrow. I know my brother would not engage in any illegal behavior. The Sheriff doesn't know that so he can't come from that premise and therefore eliminate other possibilities and concentrate on that alone. He still has to assume he might have been doing something illegal."

"If he has to leave that possibility open then it blocks out any single minded search for another answer. That's what you are saying, isn't it?" asked Jeffery.

"Yes, exactly. Jeffery, will you stay and dig into this from that frame of mind?"

"I told you I would stay and I fully agree with you about David. I am also concerned about Mary. If you are correct then whoever is involved might be capable of anything. Especially if this was not planned and even if it was."

"Mary, do you think the Sheriff will let Jeffery help?" asked Mark.

"We will find out tomorrow. We will go and see him and you ask all the questions you can and let's see. He has met Jeffery under interesting conditions that may lead him toward letting him help. He will probably understand if he doesn't, Jeffrey will be around anyhow. Better that old saying 'better the camel in the tent peeing out than outside peeing in'."

"I don't think 'pee' was the word they used Mary," Arthur said with a smile.

"Yes, I know but I didn't want to damage these young impressionable ears at the table."

"Arthur, did you ask Mary about that land in Louisiana?" asked Jeffery.

Mary interrupted, "Yes, he did at lunch today; it sounds fine. I need to check on the dates the Comp. Plan will come up; then I will be ready, sometime in the next few weeks. Mark did you look into this land at all?"

"Yes, I did and it does look good. We will know better when you and Arthur go and talk directly with the people."

"If you can get away will you come with us?"

"It will depend on how mother will be holding up. I'll let Arthur know."

"It's getting on and Mary, you need to get Jeffery settled for the night. We can pick you guys up in the morning. I don't think we will need two cars. Will 7:15 give us enough time?"

"If we leave then it should. The library is just at the end of A1A over the river. So Arthur, thank you for an excellent dinner. We all eat at my home tomorrow night," Mary said as she got up and kissed Mark and Arthur good night.

They all walked Mary and Jeffery with his luggage out to Mary's car. She gave Jeffery the keys and waved goodbye. Mary turned in the seat to Jeffery and asked, "You remember the way?"

"I do. How did Mark look to you Mary?"

"Sad and determined. Also, as if he is making a real effort to hold it together."

"He is. He is concerned about his mother. David was her baby, well, he was everyone's baby, even Mark's, truth be told. It is a family that loves well and strongly."

"Jeffery, those kinds of families manage to handle these kind of tragedies. They will all be so concerned with each other that there will be a lot of support to go around. They won't let Mark bear this all by himself when he gets home. Don't they have an uncle who is a priest and very close to the family?"

"Yes, and Arthur will be there. He is an old friend of the family. As much as I would like to be there, Mark made it clear today that he wants me here to find who killed David. Then when he heard about your near car accident, he was even more insistent that I stay. He is very fond of you."

"And I of him. We are very lucky to have him. Here we are, I'll get the gates."

"'Where are the dogs?"

"You remember, I lock them up at night; they will be all over you soon enough."

Chapter Fifteen

Friday morning

When Arthur arrived at Mary's, she and Jeffery were waiting at the gates, the dogs sitting behind them. Arthur got out and said "Jeffery, do you mind driving?"

"Not at all." Arthur held the back door for Mary and when they pulled out Mary said "Jeffery, take A1A. The Library is just a ways over the bridge and it's a pretty drive." As they drove down Palm Valley Road Mark asked, "Are these the trees you were talking about?"

"Yes, the whole area was one large oak hammock. Can you imagine how beautiful it would be if they built large homesites among the trees?"

"Yes, and can you imagine how much they would be worth? Most developers don't realize that every tree you cut down reduces the price of the land," said Mark.

"Some do but by the time the rest wake up the trees will be gone," Mary said.

They rode and chatted. Mark remarked on the houses and the beaches. He told them he had not been to this area before. Jeffery told him he must come back and go fishing with Mary, that the Intracoastal was a great place to fish. Mary told Arthur he would have to come and fish as well. He said he was just waiting for an invitation. When he said that, Mary just looked at him.

Jeffery and Mark just smiled at each other.

They pulled into the Library parking lot. Jeffery got out and walked over to Rogers' police car. Rogers told him to just follow him. The bed and breakfast was on Saragossa Street, a quiet neighborhood. The owner was expecting them.

When they walked up the steps of the bed and breakfast, the owner took Mary and Mark up to the room. She first gave coffee to Arthur, Jeffery and Rogers at a table on the porch. She had explained to Mark that she put David's clothes on the bed so he could see what was there. Then she would pack them for him. Mark went through the clothes quickly and looked at Mary and remarked that David traveled lightly. He was choking up. Mary told him and the owner to go downstairs, she would do the packing; it wasn't much.

When she joined them on the porch the owner was telling them about David's stay. How he walked around St. Augustine and what a pleasure he was for the short time he had been there. She said he was paid up through the weekend and she would give Mark a refund. Mark refused it and said she had been gracious and helpful, that David would have left a tip anyhow. They said goodbye, got in the car and headed off to the Sheriff's office, following Rogers' car.

The Sheriff's secretary, Martha, greeted them. She said Sheriff Gray was expecting them and she showed them into his office. The Sheriff walked around his desk as Major Brown came in the door. Mary introduced the men; after shaking hands they all sat around the Sheriff's desk.

"Mr. White, Sheriff Edwards in Jacksonville called a few minutes ago and said your brother's body will be released early tomorrow morning and delivered to the St. Augustine airport as you requested. Did everything go all right for you this morning?"

Mary said, "Thank you Steve, Officer Rogers was very helpful. Would you and Major Brown go over the case, as you see it, for Mark?"

"Of course." He began with the discovery of the body by the Jacksonville County employee. He told how Sheriff Edwards called them to the scene right away. He described what they found. Jeffery slowly raised his hand, "Yes, Mr. Stone."

"I'm sorry to interrupt Sheriff. I hope you don't mind if we ask questions as you go?"

"No, not at all. Be easier that way. I'm sorry I didn't think to tell you to feel free to stop me at anytime."

"Were there any signs of another car being parked at the site?"

"No, we looked for that. The area was the main entrance to the site off CR 210 and had been heavily used. Mr. White's truck was parked off the road into the trees a bit and his were the only tracks in that spot. We do believe there was someone else there, one or even two other vehicles. But they could have been left further in on the dirt road and left no sign. The county worker had also driven in." Jeffery nodded.

"We have all the pictures of the ground, blown up, of the entire area. The Jacksonville men did a good site investigation. Our men were also with them." He went on with the findings from the Zoo people, the autopsy, the truck, fingerprints, etc.

He took them through the search for Mr. Skeet and the man's background. He told them about interviewing all the parties involved in fighting the landfill. He said Sheriff Edwards had quietly checked out the whereabouts of the principals involved in the site location from Jacksonville. Except for Mr. Skeet, they had no leads yet.

He paused and looked at Major Brown. Then he said, "We have also been looking into who owns land out there and in our conference room we have a board chart of different names. How they might fit, do we have crossovers in the names of involved people, that sort of thing? I will be glad to let you look at that. The board chart was really Major Brown's idea. As you can see, we have a lot of people, a lot of possible motives. But motives for what? Why kill this man?"

Mark had been quietly listening. Finally he said, "Sheriff, with all due respect, I did not hear you ask why David might have been out there in the first place. Don't you think that is rather central to the whole case?"

Sheriff Gray looked at Mark and just waited for him to go on. Mark obliged him. "I mean do you think he was stealing gopher tortoise or even planting them? Or do you think he would kill a bear cub? Or do you think he was there to plant cat paw tracks?" He was leaning forward in his chair and staring at the Sheriff. Just like he was daring him to say yes.

"To be honest, Mr. White, at first I did not rule out any of those questions you just raised." Mark started to object but the Sheriff held up his hand and Mark stopped. "The more I have found out about your brother the less I am inclined to believe any of those things. Even the cat paw casts. Now I must admit, it was only the past day that I came to that conclusion. So to answer you, yes, I had those questions. Now I don't but anything is possible in this business of mine."

"Sheriff, do you believe he went out there alone? If so, how would he know where to go?" Mark said, in a more subdued tone but just as emphatically.

"Good questions. Before you came in this morning, I had Major Brown get ahold of our men who are out in the field asking questions. I asked them to be sure and ask the people who were at that meeting with your brother if anyone offered to go out to the site with him. They will have to backtrack a few of those people they've already questioned. One of the men told our people that your brother said he would not go on the site without city permission. So, unless he changed his mind, there had to be a reason he was there."

"David would know that if they found anything, without officially being allowed on the site, it would cause serious complications. Needless to say there would be trespassing charges and the evidence would be thrown out," said Mark. "But I can see anxious people wanting to go anyhow."

"Mary, have you been on the site?" asked the Sheriff.

"No, I am familiar with the property across from it on 210. It belongs to an old man and his wife. I looked at it a few years ago when I was still into horses. He wasn't anxious to sell then so he had a pretty price on it. So I bought the piece on Roscoe that my maid, who was killed, lived in. I'm not sure anyone has been on site. At least that they ever spoke about. There are several groups working on this and my interest has been with the civic associations on the Roundtable. Not the other groups."

"David was only doing a favor for his friend at the Guana, so I'm not sure his curiosity would have been high enough to risk even a quick look. So something and someone got him out there," said Mark. "He wasn't the kind to be afraid, in fact, he was brave almost to the point of risk taking. But in his work he was all business, very careful, very detailed and I think, since he was helping a friend, he would be even more careful. That's why this has me so bothered."

"Sheriff," said Jeffery "We talked about this at dinner last night and about the incident with Mary in her car. I don't know if they are connected but Mark has asked me to stay and see if I can be of help in the investigation. We all are a bit concerned for our feisty friend here as well." He looked at Mary and smiled. She just smiled back.

"I have no problem with that. I am sure Mark and his family will be more at ease if someone they know is looking around. As for our friend here, I fully agree she could use your company for a while. Also let me say, Sheriff Edwards and I are not sparing any men we need on this. I believe these things must be solved fast or they may never be solved." Then he went on and explained the chain of command and how he got to be in charge of the investigation. He also told them that Edwards had a loose cannon in his office he was trying to catch.

The meeting was winding down. They all went into the conference room and the Sheriff and Brown discussed the lists on the board. Brown told them he still had some more land ownership areas to fill in. Martha, the Sheriff's secretary, came to the door. "I'm sorry to interrupt but Detective Hold is on the phone. He said he had to talk with you." The Sheriff excused himself and said he would be right back. The others were engrossed with the board.

Sheriff Gray returned in about five minutes. He said, "We have a fire in the northeast sweeping toward the Intracoastal Waterway. A man fishing in the Intracoastal saw the smoke and called it in on his two-way radio. They sent fire squads in from the Palm Valley/Ponte Vedra fire station. Hold was at the bar in Palm Valley interviewing the owner when the call came in. It seems that the firemen found a shack on fire and a half-burned body inside."

"Is it north or south of the bridge?" asked Mary.

"It's south, Mary, and they have it under control. It will not jump the Intracoastal."

"Officer Port was at the landfill site and heard the call. He and Hold arrived at the same time and are there. Rogers and Cook are on the way; they had just hooked up at Ranch Road. Our evidence men and the ME have been notified. I'm on my way now. Stone do you want to come along?"

"Yes, it seems you have a suspicion who it might be."

"Yes, they seem to think it might be the man we are looking for, Bubba Skeet. Major, call the fire chief and be sure he alerts the arson people. Hold and the firemen think this looks funny."

Jeffery said, "Mark, you, Mary and Arthur go on to the Guana and meet with Martin Stack. I'm sure the Sheriff's men can give me a ride home."

"No problem," said Gray. "I'm glad we met, Mark. Mr. Steel, I can assure you we will do everything we can to solve this crime. I will keep Jeffery involved. Mark, you have enough on your plate. Go home knowing we are doing our best and Jeffery will report to you." With that he turned and walked out with Jeffery on his heels.

Major Brown walked them out to their car. Mary said she would drive since she knew the way. Brown put his arm around Mark and said, "Steve Gray will move mountains to solve this, Mark. We may look country but we aren't. I will also be sure Jeffery is informed on all our progress and he will be involved."

Mark looked at the man and bowed his head and said, "Thank you. I must tell you I never expected such cooperation. My parents will be relieved, as I am." He sat in the front seat with Mary. Arthur shook Brown's hand and said a quiet "thank you" and got in the car.

Brown watched them drive away thinking. That is a fine young man. If his brother was half the man Mark is, it is truly a great loss. He turned and went inside to bring all the forces together to move this new business along. He thought, I wouldn't be a bit surprised if we find out this guy in the shack had been killed. This was turning out to be a really nasty affair. He was afraid he hadn't seen the end of it.

He was glad Jeffery was here and staying with Mary. He laughed to himself. He was getting really fond of that lady. He remembered how he and the Sheriff had taken her for a ride in the new Cigarette boat last week. They slowed down so she could drive it for a bit. She didn't want to go far, just to feel what it was like. It was a scene, watching her standing behind the wheel, hair flying and laughing into the wind. Yes, he liked that lady and so did the Sheriff. He smiled to himself and thought and so do all three of the men who came in with her. He and the Sheriff still wondered what the relationship was between Mary and Arthur. They knew Mary would never tell them.

Mark turned toward Mary and said, "Thank you. Your Sheriff has acted like a real gentleman. I'm relieved that he is taking Jeffery with him. Will he allow him to remain involved, Mary?"

"Yes, I think so. It was Jeffery's help that allowed them to grab those drug runners last spring. He established a good relationship with some of his men as well. Jeffery is well connected in the law enforcement business at the federal level down here. There shouldn't be a problem."

"He and the Jacksonville Sheriff seem to have worked out a good relationship," said Arthur. "It speaks well for a man who can do that. Do you know Sheriff Edwards, Mary?"

"No, Arthur, I don't. But you can bet he got this murder off his hands as fast as he could. Plus, Sheriff Gray is building a reputation as a man people work well with. I heard at a recent meeting that he is well thought of in the Sheriffs' Association. Giving the control to Gray wasn't as hard as some might think. I also got the message today that they are in close contact.

"Mark, the turnoff is just up the road. This is a combined State Park and Wildlife Management Area. The park extends south of us and the preservation area north, all the way to Palm Valley." They pulled into the park management office. As they left the car, a medium sized man, deeply tanned, with brown hair walked up and introduced himself as Martin Stack.

As he and Mark talked, Arthur and Mary walked over to the dam. "Well, Arthur, how do you think it went and how do you think Mark is doing?"

"It went well, better then I expected. Gray seems to be a cut above most southern cops."

"Oh my, are we showing a bit of bias now?" Mary said.

"True. It is deserved and you know it. You are damn lucky to have a good sheriff anywhere in this country, needless to say in the south."

"I will be sure and not repeat that, especially in Steve's hearing."

"It's Steve now, is it?" said Arthur.

"Yes and you had better be glad. Better to be on the good side of the law. What with your worrying, I would think you would be pleased."

He took her hand and said, "I am pleased. I am even more pleased that Jeffery will be here. You gave us all a real scare last spring; me, especially."

Mary smiled at him, squeezed his hand and said, "I know and I'm sorry to have worried you so. I do not envy you this trip north tomorrow. I wish I could go and help but I think I am better here. I really don't know the family that well."

"You mustn't worry. It will all work out. That is a fine family and they will not let Mark bare it all by himself." They sat down by the dam and that's where Mark found them quietly talking.

Chapter Sixteen

Friday, before noon

Jeffery sat in the front seat of the Sheriff's car. Gray said as he looked at Jeffery, "Buckle up my friend. We will do bells and whistles."

Jeffery grinned and replied, "Fun. I don't get to do that often."

"Truth be told, neither do I," smiled Gray. "I also want you to know I am pleased that you are on board. This whole damn landfill issue is bad enough without killings. That is why Edwards wanted out. But he will be a real help for us behind the scenes in Jacksonville. I am not convinced the people behind this site selection have clean hands in any of this." He then went on and told Jeffery about the call he got from Hayes, the Mayor's aide. He further explained the economics involved in this particular site selection.

"Was Mary the first one to stir all the opposition up?"

"I think the people on Ranch Road were onto it first but what Mary did was bring the large homeowner's associations in the Ponte Vedra area on board. Plus, she gets good TV and newspaper coverage. She says she is not in the forefront now, except to push the Roundtable to bring pressure on the Board of County Commissioners. But you could say her name has been out there the most.

"Just between us, Sheriff Edwards is going to warn the Jacksonville crowd off Mary. He is going to say that the investigation group is looking seriously at them. That should create some nervous people. If I were them, I wouldn't go within ten miles of her."

"I agree. I'm glad you did that."

They were going west on 210. As they shot by the Sheriff pointed out the landfill site where they found the body. Around the next curve, they came upon the deputy's car and a man directing traffic. He waved the Sheriff's car to his right and as Gray slowed, he said, "You can drive in on that dirt road, Sheriff. It looks kinda bad but if you just follow the tracks through the grass you will be ok."

They moved forward slowly. They could smell the smoke and it was a bit hazy. After about three quarters of a mile, they could see the fire trucks and more sheriffs' cars ahead. Gray pulled over to the side and they got out and walked. They could see the shack ahead. It looked burned on the west side facing them. Hold saw them and walked out to meet them.

"The firemen are further south and east making sure the brush fire is out. Hi, Mr. Stone." He held his hand out and the men shook. "The body's inside, not burned very badly. The fire looks like it began here on the west side and then turned south. We have a northerly breeze. The firemen said the shack was on fire when they arrived and they had enough water in the tank truck to put it out. They said they ran inside and saw the body. They sprayed it down quickly and, when they realized he was dead, they did not move him but called us."

Jeffery and Gray walked up to the shack. They both put on gloves and walked inside, being careful where they stepped. The place smelled liked burnt flesh, hair, garbage and filth. Some of the wood was still smoldering. There were empty beer bottles everywhere. Some were broken. There was a nasty looking cot with an uncovered mattress on it in a corner that the fire had not gotten to.

"Has anyone checked his pockets for identification?"

"James went back to his car for his camera. We wanted to get some pictures before we moved him. Here he is now."

Officer James came through the door, nodded to the Sheriff and glanced at Jeffery. "Go ahead James, we will step outside until you are done. Get shots of the whole room," said Gray.

Hold said, "He is a genius with a camera. Port is here, too; he heard the sirens. He was just up the road, and was here about the same time I was."

"James is one of the Jacksonville cops working with us. Port is the other one, and he has been walking the land around here. First, the large McCormick spread next to the site. Today he was walking the Landfill site. He will do the Dee Dot Ranch Monday," said Gray.

"What is he looking for?" asked Jeffery.

"He is talking to the landowners and also looking for any rare species which must be protected. He is finishing a degree in biology or environmental science. Wants to go into law enforcement with the State Park people. He and James were the men who did the crime scene at the landfill. "James was nearby, with Cody, interviewing more people. I called them when I heard the call. Rogers and Cook were up here, too, so I told them all to come.

"When we arrived," said Hold, "I left Cody to direct traffic. James and I walked in first, and he told me he had his cameras in his trunk. We just walked up and looked around before you came. Port and Cook are out with the firemen looking at the brush to see if they can find anything. Rogers is at the fish camp talking with the fisherman who called it in. He wants to see exactly what time he saw the smoke and if he saw anything else."

"That's our whole team, Stone," said Gray.

They heard more sirens and looked up to see the Medical Examiner and the wagon and the rest of the site investigation team. Gray greeted the ME and said, "That was quick, Dr. Pool."

"I was at your office complex and Brown called us and said to move it. Is the body badly burned?"

"He's burned some but he's not charred," said Gray.

James appeared at the door and waved them in. The investigators and the coroner went in first with Jeffery and the Sheriff right behind. They all moved very carefully, not touching any surfaces. Dr. Pool saw James' camera and asked if he were finished and could he move the body a bit. James looked at the Sheriff and Gray introduced Pool to James. James told him he was through.

As Dr. Pool moved to turn the body, Jeffery bent to help him. They both stopped before they moved the man and looked at each other. "The neck looks funny, Dr. Pool," said Jeffery. They stood up and asked James if he had good pictures of the body and the neck. James told them he did, and he thought the neck looked a bit off as well. The coroner, with Jeffery's help, finished his initial examination.

The investigation men went through the man's pockets and found a little loose change but nothing else. He had no identification and the ME said they could remove him. Sheriff Gray told

Dr. Pool he needed the autopsy done as soon as possible, especially since it looked like his neck might be broken. If it was broken could he tell how that happened? "I'm sorry to rush you, Dr. Pool, but this may be a man we have been looking for in connection with another case. We have been combing the area for him for two days."

"I'm free today. I'll start as soon as we get back," said Pool.

The Sheriff's men were going over the room, packaging various items and dusting for prints when they could. One of the men picked up a coffee can they found under the cot when they moved it. He shook it a bit and it rattled. He took the lid off and carefully reached in and hooked the band of a watch on a pencil. As he held it up, Jeffery looked over. "May I see that, officer?" Jeffery asked.

The Sheriff heard him and the officer walked over to Jeffery, holding the watch up. He turned it slowly so Jeffery and the Sheriff could see it. "Its a Rolex diving watch," said Jeffery.

"Well, that's interesting. Where would a man like that get a watch like this?" asked the officer, holding the watch up.

"Where, indeed?" said the Sheriff, looking at Jeffery. "Do you think it belonged to David White, Stone?"

"I would certainly put money on it. Good thing Mark is still here in town. He will be able to identify it for you. I'll be glad to take it with me and show him. We will be having dinner together tonight. I can return it tomorrow, after I see them off at the airport."

"Can we dust it now and see whether it has any prints?" the Sheriff asked the officer holding the watch.

"Yes, Sir. Let me take it out to the truck so we can do it very carefully." The officer turned and walked out.

The investigators continued the search as the Sheriff and Jeffery looked on. They were finding very little: some empty cans of beans, old bread, a can of Spam, some sugar and half a can of coffee. "How did he heat the water for the coffee?" asked the Sheriff.

"We found a pot outside, on a grate, with stones around it. Looks as if he had a campfire. There is a well outside too, with a pump handle. It looks as though this might have been a hunting camp at one time, and this guy just took it over to live in. No outhouse around; guess he used the bushes," said Hold.

Cook and Port came through the trees from the south. "Sheriff, we found an old truck back there, and we are calling in the plates now. It is sorry looking, dirty and banged up. The inside is filthy," said Cook. Port was in one of the police cars on the radio. "It had Duval plates and there is a single-barrel twelve-gauge shotgun behind the front seat. After Port calls in the plates, we will have it towed and the inside printed."

"How come it's back in the trees?" asked the Sheriff.

"Well, we walked all around it to see how it got there. There is no road but Port noticed that the grass was disturbed. I never would have seen it but if you looked careful, you can see it drove through the grass off the dirt road we came in on. If you were following the dirt road you could miss the place he turned off on."

"Clever," said Jeffery, "He sure didn't want anyone finding his truck or seeing it and thinking he might be here. You could walk up on this place and look around and figure no one would stay here. Like you said before, Detective Hold, a hunting camp."

"We found out he can also walk through the woods, down to the Intracoastal, and fish. It's just south, past those houses on Roscoe extension. No one would see him. There is a little creek down there and an old johnboat with oars, pulled up and hidden in the trees. All a man needs if he isn't particular about the conveniences of life and paying rent," said Cook.

"What's taking Port so long?" asked Hold.

"He said he was going to wait for the plate report. Here he comes."

"Sheriff, sorry about the delay. The truck back there in the trees belongs to Bubba Skeet, the man we've been looking for. I called your office, and they are sending a tow for it. I think it's been there a couple of days."

"Thank you, Port. This is Jeffery Stone. He came down with the brother. We've had the pleasure of working with Mr. Stone in the past, and he will be joining the investigation, informally."

Detective Cook looked at Jeffery and said, "Nice to see you again, Stone."

Just then Rogers came walking down the dirt road. They waited until he joined them. "Well, officer, what do you have?" asked the Sheriff. Rogers was looking at Stone and jerked his head around when the Sheriff repeated "Rogers, report."

"Yes, Sir. I found the man who called the fire in at the ramp. He is a local who fishes down here a lot. He has a flats boat, and he was trolling up from Marker Three on the east side when he saw the smoke. He had a client on board. He is a local guide who lives in Palm Valley. He had a radio on board and called the Palm Valley fire department. He said all the folks here worry about fire and how it can jump the Intracoastal. He said he knew there was someone staying in a shack back in there. He had seen him out in a johnboat on occasion. Said the guy had a little kicker he put on the boat."

"You guys find a motor anywhere?" asked the Sheriff.

"The truck had a locked box in the back with a padlock on it. We didn't try to open it. If the kicker were small, it could fit in there," said Port. "That's where I would keep it if I didn't want it stolen."

"I guess you're right, Cook. What more could you ask; waterfront property, fish, hunt and no taxes. Our man had it made. Then, on the side, he does a little theft for beer and food," said the Sheriff. "Hold, you and the men make sure everything is finished up here and then block off the road. Was the press at the entrance when you came in, Rogers?"

"Yes, Sir. Cody wouldn't let them in and wouldn't give them any information either."

"Hold, I hate to do this to you, but I want you, Cody and James to work overtime tomorrow and finish the interviews if you can. Work in pairs or alone as you see best. I want to see all of you in my office late this afternoon. Have one of the men not on the case relieve Cody on the road so he can come in with you. Port, you are going to Dee Dot on Monday."

"Sheriff, would it be ok if I go with Port on Monday?" said Jeffery.

"Yes, that would be fine. Give you a chance to see the countryside. Cook, I want you to come with me. Rogers, when I finish with Stone, I want you to drive him over to Dr. Paul's." Just as he turned to leave, the investigator with the watch yelled.

"Sheriff, hold up a minute." He had the watch in a plastic bag, and he handed it to the Sheriff. "Not a clear print on it. Some smudges but no good to us."

The Sheriff took the watch and said, "Thank you. Please note that you gave it to me and you saw me give it to Stone to show to the brother. He will return it in the morning to our office."

He turned and walked to his car. He sat in front with Jeffery and Cook got in back. He shut the door and turned to Cook and said, "I want you to talk to Sheriff Edwards today. I want you to tell him about finding Skeet. Tell him I want you or him, whoever he thinks is better, to concoct a story about how you were told Skeet might have worked for the trash hauler. Tell them you are calling to find out if he did and if so, did he list a next of kin. It is just true enough to fly. You got the idea?"

"Yes, Sir, I'm sure we can bring that one off. Do you want me to do anything this weekend?"

"No, see where this leads you. You might find yourself looking for relatives or friends of this guy if you get a lead. Don't forget to bitch and complain in the right company."

"Yes, Sir," Cook grinned, "The Sheriff and I had a conversation about that this morning."

"Good, you call if you need help. You know where we are. Remember, we are trying to move fast but very carefully. If you can't make it in today, have Hold brief you on the meeting. I just want everyone brought up to date. Off with you now."

The Sheriff and Jeffery sat quietly for a while. Finally, Gray said, "Jeffery, I am not convinced that this Skeet guy killed the brother. I think it possible someone killed Skeet and tried to cover it up with a fire. I also think they cleaned him out but missed the watch. If he had White's watch, where are his wallet and other stuff?"

"I think you have a point. What you may not know is that David had a small gold pocketknife. It's missing too."

"Yes, I forgot about that. Cook mentioned it yesterday afternoon at our briefing. We didn't see it today, did we? I wonder if they found it and if they will keep it or toss it?"

"What do you think could have happened at the landfill? Well, I guess we can't speculate on that unless we know why David was even there. Skeet may not even be involved. He may have just found David and frisked him and hightailed it. We have one killer for sure, now maybe two. Will you call me and let me know about the autopsy? We will all be eating at Mary's tonight."

"I'll probably have that information later. Dr. Pool is fast and careful. I'll call you."

"Thank you for including me. I'll do my best to stay out of the way and not cause you trouble. It means a lot to Mark. Also, I do appreciate your telling Port it is ok if I go with him Monday."

"No problem, I'm sure you will be helpful or I wouldn't have you around."

Jeffery smiled and stepped out of the car and headed back to the shack.

The Sheriff drove out, stopping at the highway. He walked over to the reporters and gave a brief press briefing. He told them they had a dead body that they would identify in a short time. The area would remain off-limits so they might as well go home. As soon as he had a name his office would call them. He answered a few questions and waved a goodbye to Cody and drove off. He thought to himself, I'll give Cook time to call Edwards, then I'll call him myself. He half smiled; nothing like stirring the pot.

Chapter Seventeen

Later Friday afternoon

"Sheriff, phone call for you on line one. It's Sheriff Edwards," said Martha.

"Sam, how are you?"

"I'm just dandy. Best damn two days I've had in a long time," laughed Sam. "Watching smart alecks squirm makes my day. I was in to see the Mayor and his aide yesterday, and I let drop the remark about the investigation looking at the landfill site location people with a jaundiced eye concerning the incident with Dr. Paul's car. The Mayor went nuts. He wanted to know what the hell I was talking about. Hayes said nothing, just looked sick.

"I said, 'Mr. Hayes, didn't you tell the Mayor?' I knew he had the information, cause I leaked it through one of the two men of mine whom I suspected of leaking, plus the information on the brother. Instead of denying any knowledge of the situation, he said he hadn't had a chance to mention it. Anyhow it had nothing to do with them."

"You mean he made no attempt to cover up?"

"Nope. The Mayor was all over him, said if he knew why the hell hadn't he kept him informed? Hayes had no answer, just sort of shook his head. Then he repeated himself and said he really didn't think it had anything to do with them. The Mayor yelled at him and asked what the hell was he, the Mayor, supposed to do if the press asked him if they had taken a shot at Paul?"

"Oh, my, and then what happened?"

"Hayes just squirmed. Then the Mayor asked if the family of the dead man had been notified. I said, yes, a brother was flying in today. The Mayor said to Hayes to find out when he was coming in and to make arrangements to have him picked up at Jacksonville International Airport when his flight landed. Hayes was so rattled at this point, he just blurted out that he was landing in St. Augustine. I just remained silent. The Mayor actually asked him how the hell he knew that?"

"Steve, it was a good morning. I have my man pegged. I never let on that I was the least bit suspicious of his source of information. I think they may back off Paul but then this whole thing is so strange, who knows. I had Port and Cook in this morning and told them. They are not sure that the man I didn't check out is clean. So we are sure on one and have one to go."

"Did Port tell you about Skeet when he called in the plates?"

"Yes, he called me and I had them checked. I get quicker action. So I made sure the second man found out. Then Cook called, and I had him run in and we talked about your suggestion. We decided I would make the request in person so I could watch Hayes. Cook waited here for me. I went over to the Mayor's office after I called for an appointment with him and Hayes.

"I told them we had a body and we needed to find the next of kin. Then, I turned to Hayes and asked for the phone number of the trash hauler who owned DBF Haulers. The poor sucker actually turned white and asked why the hell I needed that. The Mayor just looked at him as if he were nuts. I said we heard he had worked for them and wanted to know if they had a next of kin for him in their files. Before Hayes could respond the Mayor told him to go get me the number, now!"

"Did they ask you where you found the man?"

"No, and by the time Hayes came back with the number, he was well enough together not to ask. I said to the Mayor that I surely hoped the DBF people would cooperate with us. He asked why they wouldn't. I said well, a lot of these people didn't like to cooperate with the police. He reached across the desk, took the number and dialed it himself. He told whoever answered the phone who he was and when Wood, the owner, came on the line, he told him who he was and what he wanted. He said he needed the information right now, and could Wood put him through to his personnel people.

"Wood was apparently real cool and put him through to personnel. Yes, this Skeet did some part time work for them over a year ago. He had a sister listed and gave the Mayor the number and address."

"Well, well, well, aren't we in high cotton today. No wonder you are so pleased," said Steve.

"You bet. I now have both men pegged whom I was suspicious of, and we have a connection, such as it is, to the landfill bunch. I'm even more pleased that you are in charge. Can you imagine what a mess this would have been for me?"

"Yes, I can. You think that Hayes told Wood the name your guy leaked to him?"

"Oh, yes, I do and I think that Wood is cooler than Hayes. He knew not to lie to us. If we heard that Skeet worked for him and he lied, he would look real suspicious to us. Now, if it is ok with you, I will have Cook go see the sister and bring the sad news. She lives way out on the west side."

"Absolutely, and if he needs help with this, he knows to call Hold over the weekend. What are you going to do about your less-then-loyal men?"

"I'm going to go home and savor that question over a cold beer, with pleasure, I might add."

"I'm having a meeting with the team in a few minutes and I expect an autopsy report right away. Do you want me to take Port aside and tell him your news?"

"Yes. If it hadn't been for him and Cook, I might not have checked further after I found the first guy. Do you think Skeet was killed?"

"Yes but we will wait for the autopsy to be sure. Did he fall and break his neck or did he have help? Plus, the place was cleaned out, no ID, no money, nothing. Someone was there. They missed young White's watch 'cause Skeet had it in a coffee can under his cot. Someone is getting nervous. You have a quiet weekend. If anything exciting happens, you will be the first to know."

"The city granted the opponents access to the landfill site to look for endangered species, Saturday, Sunday and Monday. I guess they found someone to look. I wish them luck." They said goodbye and hung up.

Sheriff Gray's secretary told him the men were in the conference room. The Sheriff hadn't had a chance to talk with Major Brown. Brown had been busy and out of the office when he got back. When he walked into the conference room, Brown was just coming in. "I went over the autopsy. Do you want me to report inside?"

"Yes, no sense repeating yourself."

The Sheriff took his seat and asked, "Did you finish at the shack, Hold?"

"Yes, we left one of the afternoon shift on site at the road to keep the press and other nosey bodies out."

"Good. Ok, Major Brown, what did the good Dr. Pool find?"

"The man had some beer in him but some food as well. His neck was broken. He had received a severe blow to the back of his neck. He was a skinny man and he thinks that the blow was such that it snapped his neck immediately. He did not fall and do that, according to Pool. He didn't have any broken nails or signs of skin under them. He doesn't think there was a struggle. No broken bones, or bruises, or cuts. It is as though someone was behind him and just hauled off and hit him with a blunt object. Swung hard enough, a bat or four by four would do that. He said the blow came from a bit above him, so the person was either tall or Skeet was bending over or sitting down. So, no question he was murdered."

"Jeff, would you step out and call Sheriff Edwards and tell him? I just got off the phone with him. He should still be in his office."

"Ok, Detective Hold, did the team find anything else?"

"Not much Sheriff. There were some prints but the firemen had messed up some of the areas on the door when they came in and there weren't many surfaces to leave anything on. The dirt road had too many cars and the fire trucks on it to tell us anything. If anyone drove in, he wouldn't have been seen from the road or from the waterway. We could ask the press to put the word out to ask whether anyone saw a car or truck drive in that way but I don't hold out much hope."

"James, Cody, Rogers, how did your interviewing go?" They all reported they were hearing pretty much the same thing they had been. James was able to add another name to the group that met with White. "We will probably do better tomorrow when more people will be home. I also heard they are having a meeting tomorrow, of the whole group," said James. "I think we should go and see whom we can talk to, or make plans to talk to, before the day is over."

Cody said, "Sheriff, how about we go in street clothes. Not as threatening and the neighbors won't be looking out the window so quickly. We can use our own cars or the unmarked cars of the department."

"The rest of you agree?" asked Gray.

"Yes," said Rogers and the others nodded. "Over the weekend there are more people about, and we would be less conspicuous."

"I was at the fish camp bar," said Hold. "They said everyone who came in there was against the landfill and a lot of the 210 people drank there. No one person stood out or was any more upset than another, they said. That guy Key, who called us before, came in while I was there, and the bartender introduced us. He told me about the meeting tomorrow, too. He suggested we should go. Said we could get a real feel for how upset people were."

"So the fact we are out there asking questions doesn't seem to have spread too widely. People may be a bit scared. You may hear more tomorrow," said the Sheriff. The men added a couple of more names to the board, and the Sheriff let them go. Told them to report to Hold at the end of the day and take Sunday off if they were done. He told them Cook and Sheriff Edwards, through some clever work, found out that Skeet worked for the trash hauler and got the name of a sister.

"Hold, I told him if he needed help, or had anything to report, to call you. I don't know what he will turn up, but he won't be going off by himself. Port, come into my office a minute."

He sat down at his desk and Brown joined them. Gray told Port what Sheriff Edwards had told him. Port grinned, "Good. Cook and I didn't think either one of those guys were worth a damn. Suck ups, if you get my drift. You can tell when someone isn't quite straight. They give off strange vibes to the guys who work around them. You know, Sheriff, in this business we are in, trust is imperative. I mean, it's us against them and if we aren't solid with each other we don't have a chance."

"I agree," said the Sheriff and he grinned at Brown, "I just never thought of putting it that way before. Now, I want to be sure you're ok with Stone going out with you on Monday. I mean, I don't want you to think we are sending you out with a tourist or just some guy from New York."

"No, Sir, it's fine and I appreciate your asking me. I talked to Rogers a bit on the ride down here after he took Stone to Paul's. He said Stone was a real stand-up kind of guy and as cool under fire as they come. I got the impression he was a real admirer of the man. I also did talk a little with Stone before he left. He asked me what he should wear on Monday. He also told me he was licensed to carry in Florida. He thought it best if I knew he would be carrying."

"Really," said the Sheriff.

"Yes, I like a man who isn't afraid to ask something like, what to wear and who tells me he has a gun on. Tells you a lot about a man who acts like that."

"You getting a degree in biology or psychology, Port?" asked Brown.

Port almost blushed, "No, Sir, my mother is a psychologist and she taught me about people as I was growing up. When I became a cop, she increased the lessons to, as she said, 'provide me with a discerning brain' so I wouldn't be too quick to use the gun. She is really big on knowing the people you are working with; sometimes it drives me nuts. However she isn't wrong too often. My dad is in charge of personnel in his company, and he uses mom all the time." Now he did blush. "I'm sorry, I didn't mean to get so personal."

"No, that was just fine Port. I want to know the men who work with me also; know their strengths and weaknesses. I am pleased to know Stone carries. I am not surprised one bit. Thank you for stopping. I hope tomorrow goes well."

After he left, he looked at Brown and said, "Too bad we can't hire him away from Edwards."

"Better yet, hire the mother," quipped Brown.

"Well, jokes aside, Jeff, this case is heating up and I am not pleased. Just what are we dealing with here?"

"Well, Steve, if you go back to Mark White's statements this morning about his brother and then his questions based on them, we may want to look at this whole thing from his point of view. Just what was his brother doing out there? If they couldn't get him to do anything slightly illegal, like go on site without permission, you can forget his having any role with those cat paws."

"Ok, something made him to park his truck and get out of it."

"Yes, or someone. Steve, do we have anyone trying to find out where you could get those casts?"

"Yes," said the Sheriff. "Martha is making calls. She called the Zoo. They weren't very helpful, but they did tell her that people who did window displays for fancy stores who want to put paw tracks in sand in the display would use them. So she is phoning stores. It may not even be local. It could have come from anywhere."

"I figured you had checked but it just was on my mind. How was Stone today?"

"Quiet. He listens well. He picked up on the guy's neck the same time as Pool. He did thank me for letting him join us. Hell, I'm glad to have him, especially at Paul's."

"That quietly listening must have rubbed off on him from Steel. The man never said a word this morning, but he didn't miss a thing that was said either. He watched every one of us. I had a feeling that we were all being analyzed for a job," said Jeff.

"Noticed that; he wasn't hostile, just alert and quiet. Those were his boys with us, and Mary told me he is a good friend with the family as well. He was here to listen and listen he did."

"Wouldn't you love to hear his remarks? He will probably save them until they are all together. He looks like he doesn't repeat himself too often. What do you suppose ties those people together, Steve?"

"Nothing down here. They knew each other from up north somewhere. Well, enough of this. I'll only say, I'm glad they are on our side."

Chapter Eighteen

Friday evening

"Mary, Mary, I'm home," yelled Jeffery as he started up the steps to the porch.

Mary walked out on the porch and said, "Hi. I didn't hear a car or the dogs bark. Got them trained have you?"

"No, dear. Rogers let me off at the gates. I whistled and they came and met me. I guess they don't bark until they are sure it's worth the bother." He leaned down and kissed her cheek.

"What are you doing?"

"I just finished putting the final touches on dinner. I told them to come at 5:30 for drinks and dinner at 6:30."

"Do I have time for a shower? This looks nice," He was looking at a platter of cold asparagus, tomatoes and snow peas. "What else are we having?"

"Garlic mashed potatoes and pork tenderloin. Arthur called and said he would bring the wine. Yes, you have time and no use telling me what you discovered. Save it for when the others get here."

Mary had just finished setting out some sharp Danish cheese and crackers and the wine glasses when the dogs started barking and Jeffery appeared. "I'll go quiet the crowd," he said and headed out the door calling the dogs. They came up the steps with Jeffery in the lead carrying four bottles of wine. Mary raised her eyebrows and, after she had greeted Mark and Arthur, she said, "I'm surprised you found anything in the stores to buy."

"I didn't bother. This is from the Club's cellar. They are very accommodating when it is called for, and paid for, I might add," Arthur said.

Jeffery opened a bottle and poured a bit and handed the glass to Arthur to taste. "Good. Thank you, Jeffery. Pour four glasses now, will you please." He took Mary's and Mark's arms and led them out to the combination front room and office that overlooked the waterway and sat. Jeffery served them and they toasted each other and drank.

"Now, Jeffery, can you tell us what happened?" asked Mary.

For the next half hour, Jeffery related all that they found and who the dead man was. The phone rang and Mary answered it and said, "Jeffery, it's the Sheriff."

The others chatted a bit until he came back and told them that the autopsy showed the dead man's neck had been broken; it was murder. Mary stood up and took the pork out and carved it. She said, "Enough for now, my friends, let's stop and dine."

Dinner was a great success. They finished off everything. Mary served fresh fruit and cookies for dessert. Finally, they got back to the crime.

"Jeffery, do you think the Sheriff will really ask why David was out there, I mean in a way that does not make him a suspect in wrongdoing?" asked Mark.

"Yes, he indicated as much on our ride to the fire. He was honest with us when he said he was coming to that conclusion even before meeting with us."

"Arthur, you have been quiet all day. What do you think?" asked Mary.

"I think you are all doing a very good job. Mary, I must say from what I have seen I am generally impressed with Sheriff Gray. He listens but, even more important, he can give credit to his men when it is deserved. He made it clear that Major Brown thought up the board lists. Which, by the way, is a great idea. It made me aware how many people are involved. Also, how many really do not want that landfill built. The overall loss to the larger community, needless to say those near by, is appalling," said Arthur.

"I don't mean to interrupt you, Arthur, but that is what hit me as well. I mean, I wonder if David even knew what a terrible thing this was. You say you never even talked to David, Mary?"

"No, he just left a message. I knew we would talk, so I wasn't worried."

"Yes, I understand. I still think he might not have known the extent of the problem. But they say he met with a group one evening.

The names of those people in that group were on the board. Could they have given him a total picture?"

"I looked at those names, Mark, and, depending on what they spent time talking about, they could have painted a fairly accurate picture. But I do not think they went into all the financial benefits of the landfill to the Jacksonville crowd. They may not fully understand that themselves.

"The Sheriff called me the week before because a Mayor's aide, a man named Hayes, had called him. This Hayes tried to get the Sheriff to scare me off the opposition. The Sheriff made it abundantly clear to me that the trash-hauling crowd was not to be trifled with. He was concerned. I did not take his call lightly. I had a TV interview to do this past week, and I told him that was my last public appearance.

"I must say, I don't know what any of them would have to gain by killing David or anyone at all." Mark started to interrupt, but Mary put her hand up, "Mark, I am not saying they weren't involved. I think, somehow, they are, but I don't see a motive for this particular act."

"Mary," said Jeffery, "I'm sorry, I was thinking about the man's broken neck. I forgot to tell you all the Sheriff also said, that, through some fast and clever maneuvering with Sheriff Edwards, they found out that Skeet had worked part time for the trash hauler in the past."

"What!" said Mark? "Well there you are, they are in the thick of it."

"Maybe so, Mark, but there is still no motive for the killing of David." Mark started to interrupt, but Arthur stopped him. "Mark, if that Skeet man was at the site, and I think we can say he was, it might have been him who dug up the gopher tortoise. But we don't know why. If you say he killed David because David interrupted him, you still haven't answered the question of why David was even there."

"Are you saying, Arthur, that until we know why David was at the site we will not know what happened?" Mark asked. "No matter how guilty this man Skeet looks?"

"Oh, Mark, I told you they found a watch that might be David's. I forgot to show it to you. Just a minute." Jeffery came back and handed the plastic bag to David.

David looked at it through the plastic. Finally, he looked up and said, "Yes, that's my, I mean David's watch," tears were in his eyes. He blew his nose and said, "Are you still going to say he didn't kill David?"

They were quiet for a moment and then Mark said, "I'm sorry, I didn't mean that but it does connect him to David somehow, doesn't it?" He looked at each of them so sorrowfully that it was enough to make them all cry.

Mary recovered first, she put her hand on Mark's arm and squeezed and said, "Yes, Mark, it does mean he is connected. Now they must find out how."

"Jeffery, could there have been someone else with David and for whatever reason he killed David and just left him? Maybe this Skeet man heard them and ran off into the bushes and then, when he came back he found the body and robbed it. The Sheriff told us today the man wasn't much and had a petty thief record," Arthur said, then stopped and looked at Jeffery.

"That's a reasonable scenario but it still leaves us with why David was there and with whom?"

"It also leaves us with who killed Skeet and why?" Mary said.

"Don't forget, they cleaned Skeet's shack out, they missed only the watch because it was in a coffee can under his cot," Jeffery replied.

"I don't want to complicate this but it could have been one of Skeet's drinking buddies who got in a fight with him after they had one too many, hit him and robbed him," Arthur said. They all looked at him in astonishment. He held up his hands and said, "Hey, anything is possible. The worst thing any of us can do is shut our minds to all the possibilities. By creating a conspiracy, when in fact, it might not be that complicated.

"Mark, you accused the Sheriff of not having an open mind about David and his inherent honesty. We must be very careful not to fall into that trap ourselves. If we blind ourselves to other possibilities, we may never see the truth."

Mark hung his head and nodded. "That is a major reason why my being here will not be good. Jeffery, you have always been more objective then I."

"No, Mark, that is not true. You are one of the most objective men I know. But when this is your brother objectivity goes out the window. I am going to have to be very careful myself.

There are many possibilities of what could have happened and who could have been involved. We must keep all avenues open. The message today was that the Sheriff is doing just that," said Jeffery.

"Does it help to speculate different scenarios or is it better to just ask all kinds of questions?" asked Mary.

"Actually," replied Arthur "Why can't we do both? What do you think, Jeffery?"

"I tell you what, why not sort of role play. You be the Sheriff, Jeffery, and we will pose questions and scenarios."

"Can't hurt. You are not afraid of contaminating my mind are you?"

"Fat chance of that," laughed Mark.

"I'll start with this: why the bag of gopher tortoises?" asked Arthur.

"Well, they didn't say they saw any holes or tunnels dug up at the location of the body so he could have dug them up or found them in a different part of the site. Mary, have you a pad of paper? I should write down some of these questions I want to check on. Such as, did Port find gopher tortoise tunnels? He was on the site today."

Mary went to her desk and picked up a pad and a pen. Mark asked, "Who is Port?"

"He is a young Jacksonville police officer that has been assigned to the investigation who happens to be an ardent environmentalist and finishing a degree in biology. He has been walking the neighboring properties, and he is the one I will go out with on Monday to walk or ride the Dee Dot ranch."

Mary had returned, and Jeffery was writing. Mark asked Mary, "Can we trust the Jacksonville group not to cover up if it becomes apparent they are involved?"

"Mary, let me answer that. Yes, we can, Mark. The Sheriff explained why he had the case, and today he sent Detective Cook into Sheriff's Edwards office so the two of them could set up the Mayor's aide to see whether he could find out who, in his office, is leaking information to the Mayor's aide. Before you ask, I get the message that the Mayor is not involved at all with the site. He wisely delegated it to his aide."

"Deniability it's called," grumbled Arthur.

"That may be true, Arthur, but I got the impression that Edwards not only wanted to get it out of his office for his own sake, but also for the sake of the investigation itself. I can explore that with Gray if you want," said Jeffery.

"Yes, if you can do it without creating antagonism," said Arthur.

"Ok," said Jeffery, "that is item two."

"Do we think it is possible the gopher tortoise was brought on site in that sack?" Mark asked.

"Well, we know that shovel had Skeet's prints on it. I'm inclined to think he got them on site rather then brought them to the site," Mary said.

"I agree," said Arthur and continued, "How do we explain the dead bear cub, apparently killed with the shovel, away from the site of the body? Who killed it? Skeet?"

Jeffery was writing away. Mark said, "Good question. Let's say Skeet killed it, that it came too near when he was digging. But I was under the impression it was really young, so where was the mother bear?"

Jeffery finished writing and looked at Mark," Well, where was the Mother bear?"

"Damn close by I can tell you," Mark replied. "The best question is, what scared it away? Why didn't it attack and protect its cub?"

"I will run these questions past Port on Monday. I'll bet he has the same questions and I'll bet he has been looking for bear as well."

Jeffery said, "They found a shotgun in Skeet's truck. Would he have taken it into the woods with him? If so, he could have shot at the bear, being careful not to hit it, and chased it off."

"Why not shoot the bear?" asked Mary.

"Well, let's assume he didn't want anyone to know he had been out there. A dead bear would be hard to lug off in a sack. He was also a hunter..."

"And a drinker," said Mark.

"Yes, that too. The point being, he might have thought one shot at the bear would be enough. He may have then hotfooted it back to wherever his truck was and heard David and whoever was coming in or seen David's lights. We aren't sure what time this occurred. There were houses not too far away and the gunshot noise would carry. He probably wanted to get the hell out."

"Jeffery, gunshots in the Valley aren't unusual but yes, I can see your reasoning," Mary said.

"Arthur, why are you looking so perplexed?" Mary asked.

"We still have not explained why David would be anywhere near the site," Arthur replied. "Until we have an answer to that, these will remain only speculations. Also, add one more to your list, Jeffery. Why would Skeet be killed? Not who but why?"

"I know why," said Mary, "We have two choices. One, he was a petty poacher who almost got caught and one of his drinking buddies killed him when he flashed David's cash. Or two, if he were sent out there to hide evidence of endangered species. When David's death hit the press, whoever sent him had him killed."

The men sat there and looked at her. Jeffery recovered first and wrote what she said down.

Arthur said, "Mary, whatever you do, promise me you will never repeat that to anyone at all. No one, hear?" He stared at her, his eyes boring in on hers like guns.

Mary sat there flabbergasted. Finally she said, "What's so unusual about what I said? It's only logic."

"Mary," Jeffery said, "No one knows that Skeet was killed nor what we found at the site of David's body. You must remember that you are the recipient of carefully guarded information."

Mary, looking very chagrined, said, "I won't say a word but you are right, I had forgotten. I won't again."

Arthur stood and put his arm around her, "I didn't mean to imply you would but any kind of slip could put you in danger. Now, Mark, let's take ourselves back to the Club. It will be an early and long day tomorrow. Jeffery, we will pick you up about eight. They told Mark they would have David's body at the airport just after nine. You can take one of the rentals when we leave."

Mark came around and hugged her and thanked her for dinner. She and Jeffery and the dogs walked in front of their car to the gates and let them out. On the way back, Mary said, "Jeffery, I won't say a word, not even to Clara. I keep forgetting that there really are killers at loose. I won't again."

"Good. Takes a load off my mind. Those were good questions and your remark was great. By the way, what are you doing tomorrow?"

"There is a large group meeting of the opposition I have to be at. I'm sure there will be questions. When we were at the Club, I introduced you all to one of the Ponte Vedra men, the one on the Roundtable, so they will know that I know the family. I will just stick to answers about that, if any come up. Clara will be there. How about I ask whether she and Ed want to have dinner with us?" Mary asked

"Good. I like her and Ed."

"Right, and when I get up to go to the bathroom, you two can continue to plot behind my back."

"Arthur told me you knew."

Silence followed. Mary then said, "How about we go fishing Sunday morning? The tides will be good. We won't have to leave until eight."

"Great, I'll buy shrimp later tomorrow afternoon. They will keep in the aerator overnight." To himself he said, well she dropped that in a hurry. Wonder if she settled things with Arthur. I was afraid she would find out I had talked to Clara and given her Arthur's phone number. She is so damn touchy about being looked after. I wonder if we were just more straightforward about it, like Arthur was tonight, if that would be better. I will try it.

Chapter Nineteen

Saturday morning

"Good morning, Mary, the coffee smells wonderful. How long have you been up?"

"Since about six. Happens each day, no alarm needed. After you have a cup of coffee, how about some bacon and eggs before you leave?"

"Sounds good."

"Arthur and Mark will be here at eight. Just give you time for a shower, shave and breakfast. Everything is ready. I'll just put the eggs on when you are ready," Mary said.

Over breakfast Jeffery asked when the meeting she was going to would be. Mary told him at ten; they were meeting at the Palm Valley Community Center. "There will be a lot of people, Jeffery. If you are done, just walk in, no one will notice. In fact, it will give you a chance to listen and watch. It should go on until at least noon."

"I can do that. Jeans and loafers should look about right, or do I need to put boots on?"

"No, jeans and loafers without socks will put you in the middle of the bunch. Not quite Valley but not quite button-down either. Will they be able to get the coffin on board?"

"Oh, yes, more than enough room. That is one big plane, Mary. Thank you for the way you handled Mark. I think the past two days with us has helped him."

"I like him, Jeffery, and he is very important to us. I just hope he will be ok for the trip to Louisiana. You are planning to go with us, aren't you?"

"Oh, yes. When Arthur told me about it, I told him not to leave me out. You know, 200,000 acres will take a while to look over. Arthur said there are some good trail roads and it has been managed well over the years. Mark will be very valuable to us. I'll talk to him after things settle for him. It's getting near eight. How about walking down to the gates with me so they don't have to drive in?"

"Good idea. I can pick up the paper out of the drive while I'm there and say goodbye to them." The dogs joined them in the walk. They didn't have long to wait. Arthur pulled in and stopped. Jeffery sat in the back seat. Mary hugged Mark goodbye when he got out of the car to greet her. She went around the car and leaned in and kissed Arthur on the cheek. He asked what her plans were. She told him about the day's plans and fishing tomorrow. Nothing exciting and he said to keep it that way. He would call later, when he had a chance.

Mary arrived at the Community Center about the same time Clara did, just before ten o'clock. There were two chairs in the back row. They both sat down. Larry, from Ponte Vedra came toward her and Mary stood up. Larry said very quietly, "Mary, I think you should chair this meeting. I told that to the people from Ranch Road and those other two I was telling you about."

"No, Larry, I think it would be in our best interest if I don't, especially in my interest. You are the contact person for the associations up here. Tell them I asked you to chair." He started to object but Mary stopped him and said, "If you want a report from the Roundtable, you can call on me. But it would be best if you chair."

He stood there silently for a moment, then said, "OK, I'm sure there is more behind this request of yours but for now, I'll do it." Mary returned to her seat and Larry walked away and huddled with a few people in front.

Clara asked, "Is he really good, Mary?"

"Yes, and he has the same fears I do. That if we don't keep this opposition clean and well presented, the Commissioners will be hesitant to support us. No one likes a band of rabble-rousers. Larry is well respected and no one will walk over him. He knows what is at stake and will warn them away from crazy ideas."

Larry called the meeting together and announced that there were some Sheriff's deputies with them today. They would be asking to talk to some of the people after the meeting. He explained that they had talked to a number of people already and were just finishing off their list. He had a list of names that the deputies hadn't spoken to yet and as he read off the names, hands shot up. One man said to one of the names, "He went fishing this morning. Should be home by noon." Another mentioned that a man who was named was on the golf course. They could catch him after one.

Larry asked the deputies to put their hands up so people would recognize them. He then asked Officer Rogers if he could give them a brief update on the murder of Mr. White. Rogers stepped up and told them they were talking to people who might have been at the meeting with Mr. White as well as others who were involved in fighting the landfill. They were in the data collection phase, trying to put together pieces of the puzzle.

He was interrupted by a man in back, "Why don't you look at the Jacksonville people? Why would we kill a man who was trying to help us?" Others mumbled in agreement.

Rogers kept his cool. He looked at the man, glanced around the room, stopped briefly, and then moved on, saying, "We are looking everywhere. Ponte Vedra is only a part of our investigation. We lucky four guys have been allowed to conduct it today when we knew we could get all of you together." They all laughed; Larry patted him on the back and thanked him.

Mary turned and looked behind her where Rogers had glanced. There stood Cody, Hold, another two men she didn't know and off to the side beyond them stood Jeffery. Hold had nodded at Rogers when he had made his little joke. Hum, isn't that nice, letting the junior man make the report. Or is it because he can always claim ignorance when he gets a question he doesn't want to answer. Why did he say four men? She counted five.

Larry began with reports from the various groups. The School Board member who lived in Ponte Vedra said the kids from Nease were planning a march at the landfill site for a Saturday, either next or the one after. They would get TV coverage and would ask the Sheriff if he could have some traffic control out there for them. They were telling the newspapers and hoped to get parents as well. They said they were going to talk about the future possibility of contamination of Nease's well water supply, a terrible odor close to the high school but mostly the danger of big trucks on the road with school buses and kids driving to school.

Mary leaned over to Clara and said, "Well, that should take care of the parking problem at Nease. Wouldn't want our darlings hit by garbage, would we?"

"Shhhh! Lord, Mary, what if someone heard you?"

The woman in front of Mary turned and said, "Heard what?"

"I said what a shame it would be if those trucks caused an accident with a Nease driver," replied Mary.

"Oh, yes, that is what we are all so concerned about. My son drives to Nease and next year we are buying a car for my daughter so she can drive. All her friends are getting cars and she must have one. It is a necessity now days." Clara reached down and squeezed Mary's arm and glared at her. Like 'don't you dare utter a word.' Mary just smiled.

They had a report on the letter-writing campaign. They said they were especially hitting the Jacksonville and St. Augustine papers, questioning why public officials would allow such a terrible thing to happen to Palm Valley and Ponte Vedra. It would ruin the TPC and on and on. Mary said to Clara, "I never thought of that one. That should get attention in Jacksonville. They still think the TPC is held in Jacksonville."

Clara smiled, "Well, isn't it?"

The woman in front of them turned again in her seat and said, "You two must be new here. The TPC is held where I live in Sawgrass Player's Club. It has been, just, well forever. If you like, I can get you jobs as volunteers?"

"Oh, no," said Clara, "My husband would never allow that. He thinks it's a dangerous game with all those balls flying about. Oh, no, perish the thought." Mary started to cough and covered her mouth. Clara patted her gently on the back. The woman sort of huffed and turned around. Clara looked at Mary and raised her eyebrows and shrugged.

Larry next asked for a report on the Turkey Shoot. The guys from Ranch Road reported on the money and how many people just stopped by to cheer them on; how a great time was had by all. They discussed possibilities of other fundraisers to get money for a legal fight. A couple of the lawyers present were asked what it should cost. Figures were tossed about. The bottom line was, a lot of money and few hopes of raising all of it.

Larry then told them a little about the Roundtable. A lot of people said they had never heard about it so he went into its history and who all belonged. One of those who said she had never heard about it was the one in front of them. Clara, in a stage whisper that could carry said, "They must be new here," and smiled. The woman in front of them did not turn around.

Larry then said he would like the person who was the current vice-chair, going to be the new Chairman of the Roundtable, to make a report. He said he was sure no one needed to introduce Mary, as she was the President of the Palm Valley Community Association. Mary stood up and moved to the front. Clara could see a bit of red appear on the neck of the woman in front of them. 'Good' she thought.

Mary told them what efforts had been made and what was currently going on. She said Larry was the coordinator of the associations in getting them to get a vote of support from their Boards. The purpose of this was to bring political pressure on the Board of County Commissioners so they would hire a Tallahassee lawyer to fight this for them. She said between 300,000 and 400,000 dollars was about what it would cost. That it would end up at the Cabinet level.

They asked a lot of questions about the other commissioners and why they would overrule our commissioner, who was supporting this landfill site. Mary explained that we elected all the commissioners, for one thing. For another, the Roundtable people came from all around the County. Their approach was, if you let this happen in the northeast, what next with us? They asked, why a Tallahassee lawyer. One of the Ponte Vedra lawyers raised his hand and said, "I can answer that for you, Mary." She smiled and nodded. "You want a man who is an expert in landfills first and a man who knows the players in Tallahassee. There are several like that in Tallahassee. None of us here in Ponte Vedra are that qualified." He sat down. That said it all.

Mary fielded a few more questions. One man said what a good job she had done on the TV last week. Mary thanked him and then said what great ideas they had about the children at Nease and all the letters. She thought everyone should keep up what they were doing. That people needed to know it was a total community effort, not just a few. She went to her seat and sat down.

The woman in front of them turned to Mary and said, "I'm so excited to finally meet you. I have heard so much about you. I missed the TV program or I would have recognized you right away. We must have coffee some day soon."

Mary smiled and said, "Of course, Clara and I would love to."

"When hell freezes over," whispered Clara in a very low voice in Mary's ear.

Larry then said, in spite of the tragic death of Mr. White, they still wanted to have someone of their own look over the landfill site. He told them one of the Roundtable members, who had lived in New York, mentioned a man who was down visiting and looking for a future homesite in the St. Augustine area. He was an Audubon member and a great environmentalist. He wasn't a certified expert on birds, animals and flowers but he was very, very knowledgeable.

He told them the man's name was Roger Van Ghent. He said he would go out to the site today after lunch, at one. Then spend as much of tomorrow as he could. He was leaving for New York Monday. He said he had asked Mr. Van Ghent if he minded if some of the people went with him. He had said no but they must be quiet, not smoke and wear dark clothes.

"Did we get permission from Jacksonville to go on site?" asked Mr. Gunther.

"Yes, they said we could go today, Sunday and Monday. I would suggest that we divide up and some go today and some tomorrow. Would those who can go today hold up your hands?"

Hold nudged Port and nodded. Port held up his hand, as did five others. "Ok, you people meet together at the site opposite Ranch Road. Park on the entrance road well off 210 please. Tomorrow they will be meeting at ten o'clock, be finished after one or two. Roger said you could bring an apple or sandwich or a bottle of water. Wear good walking shoes and dark clothes. It's a fairly large site. By the way, I see some of you looking confused. The dark clothes are so you won't scare the birds."

"What will we be looking for?" asked Gunther.

"Species which the state or federal government lists as Endangered, Threatened or Species of Special Concern. Roger will tell you what to look for."

"When are you going, Larry?" asked Jim.

"Tomorrow, after early mass. Why don't you come with me?" Jim said he would.

"Unless anyone can think of anything we have missed I think we can adjourn, give everyone time for lunch. Oh, and will those who raised hands that the deputies need to see, please check with these men at the door for appointments today."

Hold took Port aside and said, "Catch some lunch and go with that group. You don't mind?"

"No I'm glad you caught it. Be a chance to listen to them interact. How about I ask Stone to come along?" said Port.

"Good idea, he's over there talking to Dr. Paul, catch him now."

Port walked up to Stone, Mary, Larry and Clara. He motioned to Stone, who stepped back. He asked him whether he would come along this afternoon? Stone told him to wait a minute. He pulled Mary aside and told her. She told him fine, why didn't he take Port home with him and fix all three of them a sandwich, she would be along in a minute. The men left.

Clara and Larry were discussing the school kids' problems and the plans that had been made. Mary rejoined them and joined in the discussion. The School Board member walked up and inquired if Mary would be there to march on the Saturday designated. Mary laughed and told her no, she would beg off that one. She would do her marching before the County Commission.

You could see the School Board member was about to object. When Larry put his arm around her and said, "Mary has enough on her plate. We can let her off this time, can't we?" Larry cut quite a figure. He was well over six feet and very distinguished looking. One did not often argue with him. The School Board member said she only wanted Mary to know she was welcome and smiled sweetly. Mary smiled just as sweetly back and said "thank you."

Roy Gunther came up and said, "Excuse me, Mary." She looked up and he was with two others from Ranch Road.

"Hi, Roy, I'm glad you stopped. I have wanted to thank you for rescuing me this week."

"Rescuing you from what Mary?" asked Larry. She briefly told him about being run off the road. By that time a few others had joined them.

"One of the men said he heard a developer from the meeting in St. Augustine had done it. Maybe that Fletcher guy on his way home?"

Mary immediately said, "No, Paul wasn't even at the meeting and he wouldn't engage in such childish behavior."

"Well," the guy said, "One of the developers said it was too bad they missed you with the truck."

"How did they know it was a truck?" asked Roy.

"Hell, I don't know. You know how guys are; just say anything to sound big."

He looked at him and turned to Mary and said, "Mary, I would like to ask you to come along to see the site with us this afternoon. Or, if you can't make it, I can go tomorrow," said Roy.

"Yeah," chimed in Larry. "How about tomorrow, Mary?"

"Oh, I would love to but I have a house guest and we have plans for tomorrow and even for later today. But thank you, anyhow. Now I must get home for lunch."

She headed for the door with Clara. "Jeffery and I will pick you and Ed up at five-thirty. If we go later, we will wait all night for a table."

"Good. I want to talk about what that guy just said. See you later."

When Mary got home, Jeffery introduced her to Officer Port. "Wonderful place you have here, Dr. Paul. I like the passing boats, too, and the view of Dee Dot."

"Lunch is ready," said Jeffery. The men had iced tea and Mary had a beer with the roast beef sandwiches.

"Fast thinking on Hold's part to have you go along," said Jeffery.

"Yeah, he is pretty good. I'm glad you're going. Between us, we won't miss hearing much."

"Jeffery, I told Clara we would pick them up at five-thirty."

"No problem. I'll leave a little early to get the shrimp."

"That's ok. I have to go out this afternoon, I'll get them," said Mary.

"Why don't you come along with us?" asked Jeffery.

"I'd love to but I have a tree man coming at 2:30 to look at the big pine over the Refuge. I want some of those overhanging branches removed. This is the first chance he had to come by and give me an estimate." Mary looked down at Jeffery's shoes. He had changed to work boots and they both had navy blue work shirts on. "Officer Port, maybe you and Jeffery can see if that Mr. Skeet left any holes from digging. I mean if he was there digging."

"Someone did, I saw them yesterday. I had forgotten to tell the Sheriff. I'll show them to you this afternoon, Jeffery. I hope you don't think I'm careless in not telling the Sheriff but the fire and finding Skeet just put it out of my mind."

He looked so shamefaced Mary had to smile. Jeffery hit him on the shoulder and said, "Don't worry about it. I'm sure once we got out there today you would have remembered. Hell, I'd have forgotten myself after the afternoon we had. It's getting late, we better hustle."

Mary finished the dishes and went out to the dock for the portable aerator pail. She put a little water in it. The fish people never put in enough water to suit her. She got in the car and told the dogs to stay out of trouble, that she would be right back.

Chapter Twenty

Saturday, early morning

Wilber Wood and Robert Hayes pulled up in front of John Smith's legal offices at seven in the morning. They both had paper cartons of coffee in hand. Wood said, "I'd rather be fishing."

Hayes just looked at him and thought, bastard.

He grumbled a good morning and they went in. John Smith greeted them and said, "When your coffee gets cold, I have some brewing." They sat in Smith's office and he shut the door. He laughed and said, "I expect we will be alone but sometimes one of the younger associates comes in on a Saturday." He looked at Hayes and realized he was agitated. He said, "I'm sure we all have news, so why don't we take it in order. You start, Hayes."

Hayes pulled himself together and thought, calm down. Start in on yesterday morning. Then build up to tearing a piece out of Wood. "Ok. Thursday morning early, Sheriff Edwards had an appointment with the Mayor. One of the cops, who tells me things, had already told me about the almost accident with that Paul woman. He also told me the brother was coming in Thursday."

He did not tell them about the interchange with the Sheriff and the Mayor about why I hadn't told him sooner. Hayes did not like to remember the embarrassing moments of his life, much less repeat them to others.

He went on and told them, "The Sheriff said the investigators, I think mostly St. Johns County people, were looking at the Jacksonville landfill people with a great deal of suspicion as it related to the Paul woman. The Mayor went nuts. Yelled at me about what the hell was he supposed to tell the press if that idea leaked? I told him it had nothing to do with us."

"Well, what the hell happened to Dr. Paul?" Smith asked with some disturbance in his voice.

Hayes told them about Paul almost being hit by a truck and being run off the road after a late night meeting in St. John's County. He finished by saying, "Too bad they missed," in a grumbling voice.

Smith almost stood up from his chair. He yelled, "Damn it, Hayes, are you nuts? I hope the hell you haven't said a thing like that in front of others. Lord, man, talk about throwing suspicion on us, you can do that all by yourself with a stupid remark like that."

Before Hayes could respond, Wood jumped in. "Hey, let's not go off half-cocked. I was at the same meeting and Paul made a bunch of developers and landowners mad as hell. It was probably one of them. In fact, I heard someone say it might have been one of the large developers in Ponte Vedra. I'm sure that story will get out soon enough."

"I don't suppose you had a hand in helping it get out?" sneered Smith.

Wood wasn't the least bit offended at Smith's tone. He just grinned and said, "Well, I certainly wouldn't go out of my way to correct it."

"What the hell does that mean?" asked Smith. "You're are not implying that you had a hand in it are you?"

"No, I'm not but what the hell difference would it make if I did. She is a pain in the ass. To shut her down would be a favor to all of us."

"Oh, my God," said Smith. "What kind of idiots am I working with?"

Before he could go on, Hayes jumped in. "I agree, John, but I can't fault Wood for feeling as he does. Let me finish. Yesterday one of my cop informants..."

"You have more than one?" asked Smith

Hayes smirked and said, "It pays to have help. Anyhow, he told me that St. Johns County found a dead body in a burnt shack and a truck near it. It turns out to have your friend's name," he looked at Wood, "registered to the plates on the truck, that Skeet guy you told us about. Apparently, someone told them he might have worked for Wood."

"He is no friend but a guy who worked for us once," snapped Wood, who was ticked off at Smith's remarks.

"Yeah, well anyhow, the Sheriff gets a late appointment with the Mayor yesterday afternoon. Tells him this information and asked whether we have," he nods toward Wood, "his phone number. The Mayor himself called it and damned if you" he nodded again to Wood "didn't admit he worked for you. Why the hell you did that is beyond me?"

"What did you want me to do; lie and have them find out later I had lied? I mean, my God, man, use your head. If someone told them he might have worked for us, they could be out there in a flash with a subpoena for our records."

"That's nuts and you know it. No judge is going to give out subpoenas on that kind of information."

"What, you're an authority on subpoenas now? If you had called me when you found out, maybe I might have had an opportunity to think up a story. But when the Mayor calls and asks a straightforward question, hedging would have been obvious."

"The cop didn't mention anybody saying he might have worked for you or I would have called. Not that it would have made a difference. You probably would have done the same thing."

Wood started out of his chair. Smith yelled at him to sit down and he did. Smith looked at them both and thought, what is going on here? Hayes is loosing it and he came in edgy. Wood is being defensive as hell. "Is that all you have to report, Hayes?"

"Isn't that enough?"

"Well, yes, it is. Now let's hear from you, Wood." asked Smith.

"Nothing to say except what I just told you. I was sitting in my office and the Mayor called. No friendly greeting or chitchat, he got right to the point. Told me he needed a little help. The Sheriff had a dead man named Skeet. Someone told him he worked for me and would I put him through to our personnel people to see whether he had a next of kin listed. What was I supposed to do, ask him all kinds of questions? Look suspicious as hell if I did. I just told him, no problem, rang him through to personnel and told them to help the Mayor out."

"You're saying you couldn't have stalled?" questioned Hayes with a sneer.

Before Wood could snap back, Smith said, "Do we know how this Skeet guy died?" he was looking at Hayes.

Hayes just shook his head. "The cop didn't know and the Sheriff didn't volunteer the information."

"Smart guy, why didn't you ask him, if you are so quick on your feet?" Wood said as he leaned back in his chair with a look of satisfaction on his face. Thinking, I'll bet you were trying not to wet yourself.

"Because, I hate to admit it but, like you, I was trying not to appear too interested."

"Good, it sounds as though you two acquitted yourselves well, under pressure. Do we know where they found him?" Smith was trying to calm them both down. Neither one was acting too well today. Fear was almost oozing out of Hayes and Wood was just plain angry.

In a little milder tone Hayes answered, "No, unless it was the man they found in St. Johns County. There was no name given but he was found at the fire near the Intracoastal. It was on the late evening news."

"So we don't know whether he was killed or not. Nor do we know who went after Paul."

"You know John, they both could have been accidents. The Paul thing could have been a drunk having his brand of fun. Or, as I said, one of the developers, or people at the meeting trying to teach her a lesson," said Wood.

"Ok, but what about Skeet. We know you sent him out to check the landfill site and then we have that White guy dead. Could there be a connection there?" asked Smith. Both he and Hayes watched Wood think that one over.

"To the extent that they both were at the landfill, yes. But there is nothing to say they were there at the same time. Skeet drank a lot and I gave him a few dollars to do the job. He may have started or was about to when the White guy was found dead and got scared off and spent the money. Got drunk and accidentally set himself on fire. That is, if the dead man is him, but it seems logical it is. Didn't hear of any other deaths in the news."

"Do you know where Skeet lives?" asked Smith.

"No, he doesn't have a home. He has a sister. But you know, he didn't work for us regularly, only when we were short and it's been a while. I don't know who could have told them he was connected to us."

"If Edwards hadn't been so quick to hand that investigation over to St. Johns County, we would know a lot more about what is going on," sighed Hayes.

"Why did he do that anyhow?" asked Wood.

"Politics. He is up for reelection this coming year. I bet he didn't want to be involved in the landfill fight at all. Plus he and the Sheriff in St. Johns seem to get along, so I'm sure it was easy for him to do. At least, that is the gossip around city hall," offered Hayes. "I'm not going to find out a damn thing until Monday, you know. I really can't seem to be over-interested in those two cops who talk to me. Especially with another death on the books."

"Speaking of the landfill, how is the mess in Ponte Vedra going?" asked Smith.

Hayes said, "They gave the opposition three days to go over the site: today, Sunday and Monday. After that White fellow's death, they had to for public relations reasons."

"Why is that?" asked Wood.

"The Mayor wants to look cooperative, not as though we are hiding something," inserted Smith. "He called me and I told him to give them the weekend and even Monday. You know, even if our environmental firm finds an endangered species or one of special concern, they will have to report it or lose all credibility on jobs if anyone finds out they didn't. There is no hiding in this business or at least not much."

"Will they have someone of authority in the field to look for them?" asked Hayes.

"I heard they might have found an amateur to help them. I suspect the site will be crawling with people for the next few days," Smith replied.

"Do we need to have anyone out there with them? I mean, what if they tried to plant something there?" asked Wood.

"It's not very easy to plant an endangered species, Wood. We don't need anyone there. All that would do is make them angrier than they are currently. No, we stay away from those people," replied Smith.

"The White guy's body is being flown out today," said Hayes.

"Out from where, Jacksonville?" asked Wood.

"No, they have a private plane at St. Augustine airport. His family has some big bucks, which makes this case a bit more sensitive," replied Hayes. "I also heard the Ponte Vedra people are having a big meeting today at the Palm Valley Community Center. Plotting more trouble, I guess."

"Probably" said Smith "We'll know soon enough. For now, let's just sit tight and see how things flush out. I cannot see how any of this concerns us. The only connection we have to anything at all is Skeet and that is very loose indeed. I suggest you both go ahead and have a quiet weekend. I sure will." Smith stood up and showed the men out. He looked at his watch. It was only eight. He would finish off a few things on his desk and head out.

He sat down and thought about the meeting. Those two were sure at each other's throat. Hayes came in jumpy. I wonder if he told us everything that went on with the Mayor and the Sheriff. God help him if the Sheriff catches him messing with his men. It will be even worse if the Mayor finds out there is anything funny going on. He may seem single minded about this site, but he surely wouldn't stand for any rough stuff. If he caught Hayes lying to him, Hayes would be gone immediately. He would also have trouble getting another job in Jacksonville.

Wood doesn't even own the company; he is just the senior area manager of the firm. An out-of-state outfit owns it. They let Wood tell people he is the owner; it makes the locals feel like it's a homeboy they are dealing with. The Mayor told me that. I wonder if Hayes knows? Bet he doesn't. The Mayor said he was telling me in great confidence. Hayes isn't the big dog in the Mayor's office that he lets on to other people. In fact, without this landfill site, he is just another paper shuffler.

Wood bothers me. He was at that meeting in St. Augustine, he said as much. Wouldn't put it past him to put someone up to messing with Dr. Paul. Not that she hadn't given some of those people cause. He had to smile when he thought back to the TV program he participated in with her and the County Commissioner. If he hadn't a client's interest at stake, he would have cheered her on when she quietly went after the Commissioner about who pays taxes. Well, get with it, John or you will never get to the beach with your family.

Hayes and Wood stopped out front and exchanged apologies for their tempers. Hayes said, "I just had more than my share with the Sheriff and not being told what was going on."

Wood asked him, "Does the Sheriff usually tell them about on-going cases?"

"No, he doesn't, at least not me. But he knows what is at stake with the landfill site and I sort of hinted that we would like to be kept up-to-date. I told him the Mayor expected me to stay on top of all the issues involved in the site. He merely nodded and said he understood. What he understood and what he delivers are miles apart. Well, what the hell. I'm going home. You have a good weekend."

A good weekend, thought Wood. If you only knew. He found a phone and called his two men that he had sent out to look for Skeet. They started to explain to him what had happened. He said, "Shut up and get down to my office now, damn you. Don't talk on the phone," and he slammed it down.

He climbed into his truck and headed to his office. He looked at his watch. Good, a bit after eight. He shook his head, thinking about those guys he had working for him that he had just called. They weren't but a step removed from Skeet. Muscle with few brains. Good for trash hauling but not much else. But then, what could you expect. You had to work with what you had. If they had brains they would have his job. He laughed out loud and said "May be a good idea if this mess doesn't clean up."

Chapter Twenty-One

Saturday morning

It wasn't long after Wood got to his office that his men arrived. They lived on the west side of Jacksonville, not far from Wood's office. They both had coffee in paper cups. Ned Perkins was about six feet tall with broad meaty shoulders. He had a bull neck, small eyes and a receding hairline. Ted Baker was just as tall and big, but he had shaved his head and kept a neatly trimmed beard. They both wore jeans, denim shirts with the sleeves rolled up and work boots.

Wood told them to have a seat. He looked them over and remained quiet for a minute. He watched Baker squirm in his seat. Finally, Wood asked, "What the hell did you do to Skeet?"

Perkins, who was looking at his feet, jerked his head up and said, "What do you mean?"

"You know damn well what I mean. They found him dead in a half burned shack on the Intracoastal. Now, you two tell me what happened. Also, why didn't you call me yesterday?"

"Well, hell," Baker said, "We did just like you told us to do. We looked for and found Skeet in that shack one of his buddies told us he sometimes holed up in. He was half-drunk and not too happy to see us." He looked at Perkins for agreement. Perkins nodded his head.

"Yes, then what?" growled Wood.

"Well, it was a hell hole; a dirty cot with a filthy blanket thrown on it, rickety table and one chair. He had some empty beer bottles on the floor and some full ones just inside the door. Had some empty cans of beans and meat. He asked us if we wanted a beer. We said no, that you wanted to know what the hell had happened at the landfill site." Baker stopped and looked at Perkins.

Perkins picked up and said, "He claimed he didn't know what we were talking about. So, I jerked him around a bit; he sputtered and asked me to let him alone and he would tell us. He sat back down. He drank some more beer and then said he had gone out there on Monday in the afternoon like you asked him to. He said he needed enough light to see. Said he parked his truck way into the trees so it couldn't be seen from the road." Perkins stopped and drank some coffee.

"Go on, I ain't got all day," snapped Wood.

Baker took up where Perkins stopped and told Wood "Skeet said he started looking for gopher tortoise tracks and tunnels and other stuff you might be interested in. He finally found some tunnels but not much else and decided to dig up a couple. He said it was getting late, so he went back to his truck for a shovel and a gunnysack and his shotgun."

"Why the hell did he need his shotgun?" asked Wood.

"He said there were some bear tracks out there and he didn't want to be surprised. So, he got a couple of tortoise and heard a noise behind him. A bear cub came rushing out of the brush and he was surprised and just swung the shovel and hit him in the head and killed him."

"Oh, my God, is this a comedy act. He killed a bear cub. Didn't it occur to him that the mother would be near?" asked Wood in astonishment.

"I asked him that," said Baker. "He said it happened so fast he didn't have time to think. I think he might have been drinking."

"You're probably right. I knew I shouldn't have given him any money until he finished. I gave him only five bucks. Said he was hungry. Bet he bought beer, not food. Ok, then what happened?"

Baker went on, "He said he pulled the cub into the bushes and was on the way back with the shovel, gun and sack of gopher tortoise when he heard this crashing through the trees. He knew it was the mother bear so he waited until she came in sight and shot at her. Thinks he put a couple of buckshot in her hide. He said he wanted to scare her off, not kill her. Said he dropped the gunnysack and shovel and walked back a way to be sure she wasn't stalking him. The bear took off and he waited a minute.

"That's when he said he heard a car door slam and men talking up near the road."

"Did he say they saw him?" asked Wood in a concerned voice.

"I asked him that," Perkins said, "He said by this time it was near dusk. No one saw him. But he hightailed it back into the bushes with his gun. He left the shovel and gunnysack where he had dropped it."

"Damn fool. Didn't it occur to him they would be seen?" snorted Wood.

"Boss," replied Perkins, "We both asked him that. We were all over him. All he would say was he was scared they would see him and taking the gunnysack and shovel would slow him down. I think he was afraid he would come upon that mother bear and have his hands full."

"Ok, then what?"

"He said he heard these voices, like maybe two men. Said it seemed like they argued some. Said he couldn't hear much. Then there was silence. He said pretty soon he heard a car door slam shut and so he came back slowly. He told us he found a man lying on the ground. Looked like someone had bashed his head in with Skeet's shovel. Said he was so scared he ran for his truck and left."

"You believe that crap? I mean about just taking off and running to his truck?" Wood questioned.

"Hell no. We know Skeet is a thief and he had too many beer bottles and stuff for a man with little money," said Perkins. "So we asked him how much he had taken off the dead guy?"

Baker interrupted and said, "We asked him if the guy was even dead. He popped off and said yeah the guy was real dead. So we jumped all over him and asked how he knew that if all he had done was run for the car? I'm telling you, boss, the guy was acting real squirrelly."

"Yeah," echoed Perkins, "Really ticked me off. His thinking he could just sit there lying to us."

"Ticked you off did it Perkins? And what did you do about that?" questioned Wood quietly.

"What do you mean? What did I do? I yanked his ass out of that chair and shook hell out of him and told him to quit lying to us. I was getting around to slapping him silly when Baker told me to put him down."

"Then what?" asked Wood with disgust.

"I asked him where he got the money to buy all the beer and other stuff," said Baker. "He told us you had given it to him. But we didn't believe you would give him that much, at least not until the job was over. So Perkins yanked him back up out of the chair and while he held him, I went through his filthy pants pockets. You will not believe how dirty that man was. Hadn't seen water on him in months or his clothes washed."

"Yeah, enough with the hygiene, what did you find?"

"He had the guy's wallet with an ID and about fifty bucks plus some car keys."

"Car keys, oh boy! He hadn't even ditched the wallet?"

"No, Perkins shook him some more, he was really angry that he had lied. He asked him what else he had stolen? He said nothing. Perkins dropped him back in the chair. We asked him why in hell he had kept the wallet? He said he was going to get rid of it soon. We then looked through the room to see what else he had kept. Didn't find nothin'."

Perkins then said, "He sat there whining, saying he didn't take anything else and he wanted his money back."

"What do you mean? Where was his money?" asked Wood.

"I put it and the wallet in my pocket so Baker and I could get rid of it. I told him that. Then he said if I didn't give him his money back he would tell the cops I had it and that I had killed the man.".

"Really. I find that hard to believe. Skeet hated the cops," said Wood.

"He also said if we didn't give him back the money, Wood might be sorry."

"What did he mean?" Wood snapped.

"Boss, when he said that, I just hauled off and hit him. We can't afford to have a no-account like that running his mouth when he's drunk."

"Did you kill him?"

"I didn't check that carefully, we just figured the fire would do it. Appeared it did."

Wood sat there quietly thinking about what all he had heard. The men had a point. Skeet could not be trusted, especially now that there was a murder involved. Messing with a site was one thing, murder was another. He did not want any of that sticking to him. He looked at the men and said, "Did he say why he dug up the gopher tortoise?"

"Yeah," said Baker, "I asked him and he said 'to eat, of course.'"

"Ok, what happened than?"

"Seeing as how he is a sorry drunk, we decided if we set fire to the place it would look like he did it. So we did and beat the hell out of there. We didn't go far, just across the Intracoastal and parked by that bar. Surprised the hell out of us when less then twenty minutes later we heard fire engines. So we moved out fast."

"So you don't know how much burned or what the cops might have found? I mean, will it look natural or a murder?" asked Wood.

"It was burning really well when we left. I don't think they will look too hard. I mean, he is a nobody, why would they care?" Baker replied.

"Yeah," chimed in Perkins, "The cops haven't the time to waste on an old drunk who sets himself on fire."

"You are probably right. What did you do with the wallet and the money?" asked Wood.

"We put the wallet in an incinerator and we have the money. Do you want it?" asked Perkins.

"No. Are you sure there was nothing else that could tie Skeet to the White killing? Did you do a good search? It's hard to believe that's all he took."

Perkins looked at Baker and Baker said, "No, that's all. We don't know what stuff was found on the body. Can you find that out?"

"No, the cops have a tight lid on the investigation. Those damn Ponte Vedra/Palm Valley people are meeting today, hatching up more trouble," said Wood.

"Have you figured out how to shut that Paul woman down?" asked Baker.

"No. When she was run off the road, that should have shut her up but it didn't. We need a diversion to get people's minds off the landfill issue as well as to scare hell out of the opposition.

You know, something that will make them think twice about yelling in public about how awful the landfill is going to be."

"That environmentalist being killed hasn't slowed them down?" asked Baker.

"No, they didn't know him, so it doesn't touch them. If he had been a community member it would be different. We need something closer to home. Listen, I have someone at that meeting. I want you to go to Palm Valley and follow Paul. I want her messed up. Not killed but damaged enough to get in the papers and scare the hell out of her and the rest of them.

"I want it to look like it was done by the developers or construction workers. When you mess with her, cover your faces and talk like you had been put up to do it by a developer. Got that?"

"Yeah, we got that," said Perkins smiling.

"Perkins, you get yourself together. Get some control, I do not like the joy I hear in your voice at the thought of violence. Baker you control him."

"Hey, boss, I'm not a nut case you know. I knew very well how dangerous Skeet could be to all of us. I am not going to just go out killing anyone," complained Perkins.

"Oh, yeah, well, you better not. I want the Paul woman alive, if damaged. I do not mean damaged for life or crippled. Baker, you think you two can handle this?"

"No problem. I had experience roughing up whores when they didn't pay up. This will be the same. We will warn her off the developers and the landfill both. The message will get through."

"It better. You go out there now. It's after nine. That meeting will be about ten. Paul drives a big white station wagon and lives on the Intracoastal. Don't rush, be careful. You call me half an hour after the meeting. My guy would have called me by then. We will see if they are up to anything new. Be careful and don't screw up and don't look obvious or suspicious."

They left and on the way Baker said, "I'm glad you didn't mention that little gold knife I kept."

"Hell no, that's nothing. Just a cute doodad, enjoy it," said Perkins. "I'm just glad he didn't get into a fit about Skeet."

"Was he dead?"

"Yeah, I think so. His neck felt funny after I hit him. It looked funny, too, when he was lying there. But hell, we couldn't let him live after what he told us. If the cops ever got ahold of him, no telling what he would have said."

"I agree. I think Wood did too."

Three hours later, Wood's phone rang. The guy he had at the meeting reported on everything that went on. Wood was furious but especially when he heard what Paul was planning at the Roundtable. That was serious stuff. Pickets and letters to the editor were crap. But, if they could turn the Commissioners against the landfill and have them hire a Tallahassee lawyer that was big trouble. She definitely had to be stopped.

There was no way he could bring this to Hayes or Smith's attention. Especially Smith. He was known to be a fairly straight arrow. He may work to get the site, that's what he was paid to do but to go outside the law, no way. Hayes was real chicken shit. Look how he acted when even the smallest pressure came. Plus, he wasn't impressed with his cop sources. If Edwards ever found out, he would cut Hayes dead.

Just then his phone rang. It was Baker. They had followed Paul home. They couldn't see into the property. It was blocked with tall hedges and went back quite away to the Intracoastal. They were parked at a little convenience store up the street. They picked up sandwiches and parked so they could see down the street.

Wood told them to follow her and pick their best opportunity. He told them that she was a greater danger then he thought but to be careful. He also told them his friend heard some of the people ask her to go with them out to walk the site with the new environmentalist today or tomorrow but that she had refused. She said she had a houseguest. So be careful, we don't need any witnesses.

They told Wood not to worry. They were always careful. As they watched the drive, they saw a car leave and turn south but it wasn't her station wagon. They waited and about a half hour later she drove out and turned north. They followed her up to the beaches. She stopped at the post office and then went on to a bait store. She had a bait bucket with her. Perkins said to Baker, "You follow her inside and see what she is doing."

He came back to the car before Paul left the shop. He told Perkins, "She was getting live shrimp. She and the owner were talking about the fishing. They didn't even notice me. She told the owner she was going fishing in the morning with her house guest. She sure hoped the weather would hold."

"Well, that shoots tomorrow," said Perkins. They followed her home and slowed as they passed her drive. She was opening the gate and they saw three big dogs jumping about.

"You can forget that one," said Baker. "I'm not going into that place with those dogs." They called Wood and reported. Told him about the dogs and the fishing and the house guest. Wood said to pack it in for the weekend. They could pick up again about 6:00 am on Monday.

Chapter Twenty-Two

Saturday evening

Mary heard the dogs bark once and a car door slam. She looked out the windows toward the drive and Jeffery was playing with the dogs. They seemed to love it. They were too big for her to roughhouse with but they took on Jeffery with great glee. He called an end to it and came bounding up the stairs. "Hi, have I time for a shower?"

"Just," Mary said. "I told them we would pick them up at five-thirty."

They pulled up as Clara and Ed walked out of their house. Jeffery got out of the car. "What a handsome man," said Clara as she hugged Jeffery. "I wanted to hug you when I saw you at the meeting but it somehow didn't seem the right time."

Jeffrey got back into the car after he held the door for Clara and Ed. "Where to, Mary?" he asked as he got back into the car.

"We have two choices. The Chinese place or the Homestead. How about you two, do have a preference?"

"Chinese," said Clara, "That is, if no one minds. I can cook like the Homestead at home. Not that I'm saying it's not good but not tonight."

"Wonderful," laughed Jeffery, as he smiled at Mary. "Hot and spicy, right, Mary?"

They walked into the restaurant before six and there was a booth left. After they sat, Jeffery asked the waiter if he would ask Mr. Ho to come out. Tell him Mr. Stone would like a word. Clara raised her eyebrows at Mary and Mary just smiled and shook her head.

The waiter came back and said Mr. Ho would be there in a minute. He had just finished putting their drinks down, tea for Clara, when Mr. Ho came toward them. A short gray-haired Chinese man, all smiles and bows in his greeting to Jeffery. Jeffery stood, as Mr. Ho approached, half-bowed his head and held out his hand. "Oh, such a joy to see you again, Mr. Stone." He lowered his voice and after looking carefully around said, "No one really appreciates real Chinese food like you." He then looked at Jeffery's companions and said, very apologetically, "I do not mean to hurt your guest's feelings."

"No, they are not hurt. They insisted we come here and as you know, I needed no persuasion." With that, he and Jeffery went into a long discussion on the menu and, in consultation with Clara, Ed and Mary, they all ordered.

Mr. Ho looked at Mary and smiling, said, "Slightly spicy? As usual Dr. Paul."

"Well, yes, but how did you know," she hesitated.

"Your name? I saw you on television, and I told my wife you were the woman who came in with that wonderful Mr. Stone last spring. I never forget my best customers." He asked Jeffery about New York and where he had eaten recently. They chatted briefly and Mr. Ho bowed himself away.

Clara, still looking perplexed, asked Jeffery how he had made such a conquest. He and Mary told her about their meal there last spring and how they came to know Mr. Ho. Jeffery liked hot and spicy food and had eaten his way through Chinatown. He had been asking the regular waiter questions he could not answer. The waiter went and got Mr. Ho. As the conversation about food went on, Mr. Ho asked how Jeffery knew so much. When he found out about Jeffery's sorties through Chinatown, Mr. Ho, who was hungry for news of Chinatown and the restaurants, fell in love with Jeffery.

"How was your trip at the landfill site?" Mary asked Jeffery. She told Ed that Jeffery had gone with the group to the site.

Jeffery said, "Actually, Mr. Van Ghent explained right off that he wasn't an expert but he thought he could find the obvious. The place, like all Palm Valley, is filled with birds, Fox Squirrels, 'possums, 'coons, deer and they even have Black Bear out on the Dee Dot. It is mostly scrub oak with a mixture of longleaf, planted pine and hardwoods."

"Did you see anything that would stop the landfill?" asked Clara.

"No, we didn't but a couple of us went off on our own for a bit." He turned to Mary and said, "We found the place where that man had been digging." To Clara and Ed, he said, "We found some gopher tortoise tunnels. They seem to be scattered over the site."

"That can't stop the landfill, can it?" Clara asked.

"No but it will make their life a little more miserable, having to either move them or pay for them. There were also obvious bear tracks. We rejoined the group but I soon left to be here for dinner." He turned to Mary and said, "Port rejoined the group. I'm going out with him Monday to see Dee Dot." He then explained to Ed and Clara why he was staying on and that the Sheriff had let him join them in looking into David's death.

"Speaking of nasty goings on," Clara said, "Let me tell you what one of the men said after the meeting." She then told them about someone saying it was a developer who ran Mary off the road and that one of them had said, too bad they missed.

"Who told that story about the developer?" asked Jeffery.

Mary and Clara looked at each other and shrugged. "I don't know. He was standing around with the men, some of whom were from out by Ranch Road. I don't know all those people, Jeffery, even by sight. May not even be true."

"Right, and the Pope's not Catholic," quipped Clara. "Changing the subject a little, we got a good dose of Ponte Vedra at its finest." She then proceeded to tell them about the woman who sat in front of them. She related the whole thing verbatim. Before long, Jeffery and Ed were laughing out loud.

Jeffery turned to Mary and asked, "Is she making this up?"

"Unfortunately, no. But when she invited me to have lunch sometime and I said Clara and I would be delighted, I don't know who was more upset, the poor woman or Clara."

"Poor woman!" exclaimed Clara. "I'll have you know her kind are what makes me hate this place sometimes. Let me tell you what happened at school this week. This seventh grade girl was sent to my office because she had shorts on that were way up her butt. I told her she had to call her mother to bring her suitable clothes to school to wear. That she knew the dress code wouldn't allow what she had on.

"She used my office phone and called her mother and told her what was going on. The mother must have been busy and said something to the kid that set her off. The next thing I know the girl is yelling at her mother 'if you weren't so damn lazy and would get off you butt and wash and iron, I'd have had decent clothes to wear' and some other choice things before I grabbed the phone from her. I told she should never talk to her mother that way.

"I then spoke with the mother and before I could get off more than a word that bitch mother tells me, I have no business talking to her daughter that way. Well, my dears, that was all I needed. As you may know I had some small sympathy for the girl. I told her mother that I didn't care how her child spoke to her. She was not allowed to talk that way in school and much less in my office; that we had standards. I handed the phone back to the child. She said a couple of 'Yes, mama's, and hung up.

"She told me her mother wanted her to meet her out front. I told her she could not go out front, she could stand inside the door until her mother came. I walked out with her and suggested she may want to learn how to use the washer and iron herself. She looked at me as if I had two heads. I finished by telling her those were a few of life's skills."

Jeffery was struggling not to burst out in laughter. Ed was already laughing so he did as well. "Jeffery, this generation has serious problems. It is not just here in Ponte Vedra but all over. My daughter-in-law is a strict mother; she tells me some wild stories that her kids bring home."

"Tell them about the limousines, Clara," said Ed.

"Oh yes, that's in the same category as that woman at the meeting. We have a few dances at the school for the middle school kids. Some of the parents come to chaperone, and others just drop their kids off and pick them up after the dance; a lot car pool.

"Well, at this one dance I was outside and here comes this black stretch-limo. It pulls up and five kids jump out. The driver asked me when he should be back. My mouth was hanging open; he had to repeat the question. I sort of mumbled eight. He said but the parents told him nine. I told him, these are sixth graders, and they have to be out of here at eight. Well, he asked me, what was he supposed to do? I told him to call the parents and tell them the kids have to be out of here at eight. He just stood there and said, "You don't know these parents." I told him he could tell the parents or just pick the kids up and drive around with them for an hour but they would be out of here at eight."

"Clara, a limo. What are those parents thinking?" asked Jeffery in astonishment.

"They aren't.... thinking that is. Well, that's not true, they do think about themselves. These people are too busy to pick up their kids. Probably told the driver nine so the kids would be out of the house longer. You know I love kids. It just kills me and a lot of the teachers to see what goes on with these kids."

"But a limo."

"Well, think of it, Jeffery, when money is not a problem. I'll bet that some of the parents even chipped in to pay. Or worse, one paid to show off to the others. Let me tell you one more before dinner. It's sort of a dinner-like story.

"At lunch one day, a kid stole another kid's powdered donuts off his plate. He was sent to the Dean's office and his parents had to come in. I was there as the Dean's assistant and protector, we laughingly said. The mother told us in no uncertain tones it was the school's fault for selling powdered donuts to tempt her child to steal. Don't look at me that way, I don't make this stuff up, you know."

Dinner had arrived. Jeffery asked whether anyone wanted to taste his. Clara stuck just the tines of her fork in the sauce. After tasting it, she grabbed her water. Mary laughed and said," I tried to tell you."

"How can you eat that?"

"Clara, he is not alone in this. There are people in Palm Valley and in St. Augustine who eat Datil peppers whole. Try mine, it's only slightly spicy. You will like it." They exchanged spoons full, all but Jeffery. He ate in isolated splendor, with no fear of anyone coming near his plate.

Mr. Ho came out and asked about the food. Everyone raved about what they had eaten. He and Jeffery talked a bit more about New York and food. When they finished, Ed said, "Why don't you stop at the house? I bought this great ice cream today. We can have it for desert. They all agreed.

Once settled with dishes of pecan ice cream, Clara asked Jeffery if he could talk about the murder at all. He nicely told her no. He went on to tell her about the Jacksonville Sheriff giving it to St. Johns County and why, politically. He then told her that they were telling no one what they found. The list of possible suspects was long. He told her who, in general, was being interviewed. Clara said they missed her.

Mary said, "I'll call the Sheriff Monday and correct that. Maybe the cops will come by the school and get her."

"Right, that's all I need," responded Clara. "Thank you but no thank you. Mary, I was only at the meetings you were at. Did they talk to you?"

"Yes, I don't think I was able to tell them much. They just wanted the names of the people who were at the meetings from me. Clara, I think I forgot to give them your name. Jeffery, why don't you ask the Sheriff if he wants to talk to Clara? They can see her at home after school. Or one of them can call her at home."

"Mary, what could I add? I didn't hear anything I would call suspicious, and I wasn't at the meeting with White."

"I think you're right Clara, but I'll run it by the Sheriff; he will probably agree."

"Jeffery, was that death and fire on the other side of the Intracoastal part of this?" asked Ed. Jeffery was silent for a while.

Clara stood, smiled, said, "A little more ice cream, anyone?" They all laughed.

"Let me put it this way. All the information on this thing is tightly locked up. More so then I have ever seen on a case like this. We were all at the Sheriff's office, and he gave David's brother Mark, Arthur, Mary and me a detailed rundown. Arthur and Mark flew out this morning with David's body. So, with the exception of his tight investigation group and Mary and me, no one knows anything.

"Mary made an innocent remark at dinner last night. If it were overheard it could be very dangerous to her. We all gave her hell.

Until we jumped on her, even she didn't realize how dangerous it could be, if the wrong people heard it."

"Are you saying no one knows anything, even the Jacksonville people, like the Mayor?"

"They only know what Sheriff Gray and Sheriff Edwards feed to them for a purpose. Now, I have said too much. But you two are such close friends that I feel guilty keeping everything back."

Clara had been quietly listening. "You are hoping with no information out there that someone will get nervous and slip up, somehow. Drop something or do something to make something happen."

"Smart lady."

"That's what comes from raising kids and working with them. Your approach is old hat to parents who are trying to find out something from their kids. It's sort of similar to the old silent treatment," she said, looking at Ed and he nodded.

"Yes, come to think about it. I have never had kids of my own but I can see how that would work. Also, St. Johns County is handling this at Sheriff Edwards' request. You can imagine the politics involved for him to give up jurisdiction. Before you ask, yes, Gray trusts him explicitly. That's what gives me confidence that we will solve this."

"Ok, Jeffery, I see more now. But I want you both to know that I am concerned about Mary. At the meeting today, you were there. I saw you come in."

"Really?"

"Yes, really. Parents and people who work with kids have eyes in the back of their heads. As I was saying, Mary gave the meeting to Larry to run and played low profile. At least, to some of those people it would look like that unless you understand St. Johns County and the politics of what she said they were doing at the Roundtable. That would scare the bejesus out of the Jacksonville landfill group. They are not stupid, you know. Most of those people there were so self-involved with their little part that what she said went right past them, I'll bet you money."

"Do we know whether any Jacksonville people were there?" asked Ed.

Mary shook her head. "I didn't even know the woman in front of us or the man who made the remark about the developers. There were a lot of people I didn't know. Even Port, standing not far from you, Jeffery."

"I'd have someone there if I were the Jacksonville people. The meeting was no secret."

"Thank you for mentioning this, Clara," said Jeffery thoughtfully.

"But what we are doing is no secret. We spent a lot of time on it at the last meeting."

"That's true, Mary, but I didn't see it reported in the press. They were so concerned with the Comprehensive Plan, they ignored the Roundtable this time," answered Clara.

"Something else to worry with. I am glad you are here Jeffery. I want all of you to know I am not making light of this. We are going to be getting up fairly early to fish, so we better be off to home," Mary said as she stood.

In the car Jeffery asked, "Was that a tone of self-concern I heard in there Mary?"

"Just a touch, my friend, just a touch."

Chapter Twenty-Three

Sunday morning

Jeffery and Mary loaded the boat: two ultra-light weight fishing rods apiece and an ice chest with beer, ice tea and water. Mary had made three sandwiches with rye bread, Vidalia onions and Braunschweiger, then added a package of potato chips. The shrimp were alive and active. They put them into the portable aerator and Mary put a frozen ice bottle in with them to keep them active. The Intracoastal was tidal and at low tide there was no water under the docks therefore the boats were hung on straps and cables high over the water. They had to fish according to the tides in order to get a boat in and out.

The best fishing was at the last of the falling tide and the first of the rising tide; Mary also fished way up in the creeks at the beginning of the high tide. It was only a little over a two hour trip since she had to be back at the dock in time to have enough water to get the boat out. She took her smaller boat out since it had a shallower draft for the creeks. Today they took the bigger bow-rider boat and were fishing the usual falling tide.

"Want to steer, Jeffery?"

"On the way back will be fine," he responded. He knew she liked to steer the first thing out. Last spring she had taught him how to fish the mouth of the creeks as the water fell. She had four spots she stopped at going south. Jeffery would anchor; they would throw lines out and let the current carry them past the mouth of the creek.

After about an hour and a half, they had caught one flounder and a trout. Mary pulled the boat up to shore at the shell bluff on the west side of the Guana Park. She stepped out with a bucket and her net and walked up to a little area where the water ponded at high tide. She threw for mud minnows and Jeffery put them in the bucket. They took them to the boat and put them in the aerator.

They anchored right next to the shell bluff about forty feet from the shore. The water dropped off to about twenty feet deep. The tide was still falling, and it would be about thirty minutes before it really turned. They both put out long lines with the mud minnows on and put the shrimp on the other two rods. "Time for food," Mary said as she popped the top off a beer and handed him a beer and a sandwich

Jeffery took a bite and a drink and said, "Fishing with you is always a great exercise in good food and drink. Especially when you taught me to have a beer and chips at six in the morning."

"It is not the hour, it is what you are doing that matters. When I fish, I have two beers and the proper food that I think goes with them. I have friends who think what is proper is bacon and fried egg sandwiches. I don't know how I got started doing this but I did. It fits the mood and the activity just fine," Mary said.

"Even when it is not hot out, like today, it seems to fit. I think you have made a believer out of me," replied Jeffery

"Yes. I do not hold with drinking a lot when on a boat, especially in the hot sun. Two beers seem to just hit the spot."

"Speaking of hitting the spot, these sandwiches are wonderful. We don't get Vidalias up north. Isn't it out of season for them?"

"Yep, I buy a lot and put them in the fridge on the dock. With luck, some last almost to Christmas. Sweet onions, mayo and braunschweiger (or liver sausage as my father called it) on rye are unbeatable."

The day was warming up and they were both in short sleeves. The boat was beginning to turn back and forth as the tide began to turn. "Not many people out today," said Jeffery.

"There will be more after lunch. Trying to get in a few days before the weather turns."

"Mary, tell me about the night the truck tried to run you off the road?"

"Try? He did, I ended up in the ditch."

"I know but tell me the sequence, as you remember it."

"Ok." Mary told him everything that happened. He stopped and made her repeat parts of it.

"How about a few tips on defensive driving? Have you ever been to defensive driving school?"

Mary looked at him, "I didn't know just anyone could go to those. But no, I haven't. Actually, I never had any reason to even think about doing that. Do you think it is necessary? I hope not."

"No, perhaps not but let's go over a few simple tricks. First, let's say a car is on your bumper or had even hit your bumper. When it happens again, touch your brake pedal a little and the rear car will be reduced to pushing you."

Mary thought about that and visualized it. "That would work, I'm sure, but they may then move on to other things. I don't want to stop the car."

"No, you don't, but you should also lean on your horn all this time. No one doing illegal acts wants to draw attention to themselves, unless, of course, they are nuts.

"The next case involves the car who is driving next to you and slams into your side. Now, admittedly this is scary and doesn't do the finish of your car much good. However, aside from the bump, it won't hurt you unless they have a much bigger car then you do. If you are in a small car, they can slide you sideways off the road. It would be difficult to move that station wagon of yours off the road."

"Funny, I have always felt safer in that big thing. I drove an MG convertible when I was younger for a few months. It was a lot of fun but when I was on the highway with it I always felt as though I were a moving target."

"You were. There is another one that was demonstrated to me about a year ago. We were being annoyed and outgunned. The man driving the car I was in was well trained and even taught defensive driving at a school for bodyguards. These guys were in front of us, swerving back and forth to keep us from passing, holding us up, hoping their friends might catch up to us from the rear.

"This buddy of mine grinned evilly and just as cool as could be, said it was time to teach me a new trick. He then proceeded to do so. He said, now watch, I am going to very slowly close up on him and tap his right rear fender with my left front fender. No force is necessary just a tap. He did and that car spun 180 degrees to the right and we were gone." Jeffery was thinking back on that experience. His eyes were twinkling. He smiled and shook his head. "Mary, I would never have believed it if I weren't sitting there when it happened."

"You expect me to do these things?"

"I expect you to visualize them and if you should ever be in a situation where you are desperate, you reach into your memory banks and say, I can take care of this."

"Desperate is the operational word, Jeffery," Mary said laughingly. "Want half the other sandwich?"

"You bet. Oops, hold it." His line went singing off the rod that he had parked in the rod holder. The boat had swung around with the tide, and he had hooked up with a good-sized fish. Mary pulled the other lines in and grabbed the net and watched. About ten minutes later, he had reeled the fish up to the side of the boat.

Mary leaned over the side, "Look at that, it's going to be over thirty inches! It's a beautiful Red Bass... wonderful fish," she said as she stood up, handed him the fish hook and took his rod. He gently unhooked the fish. It turned slowly, rolled once and swam away. "Well, that calls for the last beer." She handed him a beer and half the last sandwich.

"If that were a legal fish, would you have kept it?" asked Jeffery.

"No, not unless I was starving. The eighteen-inch to twenty-inch is better eating. But that's my opinion. I'm not a great fish lover. I said something about releasing a twenty-six inch fish to my neighbor one day. He about had a fit. He told me in no uncertain terms to just bring them home to him. He cleans them, then bakes them whole or even puts them in charcoal ashes to bake. I brought him a few large ones in the twenty-two or twenty-four inch range."

"Did he ever invite you to eat some with him?"

"Yes, but I was always busy."

"Busy, huh. I don't remember you ever ordering fish when we eat out."

"Jeffery, I do so eat oysters, crabs and lobster."

"Those are shellfish."

"I fixed fish the last time you were here and ate it and I will tonight if you like. I just like it fried in my own seasoning is all."

"Yes, that's true but you are not a great lover of them, are you?"

"You're right, they do not top the list but I don't spit it out on my plate either," Mary said, smiling. "Time to move north if you will get the anchor. I'll turn us and you can steer."

On the way, Jeffery asked her whether she wanted to stop at the usual places. She told him yes and settled in for the ride. They anchored in very shallow water at the mouth of a creek and after the lines were in Jeffery told her there was one other car trick he wanted to tell her about.

"Lets say you want to reverse directions rapidly. You yank your parking brake and simultaneously, you turn your wheel a one-quarter turn. This will spin your car 180 degrees and you will be facing the direction you came from."

Mary sat there thinking. Then she said, "When I was a young student nurse in St. Petersburg, Florida, I was dating a bush pilot. He was telling about this stretch of road in the northwest of the county that had a bad reputation. The thieves would wait until a good-looking car came by and blink their lights at their buddies up the road who would pull out into the road blocking the car.

"The driver would naturally stop and the thieves would come up to the car. If the driver became suspicious and decided to turn around, when he looked back, there was a car blocking his exit. They would rob the people in the car, throw their keys way off in a field and get away. A couple of times, it was a woman alone. One was nice looking; they messed with her before they left."

"Rape her?"

"No, they apparently stopped short of that. This boyfriend of mine was about ten or fifteen years older than me and had flown bush in Canada and Alaska. He hung out at a bar that cops frequented, and they had told him these stories. He said he didn't pay much attention until one night he was driving his friend's new Lincoln. He had picked it up for him up-county. Sure enough, on this same stretch of road, he saw a car pull off up the road ahead of him. Well, he stopped immediately and was about to turn when he saw, rapidly approaching headlights from the rear. He drove a truck and kept a shotgun in the rack behind the seat, but he wasn't in his truck and did not have another gun."

"Was he a Florida redneck Mary? What were you doing dating someone that much older than you?"

Mary raised her eyebrows and looked at him. "He was not a Florida redneck. He was a man of fortune, you might say. He came from a good family, he just liked and sought out adventure."

"Yeah and young women."

"Do you want to hear the rest of this or not?" Mary said, laughing at him. "Jeffery, this happened over thirty years ago. I have always liked older men. That is, until I got older, then I reversed myself."

He smiled and realized how dumb he sounded, "Yes, please go on. In fact, I was thinking what I would have done."

"Really. Well, he put that big car in gear and drove right at them," she stopped.

"Well?" he asked.

"They backed that car off the road just as he shot by. He had his portable two-way radio in the car with him and had activated the police channel and gave a running description of what was going down. Luckily, county deputies were up the road. They caught one of them, who soon gave up the others."

"That's what I would have done," Jeffery nodded.

" Ok, you tell me why, and I'll tell you what my friend said when I asked him if he wasn't afraid of hitting them."

"Ok. First, that's a pretty cowardly way to steal. Therefore, as cowards, I would bet they would move it. In fact, I bet they did it pretty fast."

"Yes, that's what he said. They were off the highway in a wink. He told me if this ever happened to me and if I were in a big car, to ram them. If in a small car, try the ditch, if it weren't deep. But never stop! Better to just carry a gun and shoot hell out of them. I agreed but I'm not sure I could ram them. I always tried, after that, not to drive back-country roads after dark."

"Oops, got one." They paid attention to the fishing and then moved one more time, north to a cut south of Marker Three.

Jeffery laughed, "Remember this spot?"

"I'll never forget." It was where Mary had nearly lost her life last spring.

"Mary, I have a new gun I want you to carry on you everywhere you go for a while."

"Jeffery, I have my Taurus and it's too heavy to put in my pocket. I do carry it in the car and the boat."

"I agree and I want you to continue doing that. But I want you to have this one," he handed her a very small gun, "in your pocket all the time."

Mary looked at it in her hand. It was about four inches long, from the end of the tiny grip to the end of the barrel. She looked at him and said, "You're joking. What is this?"

"It's a twenty-two magnum Derringer. It's a single action five shot revolver. It's for up close, personal work."

"I didn't know they made a revolver this small. Is it yours?"

"Yes, when I leave, it goes with me," he smiled "Mary, it has been on my mind to get you one of these ever since last spring. It would be great to drop in your shorts when you walk on the beach, in your briefcase or jacket pocket. It is only for up close, as I told you. A twenty-two doesn't have much stopping power but if one hits you, you will know it."

"Ok."

Jeffery looked at her. "No argument?"

"No, I have learned my lesson. I promise I will carry it everywhere with me for the present. In the future, when this mess is over, I will be more selective. You know guns, even little ones, can't go into public county buildings so I couldn't take it everywhere. When we get back, let's go out in the woods so I can try it a couple of times."

He watched her. She took it apart and examined it carefully. She really likes it, he thought. Good, that makes me feel better. He looked up, and her rod was bent and the line running. He yelled at her and took the rod out of the holder. "You pull it in," she said, "I'm busy."

Chapter Twenty-Four

Monday morning

Again it is seven o'clock and again the Sheriff had to make his own coffee. He had just sat down with a cup when Major Brown knocked and came in. "Is there more of that, Steve?"

"Yes, help yourself. These early hours have to stop," grumbled Steve, "but the men need an early start, especially Port, and I need a rundown, so here we all are. I haven't had a weekend report. Is the rest of the County still with us?"

Major Brown laughed, "What did you do over the weekend to make you so cheerful?"

"The damn windows and screens and half a dozen other 'honey do's'." She said she was saving them up for the fall. But all in one weekend is a bit much. How was your weekend?"

"About the same except I had done a bunch last weekend and this was a finishing up day. My wife said I was safe until next month, and then I could start on the Christmas decorations."

"Those two talk together too much; it's a conspiracy."

"I talked to the weekend guys and there were a few DUIs, bar fights, domestic calls. That was about all. Not a peep out of Hold or any of the other men. I saw some of the men coming in just now."

"Ok, let's go," Sheriff Gray said and walked out to the conference room. All the men were there, and it looked as though they all had coffee. "Hold, you start. How were the Ponte Vedra people this weekend?"

"We started at the meeting at the Community Center and the man from Ponte Vedra, first name Larry, was the chair. He actually helped us out a lot. He told people we were there and needed to talk to a few more people. I read the list; all but three were there. The men and I spoke with some of them after the meeting and made arrangements with the others for the afternoon.

"The meeting was interesting. They went over their whole strategy. They want to picket the site with the Nease high schools kids on a Saturday and want a couple of our patrol cars on standby." He paused and watched the Sheriff. When he didn't respond he went on and told them about Dr. Paul's report. That got a reaction.

"She reported the activity of the Roundtable to the whole bunch?" asked Gray in astonishment.

"Yes, Sir."

"Who all was there? I mean, did you know everyone there?"

"No, Sir, the place was full. We were all there; we knew some of the people. Stone was there, too."

"Stone, did you talk to Dr. Paul about the meeting? I mean about who was there?"

"We did talk about who was there and she didn't know them all either. I think I know where you are going." He then went on and reported the conversation he had Saturday night and Clara's reaction.

"Smart woman. Good analysis. The ramifications of what the Roundtable is doing, if successful, will cause havoc with Jacksonville," said the Sheriff.

"Mary is aware of that. We had a long talk yesterday; she promised she will go nowhere without her gun," said Jeffery. The Sheriff gave him a look and nodded.

He nodded to Hold to continue. He reported on the remaining interviews. The upshot was that everyone on Ranch Road, CR210 or Twenty-mile Road would suffer not only financial loss but also serious loss of lifestyle, meaning clean air and quiet living. Everyone was very angry. They also think the Jacksonville people killed Mr. White. When asked what White was doing out there alone or whom he was with, no one had any idea. Nor could they come up with a possible motive for his killing. That question remains a mystery.

He said they had added a few new names to the lists on the board. He had also taken the liberty to make a separate list of who showed up on all the lists: property owners, people at the meeting with White and people at other meetings. He pointed out, "You can see that the people on this new list are all from out near the site. I am not sure that is meaningful but there it is." They all looked at the Board. Hold also told them about the weekend trips out to the site with the new man, Roger- something. He said he sent Port and Stone out with them on Saturday.

"Ok Port, report."

"Stone and I started out with the group. The man's name is Roger Van Ghent. He was pretty good for an amateur. Really knew his birds, foliage and animals. Stone and I walked off alone. We found where Skeet had dug up those gopher tortoises. I had seen it Friday but we went over the area thoroughly. There are several tunnels on the site. Then we rejoined the others. The Saturday group was from out around there. They all behaved well. They kept asking about Panther tracks. They spent their time looking down at the ground so hard that I'm surprised some of them didn't walk into trees.

"I went back out Sunday morning. This was more of a Ponte Vedra group. Roger explained what he saw; it was really educational, but no Panther tracks. Roger did not encourage the idea that any Panther would be found at all. But there were Black Bear tracks, all headed north and east on to Dee Dot and McCormick property. They wanted to know whether bear weren't enough reason to stop the landfill. Roger said, kind of sorrowfully, that no, they would still have enough land to range. On both days I did not hear anything suspicious nor did I get a bad feeling. Much more anger on Saturday then on Sunday." He stopped and looked at Stone who only nodded.

"Did you go Sunday, Stone?"

"No, Sheriff, Mary and I went fishing and we did well," he said smiling.

"Yeah, I hear tell she can fish." Then Brown caught his attention. "Ok, Jeff."

"Sheriff, I found out who had the option to buy that land across the way from the site. The man who mentioned it called me at home. He was told I was asking and to call me. He said it's a man named Bob Key. He has a small place off Ranch Road. He has an air conditioning business and dabbles in real estate on the side. Buys land at tax sales and stuff. Apparently he knows someone who might be looking for land for some business. He had been talking to a friend of the man who called me. He was telling him if this deal went through he would make a dollar." The Sheriff looked at the board and nodded. Key's name was already on the board.

"Thank you, Jeff."

"Detective Cook, you have been patient, tell us about your adventures," the Sheriff was smiling broadly.

Cook returned the smile, "I gather you have spoken with Sheriff Edwards?"

"Oh, yes, he said I had made his day." He turned to the men and continued, "Without going into detail, my good friend to the north was able to set a trap to get the names of two of his men who were sharing confidential information out of school. As well, he was able to cause a great deal of discomfort to the man to whom they were giving the information, without him knowing what was going on. I can only assume there is a great deal of punishment still to come," he said looking at Cook.

"Yes, Sir, I think you can safely assume that. I am sure he will share with you." He then went very serious and continued, "That kind of behavior reflects badly on all of the troops. We are a unit, and running your mouth like that can put men in harm's way. What gets me is, what for? I mean, what do they expect to gain? But I am glad we found out, we suspected someone was talking. Now we know. This case is too fragile to have those fools messing it up. We got Skeet's sister's name from the trash hauler's records," said Cook.

"The trash hauler?" asked Brown in surprise. "The company that is involved in the landfill site?"

He looked at the Sheriff, who had a half smile on his face. "I'll explain later, Major."

Cook continued, "I went out to the address. It was way out on the west side. It was a little old house set up on blocks. Had a tired dog in the yard. The house sits on about a half-acre with a few chickens in the back and a lean-to like shed. I pulled up and hit my horn. Then I got out. There was a slanting porch on the front. This older looking woman came to the door and looked out through the screen at me and asked me what I wanted.

"I asked her if she were Mr. Skeet's sister Helen Barns. She finally said, 'And if I were, so what?' I said, in as nice a way as I could, that I was sorry to inform her of her brother's death. She was quiet again for a bit. Then she said, 'How'd he die?' I told her we were still investigating that; he was found dead in a shack that had been half-burned, just that day. Finally, she said, 'Thank you and turned away.' I said, excuse me but I have a few questions, if you don't mind." She turned back and looked out at me.

"She pushed the old screen door open and came outside and sat in an old kitchen chair on the porch. She told me she may as well answer my questions, can't much hurt, his being dead and all. She admitted to not seeing him in over a month. When he was real hard up, he would come and stay a day or so with her. But she said she couldn't feed herself, let alone him for long. He had a drinking problem, that's why he couldn't hold a job long. He would get work and when he was paid, he would go drink it up and get fired. Been like that all his life.

"I asked who he worked for. She said this one and that one. I asked about him working for the trash hauler. She said yes but not for long periods. He just filled in when they needed him. He told her the work was just too damn heavy to do for long. Said he didn't much like that kind of work anyhow. Was dirty and smelled bad.

"She didn't know his friends. 'Yes, he had been in jail for some little petty crap. It wasn't like he was a big time criminal. Not smart enough for that.' She wanted to know if he left any money or anything. I told her an old truck. She wanted to know if she could have it? I told her after everything was settled someone might get in contact with her. She said she didn't have a phone, could I come by and tell her or send her mail; I was to be sure to tell her what she would get. I asked about burial. She said 'potter's field,' she had no money for living, much less worry about the dead.

"She asked where he died; I told her. She said she knew he sometimes stayed at a hunting place on the Intracoastal; that must have been it. I asked if someone wanted to give him work, did they come asking her whether he was around? She said, sometimes a man would. But he never stopped, just told her to tell Bubba to call him when she saw him. I asked her when the last time the trash man had stopped by. She said a couple of weeks ago, but it was after her brother had left. She never gave him the message 'cause he hadn't been back.

"That about covers it, Sheriff. I said a few more words and left. I couldn't tell whether she knew more and was conditioned not to talk to cops or if that was all she knew. I had a feeling that she didn't know more. There are more than a few people like that in the backcountry. You have your share. I saw some when I was out with Rogers. They just won't tell us more than they have to."

"I like your assuming that you knew all about the trash man. Good questioning. What do you suggest next?" asked the Sheriff.

"If it is all right with you, I would like to go visit the trash hauler and ask him some questions?" smiled Cook. "No disrespect, Sheriff. I would first like to ask Sheriff Edwards his thoughts about talking to the trash hauler."

"None taken, that is a good idea. This is still a politically sensitive mess. He should know what you are doing. Do you want to go alone?"

"No, Sir, I thought if Hold was free we could both go," and he smiled.

"Bringing in the big guns, huh Detective Cook?" Port said.

"You bet. I need all the protection I can get."

"Are you planning on calling first or just dropping in?" asked Major Brown.

"Sir, I thought we would just sort of drop in, casual like. Unless your guys have a better suggestion or Sheriff Edwards might."

"You can use the phone in my office, when we are done. Call Edwards from there," said the Sheriff. "Cody, you go back on patrol in Ponte Vedra and stop at the shack a couple of times and scare off sightseers."

The Sheriff looked at Rogers and James. "We have two more people to see, Sheriff."

"Fine. I want you two to stop at the man's place that Brown mentioned. Ask him if he is selling? When I was up there, I didn't see any 'for sale' signs out. You can tell him you heard he might have given someone an option on his property. I want you to be available to Cook and Hold if they should need you. Have lunch at that little bar by the bridge and listen to the gossip. I see you are in street clothes. Stay that way for today."

"I miss anything, Major?"

"No, I would like all of you to keep in close contact with me. Don't be shy. Call me with anything new you find out." Major Brown looked at each one of them. They all nodded. "When this thing breaks, it will go fast. I don't want you all to think I'm being an old lady but I have a bad feeling about this whole thing. So communicate and stay near, where we can get you in a hurry." No one laughed at him.

"Port, you and Stone ready?" asked the Sheriff.

"Yes, Sir. We are meeting a man named Francis at the far end of Twenty-mile Road. Since we are most interested in the property at the south end, he suggested we come in that way."

"What is the other way in?" asked Stone.

"Way up north at the end of Pablo road. They have a big hunting lodge up that way as well," said Port.

They all stood up, Stone said, "Sheriff, a minute please." He walked over to him and said, "Sheriff, I told Mary if she were going out anywhere today, except to shop or go to the post office, to call your office. I told her to tell you whom she is going out with, where and when. I hope you don't mind. After I heard her report at the meeting and the fact there were people there even she didn't know, I was concerned. I think a bit of caution is called for."

"I agree. Will she call?"

"Yes, after David's death and her being run off the road, she will use caution. At least tell us what she is doing. You should also know I gave her my five shot 22 Derringer Magnum to take with her everywhere."

"You're joking?"

"She said the Taurus was too heavy for her pocket. In fact, we went out in the woods yesterday afternoon and she worked with the Derringer until she felt very comfortable with it.

In fact, she surprised me. She hit a tree-target from twenty-five feet away almost as well as I can. She has great hand eye coordination. Must be the pool and golf." Jeffery laughed.

"Fine. You tell Brown on your way out. A Derringer, huh? You never fail to surprise me, Stone."

When the Sheriff walked into his office, Cook was talking to Edwards. He stopped and asked, "Can we use the speakerphone, Sir?" The Sheriff turned it on.

"Good morning, Steve. Cook told me what he wants to do. What do you think?" asked Edwards.

"Fine with me, Sam. We both agreed it was a good idea to check this out with you. Have you a suggestion for an approach?"

"Yes, go in with no warning at all. If Wood is not in, just talk to whoever is around and ask lots of questions. Hint that the coroner hasn't ruled out foul play yet. You know the play?"

"Yes, I do and I agree." Steve turned to Cook and asked, "You done?" Cook nodded. "Good. I'd like a word with Edwards. Hang on, Sam, I'm seeing the men out."

He said to Cook and Hold, "You find out anything at all, you call, and when you leave there, you call." They both nodded and left.

The Sheriff turned the speakerphone off, "Sam, I'm glad he wanted to call you. They are moving into your territory today."

"You sound a bit edgy Steve, something happen?"

Steve told him about the weekend meeting and Paul's report.

When he finished Sam said, "I understand. I'm glad you told me; gives me something to listen out for. That news will not be received with welcome around here. I hope someone is keeping an eye on Paul. I'll talk with you later in the day."

Chapter Twenty-Five

Monday morning

Baker and Perkins were sitting at the small convenience store on Roscoe Blvd. drinking coffee. "What time did he tell us to call Ned?" asked Perkins

"At seven-thirty," he looked at his watch, "about now. That car left her place about fifteen minutes ago; you drove past it; she wasn't in it. I'll use the pay phone over there and call him." Baker got out of the car and called. "Boss, it's Baker. We are out in Palm Valley and some guy just left her drive. She's still in there."

"Good, you watch her and follow her. After what I heard happened at that meeting Saturday, it is more important than ever, that we put her out of commission," said Wood.

"What happened?"

"She described plans to get the St. Johns County Commissioners to hire a lawyer and fight us all the way to Tallahassee," Wood said.

"So, you want us to kill her?" Baker whispered as he looked around him.

"No, you damn fool."

"What does 'out of commission' mean then?"

Woods, sitting in his office, rolled his eyes heaven ward. Oh, God, help me. This is the best help I have and listen to him. "I thought you and Perkins told me you understood that you had handled whores and this was no different. Only difference is you can mess up her face. She ain't like one of your whores that needs her face or body to earn a living for you. Just wear masks so she can't ever identify you. Do not let Perkins rape her. Wear gloves and leave no evidence. I want other people to know she has been hurt and scare the hell out of them. They will back off, I assure you."

"You don't want her back on the street right away either? I mean if we broke a few things would that be ok?" Baker asked.

"Yes, just don't kill her. They will not look as hard for a good mugging as they would for a murder. There will also be people who say she was asking for it and those who will say she deserved it. Just don't be seen. Call me after ten and keep me informed. You got that?"

"Yes, Sir, we have my car and Perkins truck so we can switch off."

"Good." he hung up.

Baker walked back to the car and after he sat down he told Perkins exactly what Wood had said. "So we better trade off cars frequently, and find different places to park to watch that drive."

"I was thinking the same thing. I have my CB in the truck. You have one here. Let's find a clear channel and just say go and then north or south on it. Let's split up. I'll park up near here where I can see her if she comes this way, and you go park south. We can switch around," said Perkins as he got out of the car. They found a seldom-used channel that was clear, and they both tuned to it and left the lot.

Cook and Horn pulled up at the trash haulers office at 8:30. They walked in and introduced themselves, and Cook asked his secretary, "Is Mr. Wood in?"

"No, detective, you just missed him but he will be back in about an hour. Can I help you?"

"Yes, ma'am is there anyone around who might have known Mr. Skeet that we can talk to. Skeet was a part-timer of yours. He didn't do anything wrong.... wasn't in trouble, but he met with a deadly accident Friday, and we just need to get a bit of closure on him. Our boss asked us to stop by since he worked here."

"Oh my! I'm sorry to hear that. Mr. Todd, one of the truck supervisors, is out back. He knew Mr. Skeet. I'll call him."

"No, don't you bother your sweet self, just point the way and we will walk out back."

She blushed, smiled, preened a bit with her hair and pointed to a side door and said, "Aren't you the sweet one. You just go through there and straight back. He is a big man with a bald head. You can't miss him. You tell him, I said it was ok to talk to you."

Once out of hearing Hold said in a high squeaky voice, "Oh, you are so big and strong, I can hardly stand it." He lightly hit him on the arm with his fingers.

Cook grinned, "Yep, whatever works."

"That sure did."

Ahead of them, at a tall counter, leaned a big man writing on a clipboard. The detectives walked up and introduced themselves and said Mr. Wood's secretary sent them out to talk to him. He could call her if he wanted but she said it was ok. He quickly went on to tell him who he was asking about and why.

Todd relaxed and said, "Haven't seen him for a couple of months. I hate to speak ill of the dead but he wasn't much of a worker."

"Why did you use him?" asked Hold.

"Sometimes, when we have vacations, we may need extra guys. So we call in these part-timers. Truth is, none of them are worth much. I mean part time garbage men? Most are like Skeet, work a few days, get paid and blow it on booze. We hold their pay until we are through with them. We give them lunch and sodas and one beer at the end of the day."

"When did you use him last?" asked Cook.

"Couple months ago, remember when we had that big wind, had a lot of yard trash down. Used extra men and trucks for about a week until we had it cleaned up. Haven't needed any extra help since then."

"If you needed Skeet, how would you find him?" asked Cook.

"The boss, Mr. Wood, drove by his sister's and left word."

"If that didn't work, then what?"

"Mr. Wood might send out Perkins and Baker to find him. They round up extra men for us when we need them. They also will drive if we are short of drivers. Can't let the part-timers drive or even most of the guys who pick up the cans. Most don't have a license that's good. Most lost it to DUI charges."

"Are these guys around now, this Perkins and Baker?" asked Cook.

"No, I haven't seen them today. They were in and out last week."

"What else do they do around here?"

"They do whatever the boss wants them to do. This is a big operation. I thought you were interested in Skeet?" Todd said backing up a bit and looking hard at Cook.

"We are but our boss wants us to waste our time finding out what Skeet might have been doing the past couple of weeks. Busywork if you ask me. I mean, who cares what a drunk who can't hold a job has been doing?" grumbled Cook.

"Hey, watch it man, Edwards can get right nasty if it gets back to him that you're bitching and moaning and talking trash," Hold said.

"Yeah, well I don't think Mr. Todd here is going to be calling him, are you Todd?"

Todd laughed and slapped his leg. "Fat chance, me calling the Sheriff and complaining about you, Detective."

"See, Hold, you need to lighten up, I mean you'll learn all bosses are the same. Hold here, has just been a detective with us for about a week. I'm sort of showing him the ropes."

"Well, Detective Hold, seems it would be a good idea you listen up to your buddy," Todd said. "That be all, Detective? I've work to do."

"Yes, thank you for your time. If your boss comes back, tell him we were just asking about Skeet and we will get back to him. Probably later today."

The men got in the car. Hold said, "Hang on a minute." He took a couple of steps over to a guy who was getting out of a garbage truck and asked him if he had seen Baker. After a brief interchange, he had the first names of Baker and Perkins. He went back in the car. "You want to hang around, wait for Wood? I know you heard something from Todd that I didn't. That was a great fast shoe back there with Todd," Hold said.

"Good job yourself. He was getting antsy about our questions. Sure didn't want to talk about Perkins and Brown," Cook replied.

"What are you thinking?"

"Remember, I said that Skeet's sister told me that Wood was there a couple of weeks ago looking for Skeet. Yet, this man tells us they didn't need any part-timers for the past couple of months."

"So what the hell did Wood want with Skeet?" questioned Hold. "Wait a minute, if he couldn't find him he must have sent," he paused and looked at his pad, "Perkins and Baker to find him."

"That's how I see it," remarked Cook.

"If they found him the first time, they sure would know where to find him the second time. Damn, Cook, we have Skeet tied into the landfill because of his fingerprints on that shovel. No wonder you wanted out of there so fast. Wood is not someone we want to talk to, at least not right now."

"Let's hope he comes on like gangbusters with Todd and scares Todd into keeping his mouth shut. Let's head to Edwards' office, we need to do a report to Edwards and Gray. Then see whether we have anything on this Baker and Perkins. That message about communicating that Brown gave this morning is not going to be ignored."

Mary told the dogs she had to go to the grocery store, post office and library. She would be back in a couple of hours. She reminded them to watch the house and the birds. As she opened the car door and stepped in, she thought, if anyone heard me talking to the dogs that way they would put a net over me. Oops, I forgot the little gun. She got out, went back into the house, picked up the gun and dropped it in her pants pocket. She looked in the mirror. It made a slight bulge in her tight jeans. Well, with my wallet and stuff it won't matter, she thought. I'll check out how it looks with other clothes when I get home.

She turned north and then east on Canal. Perkins clicked his CB and said north and followed her. When she stopped at Palm Valley Road, she had her blinkers on to go left; he slowed and let her turn ahead of him. When he reached the corner, he looked in his rear view mirror and could see Baker a ways back, coming up behind him. When she parked in the Publix lot, he parked several rows away. Baker pulled up next to him, rolled down the window and said, "That worked just fine. If we can't get her this trip out, let's change places when we get back. I'll go park nearer the entrance." He drove off.

Half an hour later, she came out pushing a cart filled with bags. She loaded the back of the wagon and drove out. She stopped at what looked like a small post office and then at another building and then headed back home. Maybe I can get her driving into her place. He slowed; he saw her walking back to drive her car in, after she had opened the gates. He pulled up and there were all three of the damn dogs. He took off cursing. Damn, she got those gates open fast. But maybe that was a dumb idea; if those dogs saw me and she yelled the whole neighborhood would hear them barking.

He saw Baker drive by. He followed him and pulled up next to him. They talked a while. "Let's go back to the convenience store and get a sandwich for lunch and call Wood. Who knows if we will have a chance to eat later? She ain't going anywhere until she unpacks those groceries," Perkins said.

"You call Wood, Baker. What do you want to eat?"

"Couple of hot dogs with everything, chips, candy bar, soda, and anything else that looks good." He called Wood. He had to wait; the secretary said he was out back talking to Todd. He gave her the pay phone number and said he would wait by the pay phone.

Wasn't long before the phone rang, "Hello" he hesitantly said.

"Baker?"

"Yes, Mr. Wood, this here is a pay phone and I was being a bit careful. I just wanted to tell you we set up so we can track her and not be too obvious about it. She left about eight-thirty went to the store, made a couple of other stops and shot right into the yard. The dogs were right at that gate."

"Ok. Keep on it. The cops were here while I was out. Asking about Skeet. They were out back and talked to Todd."

"What did he tell them?"

"I asked him. I'm not so sure he gave me a straight answer. He said he told them how sometimes we used Skeet like we used other part-timers. He said they asked how we contacted him. He said he thought through the sister. That wasn't his job. He just ran the truck routes and set the crew up."

"That seems ok, what bothered you?"

"They were out there with him for almost half an hour, doesn't seem that little would take so long. Also, my secretary told them I'd be back in an hour, why didn't they wait?"

"Hell boss, cops are lazy, they probably got what they wanted and cut out. Coffee time you know."

"You know Todd. He seem the talkative kind to you?"

"I don't know him well. He may not look it but he is a pretty straight arrow. He is the kind that would think nothing of bullshitting with cops. Probably thinks cops are great guys. What could he have told them anyhow?"

"Nothing, you're right. I'm just edgy about what that bitch Paul is planning in St. Johns County. That has to be nipped in the bud," Wood said.

"We'll get her but we can't go in that yard. She'll come out again. We will get her, don't worry."

"Ok, you hold Perkins in check," he hung up.

Perkins was back in Baker's car. Boy did those dogs smell good. "Let's drive down that little road across the street down to the water and eat these. She ain't going anywhere yet,"

"Ok, I'm hungry but we can't take long. Wood said the cops were out asking questions about Skeet. Said they talked to Todd since Wood was out. He said Todd seemed to be holding some of the conversation back from him."

"That's nuts; Todd don't know nothin'. He probably just likes to bull with cops."

"That's funny, that's what I told him too." They both laughed.

"Anyhow, Ned, he emphasized again how he didn't want you accidentally killing Paul. Just mess her up good."

"That's getting old. The way you guys talk, you would think I was a stone cold killer," Perkins said staring at Baker.

"Hey, don't be giving me that stare, I'm just passing on what Wood said," Baker protested.

"Well, if he is such a hotshot let him do his own dirty work. Quick to give orders then sit on his hands keeping them clean. You know, I get tired of him talking down to me all the time."

"That may be true Ned but I sure don't tire of the money. You got to admit it beats lifting garbage cans all day." They both laughed.

Chapter Twenty-Six

Port and Jeffery walked out of the Sheriff's office. Port said, "The Sheriff told me to take the four-wheel drive. You can leave your car here. Gray will want us all back at the end of the day. That is, if you want to come back."

"Wouldn't miss it for the world. But seriously, that is one of the reasons I stayed on. The family wanted me to follow the investigation. Mark is one of my best friends, and I was very fond of David. So you can say I have a special interest."

"You said one of your interests. Mind if I ask what the other is?"

"Not at all. I am worried about Mary's safety. I heard her report at that meeting and if I were with the landfill people, I'd be plenty worried."

"You think she can bring this off?"

"That's what's wrong. It isn't just her; it's all those people in that room. Port, that was a million dollar audience. They are not about to have the stench of a landfill over Ponte Vedra. If the Commissioners don't get a lawyer and get involved, they will get one, as well as make sure none of those Commissioners are ever reelected. Those are multimillion-dollar homes up there. Someone in Jacksonville badly misjudged. Mary's problem is she jumped on it first and alerted the troops. That and her service on the Roundtable."

"I see, so they might have labeled her the major problem."

"Yes, I think that is very possible."

"I understand," replied Port. He got in the car, and turning to Jeffery said, "Since we aren't meeting Harry Francis of Dee Dot Ranch until nine, we still have time to stop and get sandwiches and water. Ok with you?"

"Yes, then we won't have to stop later to eat."

They pulled up at the Twenty-mile Road gates just at nine. There was a new four-wheel drive truck with Francis standing next to it and the gates already open. They drove through and parked behind the truck. They both stepped out to help the Harry shut the gates and introduced themselves.

Harry said, "I have an aerial map for you. I copied it at the office. You can keep it. Here, let me orient you to where we are in relation to the landfill."

He laid the aerial map on the back of the truck and Port and Jeffery watched as Harry drew his finger over the map. "You can see a lot of the trail roads. Some of them are logging roads. We timber regularly on a rotating basis. I drew in the roads you can't see because of the tree cover. I can spend most of the morning with you but after lunch I have to be back in the office. Mr. Davis said you could stay as long as you want. Even come back if you like. How would you like to ride?"

"Port, if you want to ride with Mr. Francis, I'll follow."

"Sure, then we can switch."

"I thought I would show you this south end near the site. Then we can head north, go up by the Intracoastal. It is beautiful. You should be able to more then cover the whole thing by early afternoon."

"Can we get back out through the landfill site?" Port asked. "Hate to ask someone to unlock gates for us."

"No problem. We haven't put gates up into the site yet. See here," he pointed at the road, "you come back this way. You see that little logging road? It will carry you south through the site and out onto 210. I'll show you now so you won't miss it later."

Harry and Port took off, and Jeffery followed. Lovely country, thought Jeffery. I wonder if they have been approached to put this into conservation some day. Boy, wouldn't the developers love to get their hands on this. They moved slowly and pretty soon they came to a crossroad. Harry stopped and motioned Jeffery up. He stopped and walked up to the car. Harry pointed to the road through the site, and again showed them the aerial. He laughed and said, "If you get lost just drive south. With that four-wheeler you'll get out."

"Let me ask you something before you drive off," Jeffery said. He asked him if a mother bear was shot at, would she run off even if it meant leaving her cub? Harry told them he thought so and if they nicked her, with some shot, she surely would. They have bears on the ranch but they are shy creatures, and they aren't seen much. He said they don't hunt them. They drove north along the eastern edge, and the land near the Intracoastal was all Harry said it was. This is what Mary's side of the canal looked like many years ago. Jeffery knew Port was peppering Harry with relevant questions.

At about ten-thirty he and Port changed places. He asked Harry whether he hunted any out here. Harry told him the family and guests did off and on but Harry had about given it up. Mr. Davis had had a lot of buffalo, but he had just gotten rid of them. The guests hunted deer, turkey and quail.

Harry showed them several tree stands for hunters as he drove slowly through the woods. It was very quiet. He stopped and showed them a couple of cypress trees. The base was so divided a man could walk through them. Harry said he had never seen larger and older ones. Sometimes they saw deer and wild turkey.

There were a few little inlets that came up into the property from the Intracoastal. He stopped and showed them one; said poachers would sometimes come up in johnboats to shoot deer, then go back out. One time the Davis's hired men were out checking an inlet and there was a johnboat. Instead of lying in wait all night, they pulled the propeller off the motor and took the paddles; came back the next day and it was gone. The guy probably waded it out to the Intracoastal and then swam it across.

Harry had a lot of stories; the time just shot by. Soon, they were at the lodge and Harry said he had to get back to the office. They told him they had sandwiches. He told them to sit on the deck of the lodge and eat lunch and watch the ranch life go by. If they went slowly he said, as he showed them the roads back, they should be out before three.

They settled on the deck and quietly talked about the morning. Port told Jeffery that Harry made it clear that they did not sell the landfill site. It was a condemnation proceeding. Old man Davis was not happy at all. They owned the land south of 210 all the way to Pine Island Road. A landfill would not be an enhancing attraction.

Cook called and told Edwards they were on their way. When Cook and Hold walked into Sheriff Edward's office, Cook told him almost verbatim, with help from Hold, the conversation with Todd. He said that, based on what the sister had said, he believed Wood had sent Perkins and Baker out to find Skeet.

Then he told him when he and Hold were on the way out to their car, Hold had stopped and asked someone in the parking lot if he had seen Baker. He said, "No, Ted hadn't come in". He asked him how about his buddy and turned to Cook, saying, "What the hell was that other guy's name?" and before Cook could answer, the guy said, "You mean Ned? Yeah, Ned Perkins'.

"Good work, it'd be hell to find them without first names. What do you want to do now?"

"Well, we have to report in to Major Brown with everything we find. So I thought Hold could call him, and then we could start finding out something about them. Depending on what we find and what you suggest, we could go back out and visit Mr. Wood."

"Good. Get right on it. Let me call the records guys for you and tell them to move this for you. Hold, use my other phone to call Brown. We don't want that conversation overheard."

Hold dialed and asked for Major Brown. He told him what he and Cook had found out. Brown told him to hang on a minute. He came back on the line, "Hold, the Sheriff wants you to get license plate numbers, make and description of the cars or whatever they are using for wheels. He also wants you to call us when you finish your search and tell us what you and Cook find before going any further. He also wants Edwards to call him before the next step. He also said to tell Cook you both did well. Tell Edwards we will check our records as well."

"Yes, Sir." He waited until Sheriff Edwards hung up the phone and told him what Sheriff Gray requested. Edwards smiled and said, "Maybe we will strike a gold vein that will lead us to the mother lode. I just bet Sheriff Gray can feel it."

Cook and Hold left. Cook gave Hold his desk and Hold said, "I'll do the plates." They both set to work. Cook used the desk of another detective who was out. It was quiet in the office. Everyone was on the streets or in court. In less then an hour they had what they were looking for. Perkins had a late model, blue, four-wheel drive Ford truck. Baker had a black, late model Mercury four-door sedan. No outstanding tickets or warrants for either one. They both had Northside addresses.

However, Perkins name had been flagged. He was still a suspect in a serious mugging involving a hooker from last summer. No direct evidence and the hooker wouldn't talk. The only reason they had Perkins name is another hooker who brought this one into emergency room was overheard talking to her about giving Perkins up before he killed her. When they tried to get her to tell them who did it, she said she didn't see them.

Cook and Hold compared notes. Cook said, "I guess we could always ask the vice boys about Perkins. But let's go talk to Edwards first. They went back to Edwards' office. His secretary said to wait a minute, he was on the phone. Soon, he stuck his head out and motioned them in. He asked did the have anything. They told him they did. He turned back to the door and before he shut it, he told his secretary not to put any calls through, he would be tied up for a while.

Edwards called Sheriff Gray and while he waited, he told the men, 'we will use the speakerphone'. They heard Sheriff Gray say 'good morning' and before he could go on Edwards said, "We are using the speakerphone, Steve. I thought, no sense having the men repeat themselves. Also, we need both of us, I fear."

"Good, but before you continue, Sam, I did do a check. We have nothing on autos or warrants, but one of our men heard Brown asking about Perkins on the phone. He stopped and told Brown that he had heard the name before; he is one of our vice squad officers. He said he would check and get back to us."

Edwards was watching Cook grin so he said, "I have a detective grinning up a storm here so, Cook, you go ahead."

Cook told them what he had found: that there was a flag on Perkins and why. He said he didn't want to ask their vice men until he cleared it. Sheriff Gray said, "That sounds as if he were an enforcer disciplining a whore or he was working one himself."

"I agree, Steve. If he was just a John, she wouldn't be so anxious to cover it up. Hold, what did you turn up?"

Hold gave them the information on the cars. Gray asked him to repeat it again, slowly. Just then they heard Brown excuse himself, "Be right back, we may have something."

"Do we want them to go back out and talk to Wood? Ask him about Skeet and these other two?" asked Edwards.

"Sir," said Cook.

"Go ahead, Cook."

"I think we need to find a careful way to ask about the other two. I'd hate to have Todd loose his job over this."

"You don't think he told Wood everything he told you?" asked Gray.

"Well, Sir, I don't think I would if I were Todd. Mr. Todd is no dummy; he almost caught us appearing too interested in this Perkins and Baker stuff. We had to do a quick shuffle and bail. If you get my meaning."

"Cook" said Hold. "He did tell us Skeet was one of the part-timers. We could say when we asked Todd how they recruited them that he mentioned a few guys: Perkins, Baker and some others who rounded them up. Then ask whether we can talk to a few of them."

"Yeah, that might work." Cook said slowly and thoughtfully. "Have to be careful.

Edwards said, "I agree. No sense getting this Todd guy in unnecessary trouble. We can find other ways to get these guys in. What do you think Steve?"

"Hang on a minute, here comes Brown."

"Brown here. My vice guy pulled a record from last spring. A working girl got hell beat out of her out off King street and left by the side of the road half-dead. When they found her she must have thought he had come back, cause she kept muttering 'no, Perkins, no.' Later, when they asked her who Perkins was, she denied saying anything like that. 'Didn't know no Perkins.' They didn't have a Perkins in the data base so he just made a note in the record."

"Matches what we have. Could be the same guy. Don't know how many Perkins we have. Course it may not be the same guy," said Edwards. "Let's have Cook and Hold go back out to talk to Wood. It might look funny if they don't show up again. It's still before noon. Call him now and see whether he is in. Tell him you are on your way. Wait a minute, tell the secretary to tell him you are on the way. Just a few minutes down the road."

"Sam, you are a tricky one," laughed Gray.

"Whatever works. Ok, let's see what we flush out of these bushes; be in touch later."

When they hung up Steve said to Brown, "Get the car and truck description and plate numbers out to our guys in Ponte Vedra. Tell them to keep their eyes open and call us if they spot them."

"You want them picked up, Steve?"

"I'm tempted. Let's see whether they find them first. You know, Jeff, this is taking an interesting turn. Hold and Cook have done a sharp job. If this whole mess ties into the Jacksonville crowd I want to be sure we have all our ducks in a row."

"You are looking at Skeet but remember, Steve, that still doesn't tell us how come White was at the landfill and whether he was alone."

"Yes, but we have Skeet and White there at the same time or near to it. Then we have Skeet dead, and not from natural causes. I'm betting we have a third party or more. I don't want to pick Perkins and Baker up off the street. At least just yet." He paused and Jeff watched him.

"You're worried aren't you?" asked Jeff.

"Yeah, and I'll be even more worried if they show up in Ponte Vedra."

Chapter Twenty-Seven

Officers Rogers and James pulled onto the property on CR 210 that Major Brown had told them about. They had stopped on the way back to Ponte Vedra, but there weren't any cars then. This time, there was a small gray car pulled up next to the trailer. Rogers honked his horn and stepped out of the car with James. An older woman came to the screen door wiping her hands on her apron. "Morning officers, can I help you? I'm Mrs. Kane"

"Yes, ma'am, is your husband home?" ask Rogers.

"No, Jake is still at the dentist; I expect him after two. Is there anything I can do?" She was beginning to look a bit anxious.

Rogers quickly said, "No, it is nothing serious. We just wanted to ask him about whether he is selling his land."

"Oh." she laughed, "You're right, he is the one to talk to. We have been mulling that over for some time now. But I'm not sure where it is at the present, what with the landfill business and all. I guess you had better talk with him. I'm making two apple pies. I'll save you two pieces when you come back."

"I'll sure look forward to that," said James smiling at her just as sweet as he could.

Driving back toward Ponte Vedra, Rogers said, "Like apple pie, huh?"

"Oh man, you just can't have anything better than homemade apple pie." He was rubbing his hands together and nodding.

His radio came on after they had gone over the bridge and north on Palm Valley Road. "Rogers."

"Officer Rogers, Major Brown wants you to call him at the office on a land line."

"Thank you. I'm three minutes away from the annex office." He pulled into the small annex office on Palm Valley Road up near highway A1A just as Officer Cody drove up. "Hi, Cody, what's up with you today?"

"Just got a message to call Major Brown." Cody replied.

"Really, so did we. Let's go see what's up." The three officers entered the back of the building. Rogers picked up a phone and dialed the St. Augustine office. When he got Brown on the phone he said, "James, Cody and I are all here together."

Before he could go further, Brown told him to get his pad out. He gave him the plate numbers and descriptions of a car and truck belonging to Perkins and Baker. Told them they suspected they might know something about Skeet. He gave him a brief rundown. Said they were to keep a lookout for them. If they saw them to call him right away. They would then decide where to go with it.

"Do we follow them if we see them? Be kinda hard to do and not be seen in our patrol cars?" asked Rogers.

"Yeah, don't lose sight of them. We can have you relieved with a plain car. We might be getting a break today. We sure could use one. Be sure to tell Cody. Did you get to the man on 210?"

"Just came from there. His wife said he would be back from the dentist at two. Promised James apple pie," laughed Rogers.

"Right, be careful, that smacks of bribery. I'll talk with you later. Stay alert."

Rogers told James and Cody while Cody copied down the information. "Finished your interviews yet?" asked Cody.

"No, have one more here and then back out to 210. Thought we would catch lunch down at that place by the bridge. Brown wanted us to sit there and listen awhile. How's your day?"

"I was stopped outside Publix by a good citizen. She wanted to know what we were doing to stop the landfill. Now how was I supposed to answer that?"

Rogers laughed, "Well, how did you?"

"Thank heavens she was one of those who follow up their questions with statements about how we can do our jobs better. When she finished, she just nodded her head and walked off looking very satisfied. I think it made her day."

"Did she have any good suggestions?" asked James.

"You don't want to know. I'll see you guys later."

Mary had put her groceries away and was finishing her bills. She didn't put the meat in the freezer. Thought she would wait and see whether Jeffery wanted steak or chops for dinner. She straightened up the house, not that it needed much, and sat on the porch with the dogs and a book. The phone rang. "Hello."

"Mary, it's Bob Key."

"Hi, Bob, how can I help you?"

"We missed you Saturday. Roy Gunther and I were going to ask if you wanted to go out today. But he just called and said he was hung up at work. That man Van Ghent was really good. I went back for a while on Sunday and he found a Florida Scrub Jay. We're really excited about that."

"Really? I'm no expert but they aren't an endangered species are they?" asked Mary.

"No, but they are a threatened species."

"Is that enough to stop the landfill?"

"If we can find a colony of fifteen or twenty it could. They really are pretty. Have you ever seen one Mary?" Bob asked.

"No, I haven't, just pictures."

"The one we saw was back into the site a way. Mr. Van Ghent said if we had a truck and would drive in a way and then get out and walk, we could tell better how many there were. That's what Roy and I were going to do today. He said if he could break loose by two-thirty or so he would meet me out there; that I was to go ahead and he would follow. He really thought you might get a kick out of the trip. We won't have to walk as much since we will be in the truck for the first part. What do you say?"

Mary thought this might be a chance to get to know the Ranch Road guys better. Roy certainly had been a Godsend when she was run off the road last week. She hadn't been too close to that group, what with the Roundtable and all. She knew they sort of felt a little alienated from the Ponte Vedra crowd. Many of them were friends with her nephew Jimbo. She had heard him talk about Roy and Bob and the others often.

The Ponte Vedra men and women she knew were older and richer and had little in common with the Palm Valley people. This was the first time she knew they were all working and talking together. Well, not quite. She knew the Catholics all pitched in together at church doings. Many in the Valley went to the little Baptist church on Palm Valley road, not Christ Episcopal Church off San Juan. Might be fun. "Ok, Bob, I would just love to. I'll meet you out there. It's just opposite Ranch Road. I can pull the station wagon off the road and go with you in the truck. Can't stay out long, I have a house guest who will be looking for me by five."

"No problem, Mary, we should be able to find the Jays pretty quickly. Roger showed us where to look. I have a good camera to take with me. Wear boots and long pants."

'You can be sure I will, I know Palm Valley woods. I'll see you at two-thirty?"

Well, isn't that nice, dogs. I'm sorry I can't take you along. Now wouldn't that be fun. I'd never see a Scrub Jay, forget anything else, with all of you along. Might never even see the dogs either, she laughed to herself.

What to wear? The boots part was easy. She went into the bedroom and removed the cargo pants she had worn on her last trip west. Arthur bought them for her because they had a smoother surface and things didn't get caught as easily. He had gotten a pair for himself as well. She remembered how she loved all those extra pockets. Even had some smaller ones on the legs. She put them on and looked in the mirror. Oh, boy, I can even put bottled water in some of these pockets.

She put the gun in the front pocket; they'll never see that. These certainly didn't do much for the figure. I guess figures are not what you worry about in the bush. She took the gun out and dropped it in the side pocket. There was one further down on the leg. She turned back and forth. Nothing showed in those pockets. Could she reach for it easily? She tried several times. Good, that works. Left more room for water.

The pocket was big enough for her to put her hand in and cock the gun as well. Hum, hum, wouldn't Jeffery get a kick out of this display before the mirror, Mary dear. She thought about Arthur and smiled. She knew he would as well. She stopped and thought about Arthur. The funeral was today; he said he would call her afterward. She hoped he would call before she left. But there would be people at the house giving condolences. He probably wouldn't call until later this evening.

"Well," she said, "I'm all set." She also remembered that she had promised she would carry the Taurus revolver in her car whenever she left the house. "Well 'Annie' you are well armed," she said as she put the Taurus by the door so she would remember to take it with her.

Cook and Hold pulled up at Wood's office. They had called and been told by the secretary that he was in and before she could say more they told her they were on the way and hung up. There was a very clean, almost new black truck sitting near the office that hadn't been there before. Cook looked at Hold and noticed him quickly writing on a small pad. Good man, he thought.

As they came through the door, the secretary picked up the phone and nodded to them.

After a few words she said, "Go on in, he is expecting you,"

"Detectives," said Wood as he stood up behind his desk, "have a seat and tell me what I can do for you."

They had agreed that Cook would keep the lead. He told Wood, "We are looking for information about your employee, Bubba Skeet."

Wood interrupted and said, "Not exactly an employee, detective. He is a part-timer we use on rare occasions."

"Yes, one of your men told us that this morning. Have you seen or talked to him in the past few weeks?"

Wood slowly shook his head and looked as if he were thinking back, "Nah," still slowly shaking his head, "not since late summer after that big blow."

"Why are you looking for information? I was told he died. Your office called for next of kin? What did he die of?"

"We haven't all the results back. It could be somewhat questionable, we aren't sure but should know a little more before the day is out. This could be busy work, you know how that is Mr. Wood? They want us to find someone who knew him. Your man said you guys send out people to round up the part-timers. Maybe one of them could help us."

'Well, maybe, but the part-timers we get to work for us aren't exactly the kind of people you would hang out with."

Cook took out his pad and asked, "One of your men mentioned guys named Baker and Parker and he said you used others, are any of them around? They might remember something about him they learned when they were looking for him to come to work."

"The guy's name is Perkins, not Parker, but let me ask my secretary, I think they are out doing some road checking on the crews." He picked up the phone and asked. He listened a minute and hung up. He said, "Apparently they went directly into the field this morning. Some of our senior men plan out their work and don't need to stop here first. I'll have my secretary call your office when they come in."

"How well did you know Skeet?" asked Cook.

"Well enough to know not to pay him until he finished working for us. You know we only used men like him for a week or two at a stretch."

"Didn't they need money for food?"

"We gave them one big meal a day and a beer after work. That's more food then they had when they weren't working for us."

"How come you didn't pay them weekly?" asked Hold innocently.

"Cause the first money they got went to booze and we would never see them back. So we waited until the work was done."

"Gee, I sure wouldn't like that," Hold said, "wonder why they came back?"

"Well, one reason is that no one here cared what they looked like. Their clothes were usually not too clean and most hadn't seen water in a month or more. The customers never looked at them on the road and certainly never came near them. They looked like the work they did," he laughed.

"Where would this Baker and Perkins be working today?"

"I'm not sure but out near Arlington and toward Girvin landfill. We cover a large area you know. When they call in, I'll tell them to be sure they see you today before they go home. That be all right?"

Cook nodded. He and Hold stood up to go. Wood said on the way to showing them out," You know this is probably the most attention a man like Skeet has ever gotten in his life."

"Yeah, well he won't get anymore, will he?" growled Cook.

Chapter Twenty-Eight

Hold said, "Cook, can we check and see whether Baker and Perkins are working in Arlington?"

"What do you mean? How can we do that?"

"Well, can the Sheriff have one of your guys stop a truck and asked whether they have seen, well maybe they could say his buddy Baker? Say he was told he would be out there working today."

Cook was quiet a while. "Can't hurt." He pulled over to a phone booth. "Sure be glad when we can use a radio again. But Edwards said to keep off that open channel." He was put through to the Sheriff right away, told him what they learned, and then told him Hold's idea. Edwards agreed and told them to come into the office. By then he might have word.

Cook told Hold and said, "Good idea, the Sheriff's on it now. Wants us to come in. We can check that license number you copied off that truck outside Wood's office," he said with a grin.

Hold laughed, "I have this thing with writing down license numbers," and then told him the story about the last time he did it at the Pine Island fish camp.

Not long after they pulled into the Sheriff's office lot they were sitting in Edwards' office. His secretary was at lunch and his door had been open. They looked in, and he waved them in and pointed to chairs. He was on the phone doing a lot of nodding to his self. "Good job, Joe, and quick. They didn't seem suspicious at all?" he waited. "No, nothing else. Thanks a lot."

He looked at Cook and Hold and smiled at Hold. "Good idea, Hold. I was able to get to the chief detective out there. He was about to break for lunch and there was a truck right down the street from him. He went up to the driver and asked if he had seen Baker. That he was trying to hook up with him and missed him at the office. He told the guy he thought Baker had told him he would be working the Arlington area today with Perkins.

"The guy laughed and said Baker was putting him on. He didn't work the Arlington area at all. One of the other guys did. Baker and

Perkins hardly ever worked truck supervision, only when a supervisor was sick or something. He asked the guy what the hell Baker did? The guy said that he and Perkins were glorified gofers for Wood. Hunted up part-timers, troubleshot when Wood had problems with the men, that kind of crap. He asked Joe why he wanted him. He said he had a truck for sale and heard Baker might want it. Good truck, but the wife wanted him to get rid of it and get a van. He stood around and bitched a bit about the wife, and the guy said maybe he would be interested if Baker wasn't. They left it at that."

"That bastard Wood bold-faced lied to us," said Cook. "Wonder why? That was stupid."

"Well, said the Sheriff, I'm sure he didn't expect you to go looking since he said he would have his men call you. Also, you and Hold sound as though you played it cool. No rush, no big deal."

"That's true boss, but Wood also said these guys did supervision. Our detective said he was told no way. This guy on the truck has no reason to tell lies."

"No," said Hold, "But maybe Mr. Wood did, I mean Sheriff, why lie about where his men were. If he wanted to talk to them before we did he could easily arrange that. Where are his men?"

Edwards sat and thought about what was being said. Yes indeed, where were Wood's men? "Let's get Sheriff Gray on the phone." He put the call through and caught Gray just before he left for lunch. Gray asked him to wait a minute for Brown. They got the speakerphones working. Edwards related all that Cook and Hold had done and what he had found out from his man in Arlington.

There were a few moments of silence, then Gray asked, "Cook, did you or Hold think you sounded urgent when you were with Wood?"

"No Sir, I don't think so. We grumbled a bit about busy work, trying to play our inquiry down. We acted as if it were ok if he had his men call us later in the day; that we were doing as we had been told. I hinted that maybe the autopsy results might not be too clear-cut. Without actually saying it, I was hoping he might think that was why we were asking more about Skeet. He kept explaining to us what 'low-downs' the part-timers were. He has them out doing something, Sheriff. Could be anything; could be innocent, but if so why hide it? Hold, do you agree?"

"Yes, Cook, and I see it about the same way."

"Sam, I had Brown give their plate numbers and auto descriptions to our Ponte Vedra men just in case they were up there. Now, we wait. Tell the men to go to lunch and check in afterward."

"Ok, Steve, have a good lunch yourself," Edwards said and hung up.

It was almost two o'clock. Mary thought she had better call the Sheriff's office and leave a message for Jeffery where she was going, who with and when. I feel like a high school girl going out on my first date, she thought. But she was not about to put him to unnecessary worry. The office answered, she told them who she was and asked for Sheriff Gray's secretary. Soon, she heard a voice say "Good afternoon Dr. Paul. This is Martha. The Sheriff is out at the moment. Can I help you?"

"Yes, you can. You know Jeffery Stone? He told me he would be out in the field with Officer Port."

"Yes, he told the Sheriff and me you would call if you were going out."

"Yes, well you must understand I am only fourteen and this is my first date."

Martha had a wonderful laugh. It lightened up the call and she said, "I know it must feel that way. Where are you going?"

"Bob Key called me. He is one of the Ranch Road men who are working with us to oppose the landfill. He invited me to go out to the landfill site with him to see whether we can find the Scrub Jays' Mr. Van Ghent discovered on Sunday. He has a camera, and we will try for pictures. He said Roy Gunther may join us if he can get off work."

"What time are you going, Dr. Paul?"

"Oh, please call me Mary. I'm supposed to meet him at the site across from Ranch Road at two-thirty. He said I should park my station wagon off the road up by the trees, and we will go into the site in his truck. He said Mr. Van Ghent told them if they went further in they might find a colony. So we will drive back a way and then walk."

"Well, it certainly is a lovely day to be walking in the woods. I'll tell the Sheriff when he comes back and Mr. Stone when he calls in."

"Thank you so much. I just hate being a bother."

"You're no bother. I would enjoy that myself."

"I almost forgot. Tell Jeffery I will have his toy in my pocket. He will know what I mean."

Martha hung up and thought, what a nice lady, while she wrote down exactly what Mary had said. I wonder what kind of toy Mr. Stone gave her. She said to tell him, so I guess it is important. The Sheriff said he would be back soon after two.

Mary checked her pockets. She had her house keys, comb, lipstick and a gold money clip with her driver's license, gun permit and money all clipped together. She hated to carry anything she didn't absolutely need. A friend of hers had given her the money clip from California when he was there on a trip. It said Palm Valley Country Club. She treasured it, plus it served a purpose and kept her pockets flat.

She opened the downstairs fridge to get some water, but it was empty. Then she remembered she had taken the last two bottles out when she went fishing. I'll just get some at the bridge. The bar will have water. She put her Taurus revolver under the front seat with her house keys and told the dogs goodbye.

She picked up her water at the bar and was about to turn onto the bridge road when some ass in a truck cut her off. Calm yourself Mary, don't want to ruin a nice day because of a simple cut off. Maybe he has an emergency. Maybe the cops will stop him for speeding. She smiled at that. It was a lovely day in the seventies, clear sky, slight breeze, good day for a walk or better yet golf.

Perkins was getting hungry again. Hell, it was coming up on two and he had eaten at ten. But he hated to show his face at that store too often. That's how you got noticed and remembered. That damn Wood, thought he was stupid; he was smarter than anyone thought, but he hid it well. They made mistakes when they thought you were dumb. Baker knew he wasn't. It was time to change places with the cars again. It had been almost two hours. He would have Baker sit where he could see the drive and he would go check out the place by the bridge and see if they had food.

He hit his radio and said 'switch". He slowed as he passed Baker and told him to park so he could see the drive. He was going to check out the place by the bridge. Did Baker want anything? "Yeah, whatever you are having. She may just stay in all day."

Perkins was just pulling off the road at the bridge. He slowed when he saw a Sheriff's car leaving at the south end of the lot heading over the bridge. Missed them. He carefully looked around to see if any cops were around before he went in. It was more of a bar then anything. They had some hot dogs and a microwave and some pre packaged sandwiches. He got a couple of both and a couple of beers. He was just about to pull out when his radio went off. 'South,' he heard. Well how about that?

He waited five minutes and she arrived in her station wagon. She pulled in and went into the bar. Five minutes later she came out with two bottles of water. Just then Baker pulled in next to Perkins' truck. "What's with the water?" asked Baker as he watched Dr. Paul get in her car.

Perkins handed him some food and a beer through the window. "Maybe she doesn't like beer, how am I supposed to know? She's turning out toward the bridge. I'll get ahead of her, you follow. We will use the same calls," said Perkins as he started out of the lot. He shot around her and took off over the bridge.

Rogers and James pulled into the Kane's yard on Highway 210. The gray car and a truck were both there. He hit the horn lightly and stepped out of the car. A tall thin man about seventy came to the screen door. "Afternoon officers; I'm Jake Kane. My wife said you are coming for pie, that right?" he was grinning and had his hand out, and they all introduced themselves. There was a picnic table and benches and chairs under a tree by the trailer. "Let's eat and talk out here. It's too nice a day to waste inside."

No sooner had they sat down then his wife showed up with three plates of pie. "Honey, get the iced tea pitcher and glasses for me, please." She told them her name was Sophie and she hoped they liked the pie. She was of average height but obviously liked her own cooking. She said, "Jake eats like a horse but never puts a pound on." She patted her stomach. "Not like me." She laughed and went back into the trailer as her husband came out with tea and glasses.

Rogers said, "I sure hate to put you to all this bother."

"No bother. Sophie likes to have someone to cook for, now that the kids are grown and gone. Eat up and then we can talk."

James inhaled the pie and Rogers didn't waste any. Rogers started off by asking Jake how he felt about the landfill. "Hell, just like everyone else. It will ruin the property values of all of us who live out here. People don't realize that most of these people don't have much but their land and homes. Hell, Sophie and I had been talking about selling in the near future. How much less do you think we will get if we have a landfill across the road?

"The County Commissioners, it seems to me, are obligated to protect the citizens. Protect their property values. That's why I support what Dr. Paul is doing. All these marches and letters are just fine, but you must go to the heart of it and that is the Commissioners. They are the only ones that stand a chance of stopping Duval. I think all the noise the rest of us make will help the Commissioners make up their minds. But they are the one's who will make a difference. I'm sorry I'm up on my soap box, but it is a mite disturbing to me and my wife,"

Rogers and James listened. They didn't hear anything new, a lot of anxious and even desperate people who felt almost helpless. Rogers said, "Have you put your place on the market?"

"No, and I'm sure not going to now. Can you imagine what would happen to the price if any of us tried to sell now? No, I'm not doing anything until this thing is settled but pray and help the group the best way Sophie and I can."

"Does anyone know you are thinking of selling someday?" asked James.

Jake looked at him and said, "Well yeah, there is one fella, Key. He lives over that way." He waved toward the east. "He dabbles in real-estate along with his air conditioning business. Said he wanted to place an 'option to buy' on my land. I told him I didn't understand that kinda stuff. He said he wanted me to give him first right of refusal if someone offered to buy it before he was ready."

"Did he have a buyer?" Rogers asked.

"Yeah, I think he was talking to some guy looking for land for a golf course, a small course. He didn't want to commit to me if this guy was not interested."

"What did you tell him?"

"The wife and me hadn't fully made up our minds to sell. I told him that, and I told him when we did I would call him first," Jake said.

"Did you talk price?" Rogers asked.

"Nope, but Officer, I'm not stupid. I did a little investigating of my own and so I know about what land out here will bring. That is, would have brought before the landfill mess came up. I figure he knows someone who might find this place to be just what he wants, that is if he knew it was available. He plans on getting more than just a commission an ordinary sale would bring. Hell, I don't care as long as I get my money. That's why he wanted me to hold it off the market until he had this guy set up," Jake explained

"Wouldn't you get more if you sold it to this guy yourself?"

"Yeah, if I knew who he was. The wife and I put it on the market a few years ago. Went nowhere, there was one woman from New York who looked but after finding out how much work was involved in running stables, she walked away. No, letting him make a buck is no different from paying a realtor. Why you asking, Officer? Want to buy?"

"Rogers, that was the car radio," James said.

"Excuse me a minute, Jake," Rogers stood up and walked to his patrol car.

Chapter Twenty-Nine

"Hi, Martha, any messages?"

"Dr. Paul called before two and left this message for Jeffery and I guess you, too. She sure is fun. Said she felt like a fourteen-year old reporting in for her first date," laughed Martha.

The Sheriff stood there and read Martha's notes. "Sheriff, it isn't any of my business but what is Jeffery's toy?"

The Sheriff had smiled when he read that part. "Martha, that is a five shot 22 Magnum Derringer. It's a very little gun about four inches long she can slip in her pocket. Damn good idea of Stone's. He told her to take it with her everywhere."

"Did he mention church?"

Steve looked at her and she was grinning. "Clowns, I'm surrounded by clowns."

"Clowns, where?" asked Brown coming through the door. The Sheriff handed him Martha's note for Jeffery and explained Martha's question and her wiseacre response. Brown didn't laugh. Rather, he said, "Sheriff, that man she is going out there with is that Bob Key the men are checking out this afternoon."

"That's right but you know we are checking out everyone. Port and Stone should be calling in soon. Martha put the call through to Brown and me. I'll run it by Stone."

"You know, Jeff, we can't keep her locked away from everyone, but I am glad Stone got her that Derringer. It's almost two-thirty. If Port doesn't call by then, have dispatch call him.'

His phone rang; Martha said Hold was on the line. "Afternoon, Hold."

"Sheriff we waited until we got the plate checked on that truck out by Wood's office. It is registered to him, not the company. He had a record of a couple of traffic tickets, speeding, nothing else."

"Ok, I want you and Cook back in Palm Valley and Ponte Vedra. I'm going to send word out to the guys up there to look for their truck and car. You help them. We have enough to haul them in for questioning, if we find them up there. On your way in check out 210 and that area first and do it thoroughly. He told him about Paul's message. I'm going to have Cody check out that little store on Roscoe and that bar."

"What if Wood yells his head off?" asked Hold.

"Let him. As you said, he lied through his teeth to you. I'll tell him if he had been truthful he could have saved us a lot or trouble. When they find them, I want them questioned separately by you and Cook."

"Yes, Sir, we are on our way."

Brown left the office when he heard what the Sheriff said. He returned a few minutes later and told Steve, "I told dispatch to tell Cody and the others what to do. I said it was priority one and to save them for Hold and Cook. Also to call us."

"Good, now let's go over those staff reports." They both settled in at Steve's desk.

Mary pulled off 210 and onto the dirt road leading into the landfill site. She didn't see Bob's truck at first. Then she saw him walking toward her and waving her forward to the left beyond some trees and bushes. She hesitated and slowed down and looked out the window and down at the dirt and path. She pulled up a little further but not as far as he was gesturing for.

She stopped the car, and he walked back to her.

"You can pull up further, Dr. Paul," Key said.

"I'm sure you are right but I have gotten this big dog stuck in this soft dirt before. To get it out is no pleasure. This is just fine," she said as she opened the door to get out.

"Well, I guess I don't think too much about getting stuck. That big four-wheel drive of mine can go anywhere and tow anyone out. Fact is, I've had to tow many a car off the beach," he laughed.

"I'm sure parking here is ok. We don't have to hide. We have permission to be out here through today, don't we?" Mary asked.

"You're right, we don't have a problem. If Roy gets here, he has plenty of space to park," he said looking around him.

"Good." Mary reached into the car and pulled out the bag with the two bottles of Zephyrhills drinking water. "I have an extra one. Do you want it or should I just take it along in case you need it?"

"Hate to see you carry a lot, but I wouldn't mind having one handy. Do you want me to carry it?"

"No problem," Mary laughed and turned around saying, "these cargo pants have big pockets. "I don't carry a wallet just lipstick and a comb and a money clip. These will fit in these two front pockets without any trouble."

"Yeah, those are neat. I have been thinking about getting a pair myself."

"Just feel the material. The stickers don't attach themselves to it."

Key reached over and pulled on the left side pocket material and said, "Nice, how does the waist fit, is it snug?"

Mary had a dark green long sleeved cotton shirt on with the sleeves rolled up. It buttoned up the front without a collar, and she wore it hanging outside her pants. She pulled it up and turned all around and said, "See, it has Velcro adjustable tabs to take in or let out the waist. It's not one-size-fits-all but it does allow for a slight weight gain and even better you can tuck winter flannels in easily."

Key looked it over carefully and said, "Gee, do they sell them around here?"

"I don't know. A friend of mine bought it for me when we were on a trip last year. I'm sure you can take the label name down and call around." Mary said as she adjusted her shirt and the water bottles.

"I don't have a pad and pencil with me. I'll call you later today when we get home and you can tell me. He looked around and said, "Better get going. It gets dark earlier now."

They walked over to Key's truck and Mary opened the door. "Damn, that's a long way up. I don't know why they don't put running-boards on these trucks as they did in the old days."

There was a shotgun on the seat, Key reached over and put it in back and gave Mary his hand to pull her up. "Oh," said Mary, "I left my Taurus in the station-wagon. Do you want me to go back after it. You never know when you might need a gun in the woods?" She turned to get out.

"No," said Key, "that's why I brought this shotgun. I agree, these woods are full of wild boar, snakes and even bear. You don't have to hit them, the sound of the gun alone sends them running."

"Good, I certainly wouldn't want to kill any creatures today," said Mary.

"Do you always carry a gun in the car, Dr. Paul?"

"Please, call me Mary. Yes, I do at night and on trips. But since I was run off the road last week, I thought now would be a good time to have it handy. I also was told by the Sheriff, a few years ago, to have one on the boat if I fish alone."

"The Sheriff?"

"Yes, it was after I came home to stay. I was talking to some of the Valley people and they said the Intracoastal wasn't as safe as it was years ago, that I shouldn't be out there without a gun. So I called the Sheriff and discussed it with him. He said to get a revolver, take a class and get a concealed weapons permit. So I did."

"Boy, I sure agree. Revolvers won't jam on you."

They were driving very slowly down this half-grass half-dirt road. He told her to look right, and he would look left. They surprised a deer and Mary was really pleased. "You know, we see them come down to the Intracoastal at times. In late spring we see the raccoons come down with the babies following them. At low tide they have a lot of beach," said Mary.

"Did you know Mr. White who was killed, Mary?"

"Not well. I had met him up north a few years ago. I knew his brother better. Nice family. Why do you ask? Did you meet him?"

"Yes. I was at that meeting he came to. We tried to get him to come out and look at the site."

Key didn't say any more, and Mary looked at him and said, "And?"

"Well, he wouldn't come with us." Mary waited him out this time. She knew why David wouldn't go, but she thought let's hear his side. "He said he wanted to go legally, that we needed permission. Hell, I told him they were stalling us. We had been asking for a couple of weeks. I figured they were hiding something. I knew the longer we waited the more likely we would find nothing."

"Why would that be?" asked Mary.

"You know if something were here they would get rid of it and then let us come look."

"I see."

"You know that's true?"

"It's very possible." I'm not arguing with this guy thought Mary.

They had gone back what seemed to be a long way. In the trees, it was hard to tell distance. "How much further do we go?"

"This is about it. Let me turn the truck around. Then we can walk slowly, this is about where Mr. Van Ghent told us to start. We really aren't back too far. In the woods, it's hard to tell how far you have come."

"I was just thinking that to myself."

He turned the truck around, and they both got out. Key carried the shotgun cradled in the crook of his arm. "Here is the camera, Mary." He showed her how it worked. He told her he forgot to put the film in, opened a box of film and told her how to load the camera. He said he had it on telephoto; all she had to do was aim and shoot.

"It's a nice camera. I'm glad it's so easy; I'm no expert at this. My house guest is very good; he shoots pictures of wildlife a lot." She looked through the lens and fiddled around until she had the hang of it. "How about a picture of you, Bob?" she said smiling at him.

"Nah, let's get started, maybe later."

Perkins was in the lead. He saw in the mirror that Mary had her turn light on. He kept going straight. Where in hell is she going? He slowed and watched Baker slow, then he heard over the speaker, "Pull over in a drive." There was a dirt road up on the right. He turned into it. Wasn't much traffic out here, he thought. Baker pulled up next to him and rolled down his window. "I'm going to go back down real slow and see if I can see what's going on, be right back." He backed up and drove away.

Damn, thought Perkins and took a swig of his beer and opened a sandwich. This might work out just fine. Baker came back in five minutes and pulled up and got into Perkins truck. Perkins handed him a beer and a sandwich. "What did you see?"

"Could barely see her car, she pulled up a way. I did see her walking toward a guy. Then they disappeared around some trees," said Baker.

"Why are they out here?" asked Perkins.

Baker said, "Remember Wood told us that the Ponte Vedra people had three days to go over the site, looking for endangered species. Today is the last day. He told me most of them were going on Saturday and Sunday. I'll bet she didn't go with them. Remember, we saw her getting shrimp. She went fishing Sunday."

"Yeah, I remember. So she came out today with some guy. Good, probably be the best shot we get."

"What are you going to do with the guy, Perkins?"

"Same as with her. Might be even better to do two of them. Give those damn Ponte Vedra people something to really think about. You have your gun in the car?"

"Hell, no. You know I don't have a permit to carry," said Baker.

"I forgot you have some fingerprints hanging out there up north."

"Yeah, and with these Federal systems and quick sharing I can't afford to be giving the cops my prints."

"Doesn't matter. I have my shotgun in back and an old baseball bat. Might just use that bat and save our hands."

"You know this site better than I do, Perkins. Do we follow them in from back there?"

"Could have, if she had parked in further, but you said you can see her car from the road. This road we pulled in on goes back a way into the site. We can follow it. The roads sort of converge up ahead. We can drive until we see them, they won't be looking back. Then stop, split up and approach them from two sides on foot."

"Damn good thing I have my boots on. Let me pull my car up further so it won't be seen too easily from the road. I don't want to go too far and get it stuck."

"Turn it around and face it out. We'll want to be out of here in a hurry," said Perkins.

Baker drove up a bit further and carefully maneuvered his car around. He got in the truck with his black stocking mask in his hand. "Do we have everything we need, Perkins?"

"Yeah," he was smiling, "this is just going to work out fine. A real twofer."

"You really get off on this rough stuff don't you?" Baker asked

"Well, I'm no pantywaist when it comes to doing the hard jobs. If that is what you mean?" sneered Perkins.

Baker just nodded and thought, no you aren't.

Chapter Thirty

"Jeffery, what time did you want to call to see whether you had a message from Dr. Paul?"

Jeffery looked at his watch, "Gosh, it's two-thirty, better call now. Can we use the dispatch radio?"

"Sure, they can patch me through to his office. We're over halfway back from the looks of these roads. It should be a straight shoot. This is Port. Can you put me through to the Sheriff?"

"This is the Sheriff's office," said Martha. "That you, Port?"

"Yes, ma'am. Let me put Stone on."

"Good, I have a message for him."

"This is Stone. What do you have for me?"

"Dr. Paul called in before two. Let me read her message to you," Martha read the message. As she read, Jeffery repeated it for Port's benefit.

Port interrupted, "Wait a minute Jeffery. They didn't find any Scrub Jays on Sunday."

"Hold on a minute, Martha."

"Mr. Stone, the Sheriff wants to talk to you anyhow. While you and Port talk, let me get him."

"What do you mean, no Scrub Jays?" Stone asked Port.

"Just that. Van Ghent showed them Swallow-tailed Kites, there were two beauties flying fairly low," replied Port.

"Stone, you still on the line?" asked the Sheriff.

"Yes, Sir, but we may have a problem here. I'll hold the mike so you can hear both Port and me talking. Now Port, what difference does it make if Van Ghent said Scrub Jays or Swallow-tailed Kites?"

"Dr. Paul may know the difference. If she does, she might be eager to go and look because the Florida Scrub Jay is a threatened species and if they find a colony they would have a good chance of shutting the landfill down. Jeffery, she can see Swallow-tailed Kites from her dock. They are a Species of Special Concern, but that's not enough to cause problems," Port said.

"Damn it to hell, what are you saying?" asked the Sheriff. "This Key told her a lie? Why would he do that? Let me get Brown in here."

"Port, get the map out and let's figure out the best way to get to the landfill site," said Jeffery.

"Stone, I just told Brown what we are talking about. He wants to know, would Mary go out just to see the site?"

"I'm not sure Sheriff. She loves walking in the woods, but it would not be a novelty for her. If she cared enough, she could have gone with Port and me on Saturday. But to find a threatened species, that would catch her attention."

"Hang on. We have a work number for this Gunther guy she said might be going with them. Let's see if he can corroborate this. We have the numbers of all the people we interviewed. Brown is calling him now. Where are you guys now?"

"Port is checking the map as we talk, hang on."

"Jeffery, it looks like if we go south then cut west, about where Harry showed us this morning, we will come in at the north end of the landfill. About at the end of a road from the entrance opposite Ranch Road."

"You hear that, Sheriff, you have an aerial of Dee Dot?"

"Hold on, here comes Brown. I'll let him talk to you."

'Stone, Gunther is at work. Gunther said he hasn't talked to Key since Saturday. I asked him whether they saw any Scrub Jays and he said no. I then asked him what Key's attitude was about the landfill. He said he was really upset. That he had some kind of real estate deal that would be ruined by this landfill. He lived out on Ranch Road, too, and it would hurt his property values just like the rest of them.

"Then I took a real shot in the dark and told him I heard it was him who was having casts made of panther paws. He said 'no, that was Key's and some woman's job who lived in Ponte Vedra.' Said he didn't even know whether they had gotten them yet. Asked why I wanted to know? I told him we were still just checking out all the interview information and that item had been mentioned."

"Sheriff, Port and I are coming in from the north. The map we have is pretty good. Can you get someone to come in from the entrance across from Ranch Road?"

"Yeah, Rogers and James should be out near there. Stone, Brown thinks this is serious stuff. So do I. The bastard lied to Mary about the type of bird, and now we find out he lied about Gunther. He wanted her out there awful badly. Probably thought she would feel safer with Gunther along. Gunther is the man that found her on the side of the road."

"Sheriff, how about a flyover with the chopper? I know there are trees but that area has a lot of scrub oak and brush. It might just give him pause for thought and give us more time to close in, assuming we can even find them."

"No problem. Brown just asked the same thing. We have aerials of the whole County. One good thing, it seems as if Mary has your toy with her. I won't call you back. That damn radio makes too much noise. If you get close enough anyone would hear it. Just expect a chopper in. Wait a minute. What, Brown? He said about fifteen minutes. The guys are already at the airport, shouldn't take them long to get up there. Good luck."

"Sheriff, we have Rogers waiting on a separate line for you," Martha said.

"Rogers, where are you?"

"We are at that guys house at 210. Nearly done."

"Learn anything new?"

"Pretty much what Major Brown said. Key was trying to get an option on this man's place. He had a possible buyer lined up, and he stood to make some money. But he would lose the whole thing if the landfill came in. Kind of sad for all these people, Sheriff."

"Ok, we have a situation on our hands. This Key lied to Dr. Paul to get her out to the landfill site with him this afternoon. She was supposed to meet him at two-thirty and go look for some special birds. Stone and Port are approaching the site from the north. We will have the chopper in the air up there in about ten minutes. I want you and James to go into the site from the Ranch Road entrance and proceed north carefully."

"Sheriff, we don't have a four-wheel drive. I'm not sure how far we can drive, but we will go as far as we can and then go on foot. It sounds like you think he may mean harm to her?"

"I don't know why he would lie to get her out there just for a nice walk in the woods. So, I am going on the assumption he's up to no good. Remember, Rogers, someone killed White and we don't think it was necessarily Skeet. We are fairly certain someone else was out there. Also, we have men out looking for the truck and car that belong to Perkins and Baker. Hold and Cook caught Wood lying to them about their whereabouts.

"Just remember, Port and Stone are coming in from the north. I don't want any accidents. So you and James move fast but carefully. Any questions?"

"No, Sir. We're on our way."

"Sheriff, Cody is on the line. He is calling from that little store on Roscoe in Palm Valley.

"Cody, what do you have?" asked the Sheriff. He had him on the speakerphone so Brown could hear.

"I'm stopped at the little store on Roscoe. I often stop here for coffee. I was talking to the clerk, sort of asked him if anything new was going on. He said 'you know same old, same old'. So I asked him if he had seen a strange truck or car hanging around. People he didn't usually see. He said 'yeah'. There was a truck and a car in twice, once for coffee, then later for food. One guy came in while the other one used the phone. Great big guys, one had his head shaved.

"After asking him some more questions, he said they drove back and forth a few times. He noticed 'cause there isn't much else to do down here in mid-morning. Said he didn't think much about it, there's a lot of construction going on and he thought they might be supervisors or something. Said he hadn't seen them this afternoon. Said he was busy until after two so he wouldn't have noticed them driving by, but they didn't come in for lunch."

"You check that bar at the bridge?"

"'No, Sir, I wanted to report on this first."

"Go on down there and ask if a couple of big guys came in, one had a shaved head; hard to miss shaved heads. Then get back to me. Stay in touch. We have some possible trouble at the landfill site."

"Ok, I'll get right on it. Do you need me at the landfill?" asked Cody hopefully.

"Not yet. I'll call if we do."

"Hold, you know this area, where do you suggest we go?"

"Let's turn in on the Nease Road and go back north to 210. Then we can start east on 210 and check out the side roads and drives."

"Do you think they will be out here?" Cook asked.

"I don't know, but the Sheriff said to check everything. I think he may have the Ponte Vedra and Palm Valley area being covered as well."

"Lots of trucks and cars here at the high school. Let's go north, we won't find anything in this mess. Can't imagine they would be here anyhow," Hold said as Cook turned to go north. There were a few homes up that way, nothing else. Soon, they were back on 210 headed east. The first road was a dirt drive to the north leading to a trailer. They drove in and saw nothing in the yard except a couple of old dogs.

They drove past another dirt road to the north. "Hang on, Cook, you missed one."

Cook pulled over and looked back over his shoulder. "Where?"

"Just back there a few hundred feet, a small dirt grass road. I think we better check it out. I'd like to be able to tell the Sheriff we missed nothing,"

Cook spun the car around and across the highway in reverse and finished in the opposite direction. He grinned at Hold, "Sure glad there is no traffic out here. I just love that maneuver."

"Me, too. Slow down, see, off to the right, up there," pointed Hold.

Cook pulled in and opened his window and looked down at the dirt and grass. He slowly went forward and around some tall scrub and there, about one hundred yards ahead, they could just see the sun reflecting off some metal. "What's that up there?"

"Keep going slowly and let's see," Hold said. They stopped about fifty feet from the front of a black car that was facing them. "Why would that car be out here?"

"Let's get out and walk over. From here it looks empty," Cook said, as he got out and loosened the flap on his gun holster, as did Hold. The car was empty.

Hold walked around to the rear and took out his pad. The car had the plates he had listed for Baker's car. He looked at Cook, "Bingo. Let's call the Sheriff before we go further. You call, Cook. Your bunch can patch you through to our office. I'll walk up a little way and see how much further we can take the car."

Cook called his dispatch and soon had Sheriff Gray on the line. He told him what he and Hold had been doing and what they just found. "Hold is walking up ahead a way to see how good the road is for us to continued on. Hate to sink this sucker in loose dirt."

"Hang on Cook, we just received some overhead maps. Let me see if the road or trail you're on can be seen." He could hear the Sheriff talking to someone. He came back on the line. "The trail you're on can barely be seen. It looks like a ways ahead of where you are; it turns to the east and north. Cook, we have a situation out there right now." He told him about Dr. Paul. He said Port and Stone were approaching from the north toward where they thought they would come upon Paul and Key. That just a minute ago he had sent James and Rogers in on the Ranch Road entry. Also, they had dispatched a chopper.

"Sheriff, what is Baker's car doing out here?" Cook asked.

"That's what Brown and I are asking our selves. Cody called in a few minutes ago. He said the clerk at the store on Roscoe told him a car and a truck were hanging around, that a big guy, with his head shaved, came in for food. If they were watching Paul's place, they might have followed her when she left. Hang on."

Oh boy, thought Cook, we really have a good one going. He looked up and saw Hold approaching. The Sheriff was still talking in the background so when Hold got to the car he gave him a quick rundown on what he had been told. Hold looked down and was about to say something when Cook held up his hand when he heard. "Cook, you and Hold drive in as far as you can and then walk..."

"Sheriff," interrupted Hold.

"Yes, Hold?"

"I'm sorry to interrupt, but I walked back a way and you can see there are tracks from bigger tires."

"Good man. They probably parked Baker's car and drove on in Perkins' truck. That's what I would have done. I have Brown here. We agree, follow them and be careful. Who knows what's going to happen out there? I don't want any of you hurt in a crossfire if it comes to that. Port and Stone know Rogers and James are coming in, but none of them know about you.

Do you have a flare gun in your car?"

"Yes, Sir, and a short-barreled shotgun."

"Take them both. You all are out of radio communication and you may need it. That chopper should be overhead soon. Get moving."

Chapter Thirty-One

"Jeff, can you get that chopper patched through to us?" asked the Sheriff

"Yes, they should be on-line now. Mike is flying and Will is on the glasses."

"Mike, it's the Sheriff. Are you on site?"

"Just crossing 210."

"Rogers and James are coming in on the Ranch Road entrance. Port and Stone are coming south out of Dee Dot and Cook and Hold are coming from the southwest. Dr. Paul should be north, on the dirt road across from the Ranch Road entrance. There are two bad guys going in. They are in front of Cook and Hold. If you have your aerial out, mark them as you find them, if you find them. Remember, Paul is in danger from the man she is with and from the two bad guys."

"What do you want us to do?"

"Hopefully, your presence will be a distraction. Our men know you are up there. Find a place where you can set down if it's called for. I don't know what to expect, so better be prepared for anything. Keep in touch and give Brown a running account. Jeff, you take over. I'm going to call Edwards and fill him in. He may want to keep Wood under surveillance."

Martha got Edwards on the phone for the Sheriff. "Sam, we have a very complicated situation on our hands. It all broke loose about two-thirty," Gray then explained to him what was happening.

"First nothing, now the whole ball of wax. I agree, Key means Paul no good. Do you think he did White?"

"Sam, I have no idea. Why are Baker and Perkins out following Paul? Why the hell did Wood lie to us?"

"Yes, same questions I have. How about I put a team on Wood so we know where he is going to be for the next few hours? We have some serious questions for him."

"Just what I was thinking. I have Brown monitoring what action the guys can see from the chopper. I'm on my way up there in a minute. How about joining me?"

"I thought you would never ask. The quickest way is 95 south and east on 210. So with bells and whistles on I might beat you there. Don't worry, Wood, isn't going anywhere."

"Fine, see you soon. Martha, when Cody calls in, have him go out and park at the Ranch Road entrance facing west. I don't want anyone slipping past us. Also, get one of our guys at the west end of the site by that little dirt road. Brown will show you. I'm going up there now. Make sure dispatch hooks all of us in here to Brown."

"Ok, Sir, take care."

"How much further should we go, Bob?" Mary had stopped and taken a bottle of water out of her pocket and was drinking. She waved it at him and asked, "Do you want a bottle?"

"What? Oh, no thanks. He looked around and said, "I think we have gone far enough."

"I'm sorry we didn't see any of the Scrub Jays, but the others can tell the authorities and they can really survey for them. We did have permission to be here, and enough people saw them they can't just brush it away. I also have some nice shots of that deer and some hawks."

"There aren't any Scrub Jays."

Mary looked at him and tipped her head, "'There aren't any Scrub Jays? Just what does that mean, Bob?"

"Van Ghent showed us Swallow-tailed Kites, not Scrub Jays." He smiled. "That's not to say we didn't look, but we didn't find any."

Mary looked around her quietly. "Why did you tell me he found Scrub Jays then?"

"Would you have come out today if I hadn't given you a good reason?"

"I might have. I love walking in the woods and I was sorry I had to turn down Mr. Günter's invitation over the weekend." She paused and looked back the way they had come. She looked back at Key and said, "He isn't coming today, is he?"

"No, he isn't."

"I suppose you are going to tell me what all this is all about?" asked Mary.

"May as well, nothing to lose. I figure finding you dead out here ought to cause so much stir that the landfill issue will go away. That's why I gave you the camera and didn't take a drink. I didn't want my prints on anything.

"Really, I'm afraid I don't understand how that will make the landfill go away?"

"Think about it. First, a biologist helping the residents gets killed and not long after, the famous development hater is found dead out here."

"Development hater, oh my, but how does that link to the landfill?"

"It's easy. You didn't know it, but the trash hauler is a good friend with the developers and large landowners in St. John's. They all have a real interest in shutting you up. So, he kills two birds with one stone."

"Now you have me confused. How are you going to pin my death on him and how does David's death fit in?" Mary took another drink and put the bottle back into her pocket.

"Easy. They already think the trash hauler is a possibility for White's death."

"But Bob, how do you know that?"

Just then a chopper flew overhead at low level. Key looked up and as he did, Mary put her hand in her side pocket and, under the noise of the chopper, she cocked the Derringer. As she was taking her hand out, he saw her and said, "Drink all you want but I don't know what for. You won't be thirsty long."

"You didn't answer my question."

"We country people aren't stupid, you know. We sat together and shared information we got from the questions the cops were asking everyone. We gather that they didn't know squat about what happened to White, but they may be looking in more than one direction. Some of us deliberately steered them toward the trash people."

"You know what happened to David?" she asked rather dubiously.

Key was listening to the chopper noise slowly fade away north. He thought, better let it get further away. Won't hurt to tell her. He didn't like her superior attitude. Did I know? Hell, who would know better? He actually laughed a bit, out loud.

"You know, Dr. Paul, you are not the only one with brains around here. I heard you made a snide remark about the plaster casts for Panther paws. That would have worked just fine. But your little buddy David turned his nose up at the idea, too."

"David. Did you actually tell him?"

"Yeah, we told him and we were going to show them to him. But, after he told us he would not be a party to something like that, we didn't. Actually, I wasn't the one doing the talking, it was the woman in Ponte Vedra who had them made."

"What did he say?"

"Well, first he told us he would not go on the site without permission. That if we did find something out there, it would not be considered at all since we didn't have permission to be there. The owners could have any information like that ignored."

"That's true, Bob, I was at a meeting where one of the big landowners made that statement when a group wanted to do mapping of endangered species. He said they would not give permission for the group to enter his property and if they did, he would take them to court."

"Yeah, that's the crap he told us. But we were going to plant the prints just before we had permission to be out there and then find them officially, but that idea was blown, at least if we were going to use him. Knowing that he knew what we had planned, we knew he wouldn't go along."

"But surely you must have realized that he couldn't risk his reputation on an adventure like that?"

"What do you mean?"

"Bob, there are no panther in this area. In fact, there are only a few in the state and they are further south and there may be some in the glades."

"So you say."

Mary realized he was getting restless. I have to keep him talking. Surely, Jeffery would be concerned if he thought I was out in the woods. But would he be concerned enough to come look for me?

Mary then asked him, "But what does that have to do with what happened to David?"

He thought: the hell with her questions. He started to shift the gun, then he heard the chopper again.

"What the hell is that damn chopper doing around here?" He hadn't seen it, only heard it.

Mary looked up and said, "We get Navy flying overhead a lot, as well as people doing aerial photos of property. Tell me about David."

Wait, Key, don't take any foolish chances, he told to himself. "We met with him over the weekend, and I asked him whether he wanted to see the area around the site. I told him I could show him on Monday, late afternoon, after I got off work. Then we could catch a beer at the bridge afterward. I had no intention of doing more than that. We had driven all over. We were finished and sitting across from Ranch Road. I was pointing the entrance to the site out to him. We were in his truck. We were just getting ready to go when we heard a shotgun blast coming from the site.

"We pulled his truck up and decided we would walk in a bit and see who was shooting. We passed some trees and there was a truck sitting back there, kind of a redneck run-down affair. I told David it was probably poachers. We walked just a little further. It wasn't quite dark and we came upon a shovel and a bag. David opened it and was really mad. It had gopher tortoise in it. He wanted us to go back to the car and call the cops.

"I thought, like hell, so I just picked up the shovel while he was examining the gopher tortoise and bashed his head in. Ran back to the car, got the plaster casts out and dumped them in the sack and wiped the handle of the shovel off. I pulled his car in a little further behind some shrub at the entrance and walked across the road. I hid in the woods on Ranch Road and watched. Wasn't long when this old truck came shooting out of there and headed toward Ponte Vedra."

"What did you do then?"

"Walked home, what else?"

Mary quickly asked, "'But why? Why kill him?" The chopper was again fading away.

"You don't get it, do you? I will do anything to stop that landfill. I have a big deal going on some land out here. If the landfill gets stopped, I'll make some good money. This White knew about the panther paws and if we went through with that idea and he found out, or even told his buddy at the Guana, it would blow the whole thing. It just suddenly occurred to me he would help us more dead then alive, that's all. Enough questions." He shifted the gun toward her.

Perkins and Baker drove a good way into the site. Even with the truck, it was getting hard to go further. Baker said, "Much as I hate to say this, if we are anywhere close to them, they will hear us. We better walk."

Perkins looked around and said, "Yeah, if we head due east, we ought to see them."

They started walking and they were quick but quiet. Perkins was in the lead. He was a good hunter and had excellent ears and eyes. He held up his hand. Baker came up to him. He whispered to Baker, "I can hear voices up ahead."

They moved more slowly and carefully through the brush. The voices were louder now. They could just see them through the brush and trees. But they could hear what they were saying. It was a man and a woman. She was asking him questions. Then a chopper flew over. Baker whispered, "Let's take them."

Perkins whispered back, "No, I heard him mention the trash haulers and that dead guy, let's hear more first." They crept up a little closer under cover of the chopper noise and squatted down. They heard the man talking about the White fellow. Damn, thought Baker, what the hell have we here? This is not a friendly conversation. I think he is going to kill her.

The chopper came back and under cover of the noise Baker whispered to Perkins, "I think he is going to kill her."

"Good, save us the trouble," replied Perkins.

"Do we let him go?"

"Unless he sees us, what the hell do we care? She's taken care of."

"But it's on our land, we could be blamed."

"True. Let me think and listen to what else he says. Maybe a murder suicide?" he grinned at Baker. "I'll get closer. You just follow my lead."

Cook and Hold were driving as fast as the dirt path would let them and still keep a sharp lookout ahead. Finally, they could hardly move. Hold said, "Be faster on foot." Cook stopped the car. He handed Hold the flare gun and, with the shotgun in his hand, he took the lead. They heard the chopper and moved faster and came up on the truck.

They approached carefully, but it was empty. Cook whispered, "They are on foot. You can see where they have broken the brush. We better move carefully, we don't want to step on them. Also, be careful, Port and Stone are coming from the north, and the others are coming from our right side." Hold nodded. He had his gun in his right hand and the flare gun hooked to his belt.

Chapter Thirty-Two

"Sheriff, this is Cody."

"It's Major Brown, Cody, go ahead and report."

"The people at the bar said that Dr. Paul was in and bought two bottles of water. I asked about a big guy with his head shaved. They said someone who looked like that was in just before Paul. He bought four beers, sandwiches and a couple of hot dogs. I asked if they noticed which way he went when he left? They said no."

"Ok, Cody, the Sheriff is on his way up there. Edwards is coming down from Jacksonville. We have a situation at the site." He briefly told him what it was. "We want you to park at the entrance to the site, opposite Ranch Road. We have another car coming that will park west of you at that little dirt road. We don't want anyone coming out of those roads but our guys."

"You don't think I need to go in after Rogers?"

"No, we have enough men in there. You should see the Sheriff soon, got another call coming in from the chopper, get going."

"Major, you there?" asked Mike from the chopper.

"Yes, Mike, go ahead; you see anything?"

"We just made our first pass. There is a truck along the entrance road quite a way in, can't see much, just a metal reflection. Saw one of our cars coming in on the same road behind it. Going north, we caught a glimpse of one of our four-wheel drives. It was parked. Guess the guys are on foot. We are going to sweep in from the northeast and go lower and then go west and see whether we can see that truck you said Cook and Hold were following. There is a bit of a clearing north of where our guy's four-wheel drive is. If we need to set down, that will work. It's tough to see people unless they are wearing white. But we are causing a lot noise."

"Good, that's what we want. Our guys are the only ones who know you are up there."

Port and Jeffery had split up. Jeffrey was coming in almost due south and Port had veered a bit west and then south. They both were good woodsmen and moved rapidly and quietly. Then, they heard the chopper coming from the south. Jeffery looked up, and it was almost on a straight line south from him. He thought, they must have come in over the entrance road; they are heading straight toward him. When they got a bit closer, he turned on the speed. The chopper covered the extra noise he made.

Port heard the chopper as well. It was south and east of him. He watched it a minute and altered his course more southeast. He, too, moved a lot faster with the chopper noise as cover. This was surely blind aim, but we have to converge up here aways. Hope we don't miss them. I'm sure they won't get off the dirt path. He had watched Stone's face when he heard they had Paul. He sure wouldn't want to be on the bad end of that man. You would think it was his wife or mother they had. I sure better act as if I think that way, too. She sure made great sandwiches Saturday. I liked her. She is what my mother would have called a nice lady with an iron core that she wasn't afraid of showing.

Both Port and Jeffery kept on moving and soon the chopper was back. It was coming from the northeast and still a bit south of them and much lower. Jeffery and Port used the noise to pick up the pace and then slowed again and proceeded more carefully. Soon, Jeffery thought he could hear voices not far ahead. He moved toward the voices and soon saw what looked like two people talking. As he was closer, he saw Mary and the man. Must be Key. Key was facing at an angle to him. I have to get behind him.

Jeffery carefully moved to his right. He could see the man had a shotgun, and it was cradled in his arm, not in a shooting position. Mary must have had a bottle of water in her pants to drink because she was now putting one in. But she left her hand near her pocket. I hope she has that Derringer in her pocket, but she can't reach, draw the gun and out shoot that shotgun.

He was behind the man now, and moving up closer. He had a 9-mm Sig Sauer 225 in his hand. He liked the gun; it was lightweight and had a thin compact design. It had eight rounds in the magazine and one in the chamber. He had a Beretta that held sixteen rounds, but it was larger and he only carried it when he knew he might be shooting. He was tempted to shoot the man in the back, but he was still a bit far to guarantee accuracy. He wanted a better angle. Mary was almost in line with him. He must get more to the man's side and still be a bit behind him.

Port slowed down. He too heard voices and moved closer, but then he saw two guys a way in front of him. What the hell is this? He moved closer very carefully. The voices were getting louder. He could hear it was a man and a woman talking, but he couldn't make out what they were saying. Who were these guys and why were they hiding in the brush watching? Watching what? Dr. Paul and Key, that must be who is ahead talking.

Where is Stone? I sure hope he is up ahead and near Dr. Paul. Port crept closer, and now he could see that the big man in the back had a baseball bat. The other one with the shaved head had a shotgun. The one with the shotgun seemed to be whispering to the other one. They were close enough to hear what was being said in front of them, but he wasn't. He changed his angle of approach so he would have a good shot at the one with the gun. Port, are you going to shoot someone you don't know? he asked himself. Then he noticed the one with the gun shift his position and bring the gun up toward shooting position. My Lord! He is going to shoot at those people. Can't take a risk he will hit Dr. Paul.

Perkins and Baker squatted in the brush. They had been listening to Key tell how he killed the biologist and how he was going to kill Dr. Paul and blame the trash haulers. Perkins whispered to Baker. "I'm going to take him out as soon as he shoots her. Both will be frontal shots. That will make it look as though they shot each other."

Baker frowned, "I think we are a little far away for that."

"No sweat. When he shoots, I'll be on top of him. I'll yell and when he turns, I'll hit him full face."

Baker was shaking his head just a bit. He thought, I didn't sign on for this kind of stuff.

Perkins is going a bit too far for me. If he gets caught, he will take me with him, but how do I stop him? This guy is going to kill Paul no matter what we do, he reasoned. Maybe it is ok to give him a shot of old time justice. When this is over I'm going to get a transfer to Georgia.

Jeffery saw Key begin to raise his gun. He moved forward and Mary saw him and turned her head. Key saw her turn and spun around and quickly moved to the side and behind Mary on her right as he spotted Jeffery. "Drop the damn gun, mister," he yelled, "or I'll shoot her. Drop it now." He had the shotgun pointed toward Mary.

Jeffery lowered his gun to the ground when Mary said, "Oh, Bob, please don't shoot him" in a whiny but loud voice, just below a scream.

He glanced at her and yelled, "Shut up, damn it." She had one hand to her chest in obvious fear and the other hanging down at her right side.

Mary turned a bit toward Key when he yelled at her. She had her hand near the outside of her pocket. When Key turned back to Jeffery, it had been only a split second glance at Mary. She pulled the trigger on the Derringer from the outside of her pocket. The bullet tore through her pocket and hit Key's arm. The shotgun went off as he dropped the gun. But the shotgun blast missed Jeffery as he had jumped to the side and back, tripping and falling over a small log behind him.

Key turned and ran south, through the trees and brush, holding his arm. It burned like fire. All he could think of was to get away to the truck.

Mary ran toward Jeffery and as he stood up they heard, "Freeze. Drop it or I'll blow you away." They both hunkered down and realized it was coming from the brush to the west of them.

Jeffery realized it was Port. "I said, drop it."

"You ok, Mary?" asked Jeffery

"Yes, who is that?" Mary asked, taking her gun from the torn pocket and rubbing her leg.

"Stay here," he said, as he picked up his gun, and ran toward Port's voice. Then he saw Port facing a big shave-headed man with a shotgun at his feet.

"Back up away from the gun and get down on your face," Port yelled.

Jeffery ran up and grabbed the shotgun. Port handed him some cuffs, and he cuffed the guy. "What's this all about?" asked Jeffery.

"I came up behind these guys. They were listening to Key and Paul talking. I wasn't sure what was going on, or what to do, when I heard Key yelling at you to drop your gun. Then, I heard a small gun go off, then a shotgun. This sucker stood up and was taking aim at you guys with his shotgun, when I yelled. There was another big man with him who had a baseball bat. He took off like a bat out of hell through the woods. I couldn't stop him while this bastard still had a gun.

Port looked down at the man and said, "He dropped that shotgun, but not 'till I yelled the second time."

Perkins said, "I was trying to save those people. That guy was going to kill that woman."

"Sure took you long enough to decide. I don't believe a word he is saying. If he had meant to save Paul, he would have intervened long before this. It looked as if he were going to shoot all three of you. I think he would have, if I hadn't called."

"Who is he?' Jeffery looked at him. "Ok, who are you?"

"I was policing the site and we thought we had trespassers."

"Who is we and what's your name?"

"Perkins."

"Why did your buddy run off?"

"Why not? You scared the hell out of us!"

Just then they heard crashing through the bushes and saw Hold rushing toward them with his gun drawn. He yelled, "You guys ok?" as he rushed up to them.

"Where did you come from, Hold?" asked Port. He looked behind him. "You didn't see a big guy going in your direction did you?"

"Yeah, he ran right into us, bat and all. Told us he was running from a man trying to kill people up here. So, Cook cuffed him and took him back to his patrol car. The man was whining and declaring his innocence all the while. We had been following their trail for the past twenty minutes. Been looking for them all day. They were following Paul."

"That's a damn lie," swore Perkins. "We work out here, we were here just doing our job."

Hold looked behind Jeffery, "Dr. Paul, are you ok?"

Jeffery spun around, and there she was leaning on a tree listening to them talk and rubbing her leg. He walked up and put his arm around her and looked down and said, "That was a damn fool stunt you pulled."

"It worked, didn't it?"

"What did she do?" asked Hold and Port simultaneously.

"She had her Derringer cocked in her pocket and when Key looked away she pulled the trigger from the outside of her pocket and shot him."

"Through the pocket?" they looked at the pants pocket and the hole and the burned fabric.

"Smarts a bit, doesn't it, Mary?" smiled Jeffery.

"Detective Hold, you and I need to get this guy out of here. Which way?" asked Port.

"How about the way you came in, Mary?'

"That's the way Bob Key ran," she replied.

"I don't think he will be waiting for us. We have his and Perkins' gun, we should be safe. Plus, I think it is the shortest route out, isn't it Port?"

"Yes, sir."

"Yes, the Sheriff also has Rogers and James coming in that way. Key may have run right into them. Let's go," he shoved Perkins. "Move it."

"You're going to be sorry for this abuse," growled Perkins.
"Just shut up and move it, Perkins."

Rogers and James had come up on Key's truck. They had stopped driving and were walking. It had become too dense for the patrol car. They were looking the truck over when they heard the shots from ahead. "Damn, war has broken out," said James. "Let's go. We may be needed."

They moved down the dirt path at a good pace when James stopped and held up his hand. He waved Rogers to the side and whispered, "I think I heard someone running towards us. Sounds as though he tripped and fell. I heard him breaking branches. Let's split up, get off the path and move slowly through the trees at the side."

They did, and soon they saw a man stumbling toward them, holding his arm. He was bleeding. They waited until he came even with them and James stepped out of the trees and yelled "Freeze."

Key, looking scared, stared back and forth at them and then behind him. He took a deep breath and said, "Some people were shooting at Dr. Paul and me while we were out looking for birds. I ran away, after I got shot. You have to hurry and get to her before they kill her."

"Really," said Rogers. "You wouldn't be Bob Key, would you?"

"Yes, hurry, go and get her."

"I think we will secure you first, Mr. Key," said Rogers as he took his handcuffs out and cuffed Key with his arms in front of him.

"What the hell are you doing? Can't you see I'm wounded? I need help; I'll bleed to death."

James pulled Key's shirt back, tore off the sleeve and wrapped it around the bleeding arm. "See, just like new."

"James, will you take him back to the patrol car and I'll run on ahead?"

"Fine, just be careful."

Rogers was jogging as fast as he thought he could safely go, when he heard voices ahead of him. He stepped off the path, into the trees and waited. In a few minutes, he saw Port pushing a big man ahead of him with Hold, Stone, and Dr. Paul following. He stepped out where they could see him. "Oh, look Mary, one of our favorite officers is waiting to receive us," smiled Stone.

Rogers looked at them and Hold said, "Didn't happen to see a man come this way with a bleeding arm did you?"

"Why yes, James and I did. We put him in cuffs and bandaged his arm. He was not happy with us. Told us he was an innocent bystander to a terrible shooting. He thought our treatment of him was outrageous."

"Yeah," said Port, "seems to be a lot of that lately. This charmer," he pushed Perkins, "has complaints as well."

Chapter Thirty-Three

The Sheriff and Cody arrived at the site entrance about the same time. Cody walked over to the Sheriff's car when they heard gunshots north of them. The Sheriff had Brown on the radio, "We just heard gunshots. Tell Mike to keep an eye out for a flare. Tell him to fly by again and stay on site."

"You want me to go in, Sheriff?" Cody asked.

"No, hard as it is to do nothing, that is exactly what we are going to do. We have six men somewhere in there and I can only pray they are not caught in their own crossfire. One more won't help. They know about each other. They wouldn't know about you, Cody. We wait."

In the distance they heard a siren coming from US1. They looked that way and saw flashing lights coming toward them. "He sure made good time," the Sheriff said smiling.

Edwards pulled up and parked. He jumped out of his car and walked over to Gray's. "Not bad time, huh? Scared the hell out of everyone on I 95 and 210. Slowest they've driven all day. What's going on?"

"Sheriff Edwards, this is Officer Cody. We just heard two gunshots a few minutes ago, but as I was telling Cody, we have six men in there and they know about each other. I'm not going to muddy it up with putting anyone else in there. Our guys in the chopper will take another fly-by. We get the tough part, waiting."

"Good call, Steve. I see you have someone at the dirt road to our west. That about covers it unless someone takes off on foot cross-country. I have two cars on Wood. He's in his office. I told them to pick him up if he looks as if he is leaving. Tell him we have a few more questions for him, downtown."

"Looks like the whole thing is coming down one way or another. Something has been bothering me on the drive up. Let me call Brown." He got Brown on the radio, "Jeff, when they went over David White's truck, did they get prints other than his?"

"Hang on a minute, let me look. Yeah, they found prints on the passenger side on the door handle and on the outside where you would reach to slam it shut. Good prints on the outside. We ran them and found nothing. What's going on up there?"

"We wait. Should hear or see something soon. Sheriff Edwards has Wood under watch. If he moves, he will pick him up."

"Steve, we are pretty sure what Wood's men were doing."

"Yeah. Looks like they were following Dr. Paul. Cody had them in the Valley today until just before two. Then, as you know, Cook and Hold driving in on that west road found Baker's car. So we have Key tricking Paul into going into the woods with him and those two following them."

"Sheriff, I have Cook patched through. He just arrived at his car with Baker cuffed. He is bringing him down to you now. He searched him at the car and found a very interesting item on him. I'll let him tell you about that. He did say, after the shots, that they found him running towards them in the woods. They grabbed him. Cook took him to his car and Hold continued on."

Steve repeated what Brown told him. They looked up the road and saw a police car pulling out and coming toward them. Cook pulled to a stop on the side of the road. They all walked up to his car. Cook got out, stood by the open door and said, "Sheriff, remember, David White's brother told us his brother's gold knife was missing. Well, guess who had it in his pocket?" Cook held it up in a clear plastic bag.

"Well, isn't that just dandy. You like knives, Mr. Baker? Where did you get it?"

"It's just a knife, there's a lot of knives like that. It's nothing. I can't help it if someone else had one like it. Doesn't prove a damn thing."

The Sheriff looked at Cook. Cook had the knife's small blade open in the bag. He turned it so the Sheriff could see the engraving. There was a clear 'D.W.' The Sheriff looked at Baker, then at Cook. "Looks as though you bagged yourself White's killer, Detective. Good work. Should have examined the knife more closely Mr. Baker."

"Hey, wait a minute I didn't kill anyone. Who the hell is White?"

"That's the nice biologist whose head you bashed in at the landfill site last week. You didn't bother to see that his initials were on his knife that you kept."

"I didn't kill him. I wasn't even there. Bubba said someone else killed him, and he found the body," he shut up and looked down.

"Mr. Baker," said Sheriff Edwards, "it doesn't matter if you killed White. For sure, we have you on killing Skeet. Maybe we can make it a twofer. You see, we didn't tell anyone but Skeet had his neck broken."

"Sheriff, we found him with a bat in the woods. Seems he likes hitting things," chimed in Cook.

"I damn well didn't kill that biologist and I didn't lay a hand on Skeet; Perkins did. We were only doing what Wood told us to do. He didn't tell Perkins to kill Skeet, just to find out what happened and to shut him up. It was an accident."

"Setting the place on fire to burn the evidence was an accident, too, I suppose?" asked Gray.

"I didn't do that. Perkins did. After he hit Skeet, he wanted to be sure no one found anything."

"You planned to kill Dr. Paul today, too." Baker started to object but Gray went on, "Don't lie to us, we have you placed in Palm Valley and following her today."

"We weren't going to kill anyone. That guy she was out there with confessed to killing the biologist and said he was going to kill her. We were going to rescue her. Until some other big sucker stuck a gun on us and I ran."

"You believe that, Sam?"

"We will know shortly when that other big guy he is talking about shows up. You see, Mr. Baker, he was probably one of our officers. I tell you truthfully, one more lie out of you and I will pin all of it on you."

"I didn't have the gun, Perkins did. He stood up to shoot at them, and this guy came up behind us and said 'freeze'. While he had his gun on Perkins, I ran out. I didn't want any part of this rough stuff. Perkins gets off on it."

"You willing to give us a statement? Maybe when they all get here, we will hear another story. Maybe even Wood will tell us another story about you?"

"Listen, I'm not taking the fall for Perkins or for Wood. I'll tell you just what I said here."

"Excuse me a minute, Sam." He took Cody aside. "You have a tape recorder in your car?"

"Yes, Sir, we were using one over the weekend on interviews."

Steve walked back to the men and said, "Sam, let's take him in. Cody, you ride with him in the back seat of Cook's car and get his statement. It sounds like Mr. Perkins isn't such a nice man. Cody, have him booked on suspicion of murder until we can clear him. Let me warn you, Mr. Baker, it isn't looking too good for you."

"I tell you, I didn't do a damn thing. I'll tell you who did." Edwards and Gray stepped aside, and Cody got in Cook's car and they left.

"How about that, Sam?"

"Let me call my men. I want Wood picked up now and held until we get the whole story. These guys didn't act on their own, Steve."

"Fine, let me tell Brown to expect company, and send us a couple more cars."

When they finished they looked up and James was coming with a man stumbling along beside him. James said, "Sheriff Edwards and Sheriff Gray, look who we found coming down the road. He said someone was trying to kill him and Dr. Paul, so he ran to get help. It's Mr. Key. Rogers went further on to see whether they needed help. We don't know what happened."

"Well, Mr. Key, did you leave Dr. Paul dead back there in the woods or just laying there wounded, while you ran?"

"I'm wounded and bleeding and this guy," he gestured rudely toward James, "and the other one, were abusive to me. They pushed me around and handcuffed me and let me bleed."

"Mr. Key, it looks as though they bandaged your arm. It's called first aid."

"Did you look at the wound, officer?" asked Sheriff Edwards.

"Yes, Sir, the bullet went through the fleshy part of his arm. It's almost stopped bleeding. It must have been a very small caliber bullet, it didn't do much damage."

"Small caliber, not a shotgun blast or a thirty-eight or larger. Do our men carry tiny guns? Who shot you, Key?"

"I'm not answering any of your questions. I need medical attention. What kind of cops are you? A man gets shot, abused by your men and tries to get help and you treat him like this. I'll sue, you see if I don't."

"Where is your car James?"

"I left it for Rogers. I didn't know what he would find."

"See, he wouldn't even take me back in his car," complained Key.

"Look what's coming, Mr. Key." The fire rescue truck from Ponte Vedra pulled up, and the men rushed over.

"Gentlemen, I want you to look at this man's arm and put a clean bandage on it. Do not remove his handcuffs. You go with them, James. When he is bandaged, we will take him in and book him."

"Book me, for what? You can't book me, I need hospitalization."

As they lead him over to the truck, grumbling, Sam turned to Steve, "You don't much like him, do you?"

"Nope. He is either a coward, an attempted murderer, a murderer or all three. We should know in a few minutes. Leaving Dr. Paul out there and running. God, how sickening."

"Seems my Officer James is in full agreement with you. Key doesn't do much to endear himself, does he?" Sam grinned.

"Let me update Brown." Two more patrol cars pulled up. "Sam, when they have Key bandaged, have them put him in the back of a car with an officer in it. I think we will wait for the others; then we can take him in and book him. I'm sure that won't be long."

"Brown, have the chopper guys sent more information?"

"No, Steve, they can't see much and there have been no flares. Cook said Hold had the flare gun on his belt and Cook's shotgun."

Steve then told him about James bringing Key out. "He was shot with a small caliber gun, but it wasn't serious. They are bandaging him now." Then he told him Key's story.

"The bastard ran and left Dr. Paul there?" exclaimed Brown.

"My reaction, completely. I'm keeping him here until the rest come out. Thanks for sending the rescue people. Key said he was going to sue us if he weren't taken to the hospital. I'll see what the rescue guys say. Sam ordered his men to pick up Wood and hold him.

"Baker is singing up a storm in the car on the way to you with Cook and Cody. Cody has a tape going. Thank God he agreed. Sam and I scared him into talking. But he needs to be Mirandized and get it all official. He claims innocence, that he never wanted to be involved with Perkins ... no honor among these guys. I'll call when the rest come out."

One of the rescue officers came over, "Key will need a few stitches and a tetanus shot. But we dressed it well; he can wait. Doesn't need to be rushed to a hospital. Officer James put him in one of the other officer's cars and told them to stay with him. If you are taking him to Flagler, do you need us to stay?"

"Just a little bit longer, until the others come out. We need to see if your services will be needed. Thanks for your work."

Gray and Edwards, along with James, were leaning on Gray's car and watching the entrance. "This waiting is not easy, is it?" asked James.

"No, it was a lot easier when we were the ones in the center of the action. Now Sam and I just stand around and pray."

It wasn't much longer when they saw the patrol car coming down the dirt road. Rogers was riding on the hood with Hold. Stone was driving with Mary in front, Port and Perkins in back. They were going slowly. They pulled up and stopped. Hold and Rogers jumped off the car and said, "Everyone is fine, no one is hurt. Well, no one who shouldn't be." He looked over at the patrol car with Key in it.

Stone and Mary stepped out of the car and walked toward them.

"You all right, Mary?" Gray asked, then he looked down at her pants and saw the hole and burned material. He looked back at her and then at Stone. "Do I want to know what caused that?"

"I would assume so," Mary replied. "I shot that man." She pointed at the car with Key in the back seat. "Officer Hold wants my gun. I told him, not until I'm out of these woods." She reached in her pocket and handed Officer Hold the gun. He had quickly taken a plastic bag out, and she dropped it into the bag. "Now, Sheriff...."

He held up his hand, "I know, you want your gun back as soon as we are through with it. I will guard it carefully. Will you please tell us what happened?"

Mary told him about Key's call and the Scrub Jay story and finally how he admitted he had killed David. "But why did he go after you?"

"He said if I were killed, it would cause so much trouble the landfill would go away. He said because David knew about the panther paw casts that they couldn't have used them. David would have told on them. I think he killed him without thought. Anyhow, Jeffery was coming up behind him and I turned my head a bit and he saw Jeffery and he made Jeffery lay his gun down and I shot him."

"How did you cock the gun through you pants pocket?"

"I didn't. I had cocked it a few minutes earlier when the chopper went over, so he couldn't hear the click. He looked up at the chopper. But when he looked back he saw my hand in my pocket and I couldn't have drawn it quick enough. So, I casually took my hand out of my pocket. I left the gun and just kept my hand near the pocket."

Steve rolled his eyes. He thought, she cocked a gun and left it in her pocket. He was about to say something about that when Stone said, "Don't ask, Sheriff."

Steve thought, he's right. Instead he asked, "Didn't he search you?"

"No, I told him I had my Tarus in the station wagon and did he want me to bring it? He said, no, he had a shotgun."

"But we heard two shots."

Stone put a hand on Mary's arm and replied, "Key dropped the shotgun and it went off when Mary's bullet hit him. If I hadn't tripped and fallen, I would have been hit. He ran. Simultaneously,

Port froze Perkins in the bushes with Baker. Perkins was just taking aim to shoot Mary and Key. Port stopped him, but Baker ran."

"How did Port find them?"

"We spread out and came in at an angle. Perkins and Baker were right near Mary and Key, listening to them talk. Perkins said he was going to save Mary's life and shoot Key. But Port doesn't believe him. Neither do I. But he does corroborate Mary's story that he and Baker heard Key admit to killing David."

Gray looked at Edwards and said, "I'm sorry, Sam, I forgot," he introduced him to Stone and Mary. "Mary, we are going to need your full statement today I'm afraid. Is your leg bad?"

"She won't let us look at it," said Stone.

"I do not take my pants off in front of strange men."

"Mary, you go over to the back of that rescue truck, and let them look at your leg now," said Steve in no uncertain terms. She glared at him, paused, and than walked over to the truck.

"That's a first," said Stone.

Chapter Thirty-Four

"That's your Dr. Paul, very interesting," said Sheriff Edwards, with a big smile on his face. Stone and the rest of the men were smiling as well.

Gray looked at them, shook his head and smiled. "Sheriff," said James. "Rogers and I have a tape recorder in our car. We were using it for our final interviews today. We can, with your permission, of course, take Dr. Paul's statement up here and save her a trip to the office today."

Gray looked at his watch. It was four o'clock. He looked at Edwards, "You have any objection, Sam?"

"No, sounds like a good idea. Probably won't get it all typed up today for her to sign anyhow. Have Rogers and James both do the interview. They weren't there, so the questions will be more natural."

"Good suggestion. James, get the recorder out of your car. You and Rogers get started when Dr. Paul is done with the rescue men. Actually, do this at the annex in Ponte Vedra. It will be close to home for her."

They all walked over to James' and Rogers' patrol car. Port opened the door as they came up to the car. James opened the trunk to take out the tape machine and new tapes. Gray interrupted him and said, "Hang on a minute, leave them there. You can take your own car. We can transfer him in one of the other cars. Get him out, Port."

Gray motioned Edwards aside. In a low voice he said, "let's walk him by the car with Key in it and see what he says." Sam gave him a half smile and nodded.

"Port, has he said anything to you?"

"Only what he said at the start. When I took his gun away, he said he was trying to save Dr. Paul. But, Sir, I was behind him and he was pointing the gun at her, not Key."

"That's a damn lie," Perkins jerked his head up and toward Port, who was a bit behind him. They had his hands secured behind his back. Port had pulled his arms as far back as he could so Perkins was a bit bent forward. He had also secured his upper arms. "He has me tied up like a pig. No cause to do this to a man."

Edwards looked at Port. "He's a big man, Sir, he tried to break away from Stone and me so we added a precautionary tie."

"You know, Mr. Perkins, I have to read you your rights before we can talk to you." The Sheriff proceeded to Mirandize Perkins.

"You want me to tape this, Sir?" asked James. Gray nodded.

"This is Sheriff Gray," he began. Then he went on to say where they were and whom he was questioning. He read him his rights again. He asked Perkins if he understood and to repeat his name. Perkins did, and then said he was innocent and being held for something he didn't do. He then repeated his story. Port said nothing.

Perkins kept looking up and over, toward the car that held Key. Edwards could see Key wasn't quite visible. He walked over to the car and told the officer to casually open the back door when Edwards walked away. Edwards then rejoined the group. Gray was asking Perkins, "What were you doing in Palm Valley and how come you were in the woods?"

Perkins said, "We were told to do supervision up there and check out the site. We just happened on Key and Paul when we were walking the site."

"Who is this we, you are referring to?"

"Baker was with me, but when this guy pulled a gun on us, Baker took off. Hell, I would have, too. Scared the hell out of us."

"Why did you have a shotgun?"

"No one walks in these woods without one."

"Who told you to walk the site today?"

"The guy we work for, Mr. Wood."

"He told you to follow Dr. Paul today as well?"

"Hell, no. Why you harping on that. We were out here working, not following anyone. I'm not saying anymore."

"Ok, Port, take him in."

"I'll help you, Officer Port," said Edwards. He took Perkins other arm and steered him toward the car with Key in it."

"Wait a minute," yelled Perkins, "that's the guy."

"What guy?" asked Edwards, waving James over with the tape recorder.

"The one there in the car. He's the one that was talking to Paul."

"You're on tape, Mr. Perkins."

"Good. I want this taped. He is the one that told Paul he killed that biologist. He said he was going to kill her and pin it on the trash haulers. You get Baker, ask him, he will tell you."

Key just sat there and stared at the man. Then he turned his head away and said, "He's nuts. I never saw this guy before."

"No, sucker, but I saw you and heard it all."

Edwards and Port pulled him away. "Come on, move it, Perkins," said Edwards. They put him in a car. "Take him to the County and book him for suspected murder and attempted murder," he said to Port and one of the St. John's County deputies. Perkins clamped his jaw shut and just stared at Edwards.

Edwards walked up to Gray. "Well, Steve, we have two verifications of Dr. Paul's story."

"Yes, we do. Hold, take Key here in and book him for murder and attempted murder. Then check his prints against those we found on Mr. White's truck. Wouldn't be at all surprised if there will be a match."

Mary had walked up behind him and said, "Sheriff, he was very careful not to touch the camera or even the film. He also wouldn't take a bottle of water; strange man."

Gray put his arm on her shoulder and steered her away from the patrol car with Key in it as it pulled away. "No, Mary, he was just trying to be careful not to leave prints. He should have searched you. But I guess he just didn't think you would be packing two guns. How was her leg?" he asked one of the rescue officers who had walked over with her.

"Actually, pretty good. It looks like a bad sunburn. We sprayed a little Solarcaine on and put a bandage on it so it wouldn't rub on her pants."

"Yes, they did good," smiled Mary at the young rescuer.

"Mary, we want you to go with James and Rogers to the annex to give a full statement. They can tape it, and we will get it typed up for you to sign tomorrow."

"I have my car here. I can ride with Jeffery."

"No, you go with my men. Jeffery is going to stay and talk with us a minute. He can bring your car and pick you up."

Mary looked at Jeffery. He nodded and she went off with the officers.

Gray took Jeffery over to Edward's car where he was on the radio. He held up his hand to stop them. "Yes, tell Wood I am on my way in to talk with him. Tell him I'm sorry to inconvenience him, but I'll be right there." He stopped talking and turned, "Steve, this is still a joint case. I want you to go with me."

"I wouldn't miss it for anything. Let me talk to Brown and make sure he has it all under control. Baker's no problem since he spilled the beans. I would like to have Perkins sit a bit and worry. Key is a goner. I'm going to have Brown call the State's attorney and have all three charged, right now. Do you want to charge Wood or shall we?"

"No, you charge him on conspiracy to commit murder on Skeet and on Paul. That should hold him until we get it all straightened out. Have one of your men come with you and when we are done you can take him back with you."

"We are lucky we missed the press; time enough tomorrow for that," Gray said. Then he turned to Jeffery. "Is that Derringer registered to you, Stone?"

"Not exactly."

"What the hell does that mean?" asked Edwards.

"It's my gun, but not registered. I would like it back without too many questions asked. I will be buying Mary another one in a day or so. She can't have that one, it hasn't any numbers on it."

"What?" exclaimed Edwards.

"Don't ask, Sam. I'll try to explain later. Stone, I'll have one of the men bring your car up in the morning. I'll come as well so we can all talk. Let's go, Sam, I'll follow you, bells and whistles all the way."

Jeffery had picked Mary up at the annex. They were sitting on the porch with glasses of wine. He was smiling at her. She said, "I know it was stupid of me to go out there with him."

"Yes, it wasn't wise but understandable. There was no way for you to know that Gunther wouldn't join you. When did you first get suspicious?"

"When he wouldn't take any water. Everyone drinks on walks like that. He was pleasant but just barely. I am sorry I glanced at you, but you startled me."

"No problem. He was so anxious and nervous that it didn't take much to spook him."

The phone rang. Mary answered it and said, "It's Arthur, pick up on the extension."

Arthur told them about the funeral and asked how things were there. Mary said, "Let me refill our glasses and Jeffery can tell you."

All she heard as she hung up was, "Tell me what?"

Jeffery finished explaining to Arthur what had been happening, just as she came back with fresh glasses. "Here she is, sir."

"You need new pants, I hear. I think we are lucky it is not a new leg. Now, don't interrupt. I am glad you are safe and that this thing is over. I am flying in tomorrow, early. I'll be there for breakfast at nine. Can you oblige me?"

"You know I can. Can you stay and play a little golf?"

"Of course, and even fish."

"Wonderful."

The next morning at ten the Sheriff drove up in Jeffery's car. Mary greeted him and asked whether he wanted coffee or a late breakfast? "Coffee is fine. Mr. Steel, nice to see you again."

They all sat on the porch and Mary said, "Can you tell us what happens now?"

They all grinned. "She is not noted for her patience, Sheriff," said Arthur.

"No, you all have a perfect right to know. I have your statement for you to sign, Mary."

Mary read it and signed it with Arthur's pen. She looked at Arthur and handed the statement to him. Arthur looked at the Sheriff. Gray smiled and nodded. He quickly read it and handed it back to the Sheriff. "Personally, I prefer golf," Arthur said as he crossed his legs.

"Can you tell us what happened with Wood?" asked Jeffery.

"Yes, that was interesting. Edwards decided we had enough on him not to fool around. So Edwards told him he was a very careful man and so he wanted to read him his rights and tape the interview. He really had Wood in a tricky position. If he refused, he was admitting he had something to hide. He must have thought we were just going to press him on the whereabouts of his men.

"The first question was, where are your men, Perkins and Baker? He went right on with what he had told Cook and Hold about working in Arlington. Edwards asked him whether he meant Ponte Vedra? He became very quiet and said, no. He asked why, were his men out there and were they in trouble? Edwards said they had been seen hanging out in front of Dr. Paul's home. Did he know why? He said, hell, no. Were we sure?

"Edwards told him Baker said Wood had sent them out there to follow Paul. We would like to know why you did that? He said he didn't and what the hell was going on? What did the men do? Edwards asked a few more leading questions and got nowhere. So he told him we had been told that Wood had ordered Skeet's death. That they also told us that they had been ordered by Wood to hurt Paul, very seriously hurt her. When we caught them in the act of attempted murder with a shotgun, they informed us you told them to put her out of commission.

"He flipped out and said they were damn liars. He never told them anything like that. Yeah, he told them to find Skeet. They said they did, and he was drunk. He set the place on fire. They couldn't get him out and he died in a fire. That's all. He insisted he didn't know anything about the rest of that stuff. He said he wasn't saying anything more and wanted a lawyer. Edwards told him he could get one after he had been booked for conspiracy of murder and attempted murder; that it was lucky for him Dr. Paul was still alive.

"We cuffed him and took him to St. John's County. Perkins and Baker both stated that they were following Wood's orders. Baker is probably closer to telling the truth. When Wood has a chance to think it over, he will probably change his story and pin it on Perkins as well."

"What will this do to the landfill?" asked Mary.

"Nothing, I'm afraid. Edwards talked to the Mayor to warn him what was happening. He doesn't think the Mayor knew a thing. He delegated the whole thing to his aide and the attorney. This business had nothing to do with the city. In fact, he made it clear that Wood was a hired hand of a big out-of-state company. The company would cut him loose in a minute if he were in trouble. No, Mary, the landfill goes on, I'm sorry to say. Finally, Mr. Key's fingerprints were the ones on David White's truck. He may try to call it an accident but his confession to you and two other witnesses and his attempt on your life will sink him."

"My gun?" asked Mary.

"I'm sorry, it is not your gun. It was someone else's, and I will return it to that person soon." He smiled at Jeffery.

Arthur patted her hand and said, "We will buy you a new one and some new pants as well. More coffee anyone?"

Postscript:

Not quite a year later, after St. Johns County hired a Tallahassee lawyer, the County won the day when the Florida Cabinet ruled against Duval/Jacksonville locating a landfill on the St. Johns County line.

The Author

The author, while a professor at New York University, spent a good part of each year at her home on the Intracoastal Waterway in Palm Valley, Florida. The love of the waterway lured her into early retirement. She began a new lifestyle, becoming active in her community when she wasn't fishing, working in her large yard and tending her German Shepherds, until she was elected as a County Commissioner.

She is an advocate of the environment and has worked to preserve the wetlands, birds, animals and trees. She fears the rapid growth in Florida will leave little of its charm for future generations. After her term in office, she again retired to her fishing, increased her golfing and began sharing her love of Florida and its inhabitants, even the two-legged ones, in these fictional stories.

Watch for:

She Said "Incorporate What?!"

*The third Dr. Paul in Florida Mystery
will be available in early of 2007*

A group of citizens want to incorporate the community of Ponte Vedra, including Palm Valley. Dr. Mary Paul and others in Palm Valley are adamantly opposed. Many in Ponte Vedra, for financial reasons, do not want to incorporate. They join together to try to defeat the referendum in September.

The local county commissioner, who actively supports incorporation, decides not to run for office again. Dr. Paul is encouraged to run for the seat at her boat parade party. Shortly after the party, one of the guests who had committed to work against incorporation is found dead in her pool on the ocean front.

The woman's husband had been killed in London a year earlier. She willed her estate in Ponte Vedra to St. John's charities to be administered by Dr. Paul, who arranges an estate sale of her belongings. The woman's homes in London and New York are broken into and files searched, but nothing else is disturbed.

The plot revolves around the investigation into the woman's death, the estate sale and who may have been involved in the husband's death. Who is looking for the husband's papers; what is in the papers? The beauty of the Intracoastal Waterway and the oceanside community of Ponte Vedra make a wonderful setting for this fast-paced Florida novel.

Designed on an Apple Macintosh computer using
Adobe *InDesign CS* and *Photoshop Elements*

Printed in the United States
62121LVS00005BA/13-15